ROUGH & READY COUNTRY

ROUGH & READY COUNTRY

BOOKS 1-3

COWBOY MOUNTAIN MAN / CURVY GIRL ROMANCE

ENGRID EAVES

JOIN THE ENGRID EAVES COMMUNITY!

ALPHA-EMOTIONAL HEROES.

HEADSTRONG, CURVY GIRLS.

SAVAGE ROMANCE.

GIVEAWAYS. FREEBIES.
NEW RELEASES. LATEST NEWS.

Subscribe to my newsletter today to never miss out on a
new steamy, small-town read.
SIGN UP FOR MY NEWSLETTER

CONTENTS

LOVE AT FIRST BLIZZARD

LOVE AT FIRST CAMPFIRE

LOVE AT FIRST RESCUE

LOVE AT FIRST BLIZZARD

A COWBOY MOUNTAIN MAN / CURVY GIRL ROMANCE

PROLOGUE

MAKSIM

"Looks like you've got yourself in some serious trouble this time, son. You better start talking," Sheriff Clyde "Roughneck" Colletti frowns, glaring at me.

We've been at this for hours now, but I know I'm more stubborn than he is. I shake my head. "I'm waiting for my attorney."

"What's taking Flynn so long anyway? You know we found her car on Federal land, which means I have FBI agents breathing down my neck." He slams a newspaper on the desk to emphasize his point. It's the *Chronicle*, and it has a photo of Alex on the front page and reads "Kidnapping Feared in Case of Missing Classical Musician."

"I didn't do anything wrong."

"Then, why aren't you talking?"

"Because I know my rights."

"Your records may be sealed, Maksim. But don't think for one moment that I don't remember in excruciating detail what a fucking troublemaker you are. Now, start talking. You're only digging a deeper hole for yourself."

3

I cross my arms, yawning as if I'm bored. It only makes the old sheriff angrier. In truth, my mind's racing, wondering what's going on with Alex. If she's okay ... if she's going to leave me.

The sound of the door crashing open catches us both off guard. My foster brother Flynn rushes into the room where the sheriff's been questioning me. From his ebony skin to his neatly trimmed beard and lean, muscular build, Flynn looks especially formidable as he stands there, staring at Colletti, a muscle feathering in his jaw.

I frown, saying drily, "It's about time, bro. What was the hold-up?" He ignores my question.

Instead, Flynn's eyes remain trained on Colletti. "My client has no further comment. Now, unless you've got some evidence I don't know about, you have no grounds to hold him any longer."

Sheriff Colletti's face turns bright red, and his breathing picks up to a pant. "Flynn, they've got me in a bind here. Because she went missing on Federal lands, the FBI's already involved. And you know what a shit show this has become with the media."

Flynn nods. But he never removes his white cowboy hat, which tells me everything I need to know. I grab my black Stetson, preparing to leave. Colletti grimaces.

"Yes, it's a shit show," Flynn answers. "Why do you think it took me so long to get here? Journalists are swarming around this town, around this building. I had to park at the Search and Rescue Office and walk over here. Don't you think you should set up a perimeter or something? Put my brother Christian's ass to work along with your other deputies. It may be a shit show. But it's a shit show you're in charge of."

The old plump man with a handlebar mustache looks

beside himself as he grumbles, "Between the FBI, the media, and her parents, I've had one hell of a past twenty-four hours."

Ironic. Thinking back to the last twenty-four hours, they've been the best of my life.

"What's the deal with all of this media attention anyway?" Flynn asks.

Colletti looks confused as he says, "She's a famous pianist or something."

"Cellist," I correct.

"What he said," Colletti says, pointing at me.

Flynn shakes his head, "Sheriff, you and I both know you've got no grounds to hold my brother on kidnapping charges. Either book him or let him go."

"It's not that simple," Colletti says, but Flynn cuts him off.

"This is a missing person's case, not a kidnapping. If anything, Maksim's the hero of this story and will have his reputation fully vindicated shortly."

"And how do you know that?"

"Because I just spoke with Ms. Petkova, and she told me she won't be pressing any charges. She also emphasized how my client saved her from freezing to death."

"That's not what her parents think happened," the sheriff counters, looking more agitated by the minute. "Besides, it could be Stockholm Syndrome or something. You know how people sometimes get when they've been kidnapped."

Flynn laughs. "You're funnier than usual, Sheriff. Ms. Petkova is twenty-one years old and no victim of this supposed crime. What her parents think is quite frankly irrelevant." Turning briskly to me, Flynn orders, "Come on, Maksim. Time to go. They've got no reason to keep you."

"Can I see Alex?" I ask.

My brother shakes his head emphatically. "Please do me a favor and avoid Ms. Petkova on our way out. The last thing we need is to add flames to the media firestorm brewing outside. You should draw the blinds, Colletti. I don't know how you can stand working here with all those faces staring through the glass. Makes me feel like I'm in an aquarium—on the fish side of things."

ONE

ALEX

THREE DAYS EARLIER

I peer through a dizzying swirl of icy flakes, unable to see yellow lines, car tracks, or guard rails. My indigo Mazda CX-5 crunches along the snowy road. I have to remind myself it's March and not December.

The twisting white flurries intensify, growing as opaque as potato soup. The glare of my headlights thickens the atmospheric broth as I squint into feathery sheets of frozen rain. The snow defies gravity, smashing into my windshield at haphazard angles, and I feel uprooted, floating.

Can snow hypnotize you?

The Third Movement of the Herbert Cello Concerto blares in the background, and my fingers itch to change it. But I can't break the double-fisted, white-knuckle grip on the steering wheel. Ahead, thousands of individual snowflakes meld into an impenetrable milky wall.

"Proceed to the route," the car GPS demands.

Am I even off route?

A sudden jolt forward ... a sickening falling sensation ...

increasingly urgent thuds, and I come to a jerky halt. Tremors rush through me like waves at high tide.

Am I alive? Yes. *Is my baby okay?* My eyes scan the backseat, resting on the hard white case of the priceless cello. Although jostled, it shows no visible signs of damage.

I register my ragged breath as though from a distance. It keeps time with the windshield wipers ... pound squeak, pound squeak, pound squeak.

"Proceed to the route."

Herbert Cello Concerto.

I pry my shaking hands from the steering wheel. Two pause buttons later, silence and fear congeal around me. I've never felt more alone.

My fingers clumsily dive into my purse. Lipstick, ibuprofen, a pack of travel Kleenexes, Chapstick, my wallet, a concealer compact, and a concert program. *Everything but what I need.*

Hot air blazes from my car's heater, and I twist the controller off. I'm burning up. My shaking hands head back into my purse, finally finding my cell phone.

Blinking in disbelief, I stare at a screen with non-existent bars.

The windshield wipers thump in time to my pulse. I take a deep breath, cold fingers of panic crawling up my spine.

Shifting into reverse, I press my foot tentatively on the gas pedal. Then, a little more. And more.

Soon, I smash the gas to the floor. The sickening whir of tires against slick ice taunts me.

Don't panic.

A seatbelt click and door click later, air thick with cold assaults my cheeks and bare arms. I close the door behind me, immediately falling to the ice-rink slippery ground hidden beneath new layers of powder.

Moist, heavy snow clings to my jeans and t-shirt, making my arms icy and my clothes damp. Clumsily, I scramble to my feet, hanging onto the door handle as my legs sprawl out from under me again. A newborn giraffe has more grace.

After regaining a precarious balance, I shine the flash-light from my cell phone at my back tires. Light glints along the pearl-shiny ruts polished in the snow by my tires. I nearly fall again.

Looking up into an unending fall of snow, fat flakes drop from the sky, plastering my face and filling my nose. The winter wonderland of an hour ago feels ugly, suffocating.

I scream for help, but who am I kidding? I'm the last person on the planet. A sore throat and crumbling hope are the only rewards for my efforts—*and* an uncontrollable, teeth-chattering cold.

Great white puffs escape my mouth as I go from screaming for help to angry cursing and finally resigned crying. I scramble back inside, shaking the snow from my shirt and mane of curly black hair. Turning the key in the ignition, a burst of hot air fills the car. My teeth chatter like the motor of a lawnmower.

What do I do now?

I've got to conserve the heat in my car for my cello's sake. I shudder at the imagined sounds of cracking seams, popping wood, and slipped tuning pegs.

Besides the cello, I have a lukewarm grande white chocolate mocha, a bottle of water, an unopened box of chocolates, and a dozen roses. Even McGyver would have trouble getting creative with those items. In the backseat next to the cello, a rose gold aluminum edition Samsonite contains a week's worth of my clothing in neat piles, and a garment bag holds concert clothes. A smaller matching Samsonite carry-on in the trunk has sandals, sneakers, hiking boots, and high heels. *Ill-prepared doesn't cut it.*

My hiking boots might feel better than the low-top Vans I'm currently wearing. At least, they'd keep out more snow and have better tread. But it's not like I plan on walking out of here. Instead, I raid the luggage in the back-seat, striking out on winter-ready clothes. I layer shirts, pants, and socks, hoping to conserve heat until rescue workers arrive—*if* they arrive.

The blue and red lights on my dashboard blaze: twenty-two degrees Fahrenheit, 10:37 p.m., and half a tank of gas. My stomach churns as I bite my lower lip, weighing non-existent options.

CHAPTER
TWO
MAKSIM

Nothing beats the exhilaration of a dog sled on fresh powder. I strategically chose the thirteen-strong team of malamutes and huskies, placing some of my most skilled race dogs—Alfie and Scooter—with the newbie nine-month-olds, Squirt and Boots.

Other dogs of varying experience round out the ranks, with Kaya as the lead dog. At first, they strain against one another. But within the first thirty minutes, the team takes on a single-minded spirit, pulling for the first time as one.

The world sparkles, bathed in mid-morning light and fresh air. Fortunately, the flaps of my fur-lined aviator keep my ears happily toasty, even when the dogs gain speed.

In the lead, Kaya lets out an unusual yelp, dropping her nose to the ground. She throws her head over her shoulder, looking back at me. The team slows. My swing dogs, Lou and Sting, are still raring to go, and the rest of the group clumps up behind them. I need to get this train moving.

Impatiently, I call, "On by!" But Kaya's not listening. "Hike!" Still, nothing.

"Shit." I knew this would happen. *How many times have I*

told Logan he would ruin her with avalanche rescue training? Too late now.

The sled stops, and she furiously sniffs at the snow. Younger pups are getting tangled up, and this whole ride is shot to hell. I grab my snowshoes, tightening the bindings before jumping off the footboards. I'm resigned to getting her back on track manually. Logan's going to catch hell for this. I resist the urge to untangle the younger dogs, talking them through it instead. This is a learning experience they need, even though it's tedious.

The gray-and-white-patched beauty with crystal blue eyes looks up at me. "What's the deal, Kay?"

The other dogs yip and whine restlessly. Scooter turns impatiently in the rigging, and Squirt nips and growls at him.

Fur's about to fly, so I throw myself between them with an intense glare and command. Kaya moves forward again. The sled lurches slowly behind as the other dogs fall in line.

"Dammit!"

But anger gives way to curiosity as her front paws go crazy and snow shoots up between her back legs.

I grab the snow shovel on the front of the sled and head towards the white mound, where she whines and tears at the snow. The first thrust of the shovel collides with something hard and metallic. A couple of shovel loads more, and I'm staring at the tail lights of a navy blue SUV.

My shoulders and back strain into the work. Soon, my Carhartt, hat, and gloves come off as the exertion flushes me with warmth. My white thermal grows damp with sweat, covering my torso with goosebumps as the wind whips around me.

The dogs yelp impatiently.

Peering through the back window of the icy vehicle, I see a blurred form.

Kaya howls excitedly, her tail going 50 miles per hour. I unbuckle my snowshoes and clamor into the ditch I've cleared, tracing the driver's door. The handle won't budge. Whether it's frozen or locked, I don't know. But there's still plenty of snow to clear before I can swing it open, so I put my back into shoveling and pitching snow.

Kaya nearly dives into the hole after me. She risks bringing twelve other dogs and a seven-foot-long, one-hundred-pound touring sled behind her.

"Whoa!" I bellow, holding up my hand.

Her front paws prance frantically, and her thickly furred body shakes with excitement. Behind her, I survey menacing clouds, darkening as they descend the mountain slopes towards us. The wind twirls around me now, driving white powder into my eyes and face.

I'm out of time.

I throw everything into clearing a path for the door. A few more attempts at the handle, and I'm sure it's locked. *Who the fuck worries about carjackers in the middle of a blizzard?*

I hesitate momentarily, weighing the potential legal consequences of breaking the window with my shovel. It wouldn't be my first brush with the law. It sure as hell would be the stupidest one, though. But a person's life could be on the line ... *if they aren't already dead.*

Action wins out, attested by the high-pitched crash of shattering glass. I reach into the car to open it from the inside. An icy hand reaches out, grasping my arm, and my heart leaps out of my chest.

A pale face and purple-tinged lips look up pleadingly at me. Chattering teeth override talking. "Ch-ch-ch-," the woman stammers, letting go of me and crossing her arms tightly over her chest.

"Ch-ch-ch-," she attempts again. Her movements are clumsy with hypothermia. But at least she's still shivering, a sign her body hasn't shut down.

"Ma'am, I'm here to help."

"Ch-ch-cello."

Did I hear her right?

"Cello."

Leaning in towards her, sure enough, I see a large white case that looks like it's for a giant guitar. It'll have to wait.

Instead, I go to work, pulling the girl from the car and heaving her into my arms to carry her out of the ditch. I crest the top of the snowbank, and now I regret having removed my snowshoes. My legs sink waist-deep into the snow, and I feel like I'm swimming through powder back to the sled, clutching a block of ice to my chest. The dogs yelp and clamor around me.

I climb onto the snow's surface on my knees, careful not to break through with my feet, and place her on the sled before sinking back down and gulping air. I swim back through the thick waves of white to retrieve my snowshoes, coat, hat, gloves, and shovel. There's also the matter of the cello in the white case.

After everything's secured, and the woman's wrapped in all my extra blankets and furs, I stalk to the back of the sled. I'd much rather take her to the hospital than my cabin. But it's too far away, and we're out of time.

Frigid snow-laced gusts announce the arrival of the dark clouds and another storm. The peaceful winterscape of this morning yields to icy rage. Cold pierces my hands as I slip my gloves on, and my pulse pounds to stay warm.

With a few percussive commands, I turn the dogs and

sled around, lining them out before sprinting full-throttle toward my cabin. I can't see where the fuck I'm going and have to leave it to the dogs. Hopefully, Kaya won't get side-tracked again. Racing into the storm across white plains bounded on all sides by frost-tipped stands of evergreens, I grit my teeth as sheets of ice slash my face.

THREE

ALEX

T turn to the right, pulling soft flannel covers over my head to shut out the gentle warmth of light. Every muscle aches, sore and raw. And my hands and feet burn. Yet, I feel warm, deliciously wonderfully warm.

I yawn, nestling further into the blankets and pillows as my senses wander back toward reality.

Tick tock. Tick tock. The sound of a grandfather clock fills my ears. Hovering above consciousness, I'm a child again at my grandparents' house in Bulgaria.

Soft guitar strumming and snippets of a rich baritone greet my ears next. *When did Grandma and Grandpa start listening to Chris Stapleton?*

The crackle of fire catches my ears, almost lulling me back to sleep—until I hear a tap, tap, tap. The sound of someone's boot on a hardwood floor.

My grandparents' house had carpet, not wood. *Where in the world am I?* I struggle to sit up.

A rumbling voice cautions, "Careful there."

My heart jumps into my throat, and I squeeze my eyes shut. The tapping of the foot has stopped, but the country crooning continues, as does the ticking of the clock and the sounds of fire.

Steeling myself, I open my eyes, peering from the red, black, and gray flannel covers in the direction of the growl. The dark, lustrous wooden walls of a cabin shine back at me, illuminated by the flashing of a fire.

Floorboards squeak, and a man looks down at me. Dark blond hair, a neatly trimmed beard, and dark blue eyes meet my gaze. His brow furrows in concern, and I catch my breath. The rugged cut of his face is all mountain man. But his eyes have the disaffected coolness of James Dean. *Am I still dreaming?* My aching body protests otherwise.

I can't break my eyes away from his simmering gaze. My lips form a question, but nothing comes out.

"Take it easy," he commands again gruffly.

I open my mouth, squeaking out, "Where am I?"

"My cabin." The voice is rich and dark, audible molasses.

"And where is that?"

"Easy now," he scolds again, leaning over me to feel my forehead. He smells of pine and soap, and his electric touch sends sparks from my forehead into my chest.

"Thank God, you've warmed up a bit. But you're still not out of the woods. Don't move around too much."

"Warmed up? Wait, what?" My voice cracks.

"What do you remember?"

I press my fingertips to my temple, concentrating. "Playing a baroque concert in Ophir City..." My fingers fly over the strings as I perform the Vivaldi Double Cello Concerto, the sonorous richness of the orchestra and the other soloing cellist washing over me.

"I remember flowers and chocolates..." A dozen scarlet roses brought to the stage by a glowing patron and a box of

Belgian chocolates gifted by our conductor, Remi Jourdan. I try to sit up, but the hand moves from my forehead to my shoulder, holding me down gently yet without compromise.

This time, the voice has a sharp edge to it. "Do you have a hearing problem? I said don't move too soon. I've been warming you up for hours now. Last thing you need is a shock of cold blood to your heart."

"Huh?"

The bed dips as the man sits beside me, his hand resting on my shoulder. "Where are you from?"

"San Francisco."

His face grows stern, icy. "Talk me through what happened."

"Driving and a blizzard. The snowflakes hypnotized me..." I feel immediate regret. *Snowflakes hypnotized me? Does that even make sense?*

But his face betrays no traces of judgment.

"You drove into a ditch during the blizzard. I'm not sure how long you were there, but I found your car completely buried in a drift. And you were hypothermic."

I concentrate, trying to remember what happened. But so little of it makes sense. The barking of dogs? Like a howling choir? And a world of white flying by, bundled beneath blankets and furs. Lying in a bed with warm bands of steel encircling me and the heat of a man's hard, angular body pressed against my back.

My mouth opens in alarm, and I search his face in horror. *Did I sleep with this stranger?*

He knits his brows again, looking at me out of the corner of his eye. "What?"

"We were in bed together," I whisper, my voice shaking accusatorially.

He frowns. "I had to warm you up."

My pulse pounds in my temples as I pat my body. I'm wearing an oversized flannel button-down shirt. "And you undressed me, too?" I pat my breasts and crotch, thankfully feeling the black satin of my bra and underwear.

"I had to get you out of those cold, damp clothes." He shrugs. He almost looks bored, as if he does this all the time.

My mouth hangs open, and I have no clue what to say.

His hand comes up, gently palming my cheek, and I feel fire ravaging a path where his warm thumb traces soft circles. "You're blushing. That's a good sign." His hand drops, and a part of me feels disappointed. But I don't know why.

My mind races with questions, but I can only manage a raspy, "How?"

"How is that a good sign?" he clarifies, raising his eyebrows.

I nod, feeling confused and dangerously close to tears.

"It means your circulation is coming back. Honestly, when I found you, I wasn't sure you'd make it. You were cold as an ice cube."

He would know. I feel my cheeks heating even more as I remember the delicious feel of his arms and naked skin next to mine.

"Were you naked? Was I naked?"

It's hard to tell in the fire's flickering light, but I almost swear his cheeks have reddened. The firelight makes his hair glow like dark bronze and bathes his aquiline nose and angular face in golden light. He shifts on the bed, and I feel it dip in a new spot. "Nothing funny happened. I promise you. But I had to get you warm—"

My mouth hangs open.

His eyes narrow, and his lips draw a hard line tipped down at the ends. "You were colder than a fucking witch's titty. It's not like I enjoyed it."

I squeeze my eyes shut, letting out a sigh.

"Seriously, relax."

"But I don't know who you are," I whisper, my voice weak and shaky.

"I'm the guy who saved you from freezing to death," he replies, a hard edge to his voice.

Suddenly, it hits me. "My cello!"

"You mean the thing in the white case?"

"Yes, where is it?"

"Your cello is fine."

"It last appraised at $600,000," I blurt out.

His eyebrows raise, and he lets out a dark laugh. "Seriously? How could a hunk of wood be worth that?"

"It's a Giovanni Francesco Celoniato from 1730. The twin copy of another cello at the Royal Academy in London, England."

Letting out an exasperated sigh, he asks, "And how can a cello have a twin?"

"They were made from the same tree."

"Whatever. Seems like a lot of money for an outdated woodworking project to me."

I gasp. No one has ever spoken of the instrument that way. "It's priceless, you dimwit!"

He shrugs. "Good thing it fit on the sled, then."

Sled?

My head's pounding, and everything aches when I move. I'm angry he's making me talk, and even angrier he's making stupid jokes about something that isn't funny. He has to understand that my cello is irreplaceable. Losing it would be like losing my soul. "It can't handle extreme temperatures. The cold will destroy it."

"I guess I should bring it inside, then?"

"What? It's outside?"

He grins. "It's called sarcasm."

I should feel angry or annoyed, at the very least. But I've never seen a more gorgeous face in my life. He takes my breath away. My eyes search him hungrily, wanting to commit every detail of my rescuer to memory. My core tightens just thinking about his arms around me.

"It's not outside?" I ask again.

"Your cello's fine. Nice and toasty in my living room."

My muscles relax as I exhale, sinking into the softness of the pillows. But then my body goes stiff again as I scrutinize the scowling stranger. I can't let his drop-dead good looks color my judgment. My best friend, Jess, is a true crime journalist, which means I'm well-versed in the handsome man turned kidnapper, rapist, or serial killer theme. As it currently stands, I know nothing about him.

Then, it hits me. *Why did I confess the dollar amount of my most precious belonging to him?* I might as well hold up a sign inviting him to rob me ... or worse. After all, who would know?

"You'll be well compensated for saving my cello."

He grunts, his face hardening. "Honey, I don't need your money."

"Seriously," I emphasize, taking a deep breath to calm my shaking voice. Living in San Francisco, I know nothing's for free. The piper always has to get paid. I try to sound nonchalant, saying, "I can assure you, the reward will be a lot more money than you'd get from pawning or keeping it."

FOUR
MAKSIM

D espite measuring my next words carefully, I sound like I'm snarling as I reply, "Let me get this straight. I save your life, put myself and my dogs at risk to rescue you and your damn oversized guitar, and then you accuse me of being a creep, a thief, and a dimwit?"

She looks down.

"This shouldn't surprise me, considering you had your car door locked in a damn blizzard. Who does that? Just for clarification, carjackers are the least of your concern in the Sierra Nevadas."

"What should I be concerned about then? Mountain men who cart women back to their isolated cabins?"

"That's one helluva thank you, City Girl."

I'm seeing red as I fantasize about throwing her fucking cello into a snowbank. After all, it caused nothing but trouble on the drive back to the cabin. How many times did I have to stop to reposition it as I drove?

I take a deep breath, steadying my voice, "As much as

I'd love to pawn your cello in the middle of a blizzard, I'll pass. Same goes for throwing your ass out in the cold."

Her eyes widen, and I can't hold back a laugh. Helping her has already been the epitome of damned if I do, damned if I don't. And it's still not over.

"Are you laughing at me?

"Maybe."

"Are you mocking me?" Her icy blue eyes pierce me.

"Look, just because your pretty little city ass ended up in flyover country doesn't mean this is *The Hills Have Eyes* or anything."

"*The Hills Have Eyes*? What's that?"

Where's this woman been living? Under a rock?

I rub my face in my hands. A mixture of annoyance and desire course through me. Even in her disheveled and berating state, the woman is breathtaking. I can't take my eyes off her lush pink lips. And her skin flushes rosy with outrage, stunningly contrasting with her ebony curls. I long to run my fingers through those lustrous locks, to cup her blushing cheeks in both palms.

"Are you even listening to me?"

I shake my head. "Look, your cello's safe. You're safe, and thank God my dogs are safe. We're all good, so quit freaking out. You've been through a lot, and you need to rest."

I can't look at her anymore. Her heart-shaped face, her bright cheeks, her full lips. I can't trust myself around her. I stand, moving away from the bed, but her hand seizes my wrist, sending flames licking up my arm.

"I'm sorry... I mean, thank you for your help. I shouldn't have assumed the worst. It's just hard to trust people ... especially strangers."

I nod, savoring how her hand lingers on my skin,

searing me. *I should be angry at her. What the fuck's wrong with me?*

"You hungry?"

Her look transforms from fierce to sheepish. "Ravenous, actually."

"Good. I like a woman with an appetite."

She beams at me, and my pulse pounds.

Tendrils of guilt crawl from the pit of my gut up my spine. I lied to her earlier. I had to. But I didn't like it. Deceit never sits well with me. Yes, she was frigid when I first laid under the covers with her, and I had to force myself to cover her body with my own.

But once she started warming up and snuggling back into me, soft and yielding to my touch, molding her body to mine, tangling her legs with mine, it felt fucking fantastic. My cock twitches just thinking about it, and I have to get out of the bedroom and away from her.

Her fingers grasp my wrist harder, and I look over my shoulder at her. She presses her generous lips firmly together in something between a straight line and a frown and says, "Thank you for finding me. Thank you for everything."

Her pale eyes are wide as they meet mine. Everything about her is gorgeous. *Too bad I'm such a fuck up.*

I grumble, "Glad the dogs and I could help."

"Dogs?"

"You don't remember?"

She lets go of my wrist, placing her forehead in her hands. "I kind of do. I remember barking ... a lot of barking..." Her voice trails off.

"Stew's ready, so we might as well talk over something hot."

She tries to rouse herself, and I stand up, pulling pillows

behind her so that she's sitting up. I take a deep breath, enjoying the faint smell of vanilla perfume lingering on her skin. I fight the urge to press my lips to her forehead, her cheek, to trace kisses down her beautiful neck, send a hand roaming through her thick hair. *Fuck, having this woman here, so close and yet unattainable, is torture.*

"You okay?" she whispers, staring up at me.

Snap out of it, Maksim!

"Yeah," I mutter trying to sound casual, but I've got to get out of the room now before I make myself look like an actual creep. I stride to the door with a single-minded purpose, finding my cell phone.

I have to talk to Logan or Christian ASAP. Sure, my brothers'll never let me hear the end of this, having a smoking hot babe in my house and doing nothing about it. But she's made it clear she's not interested, and even though my cock hasn't gotten the message, the rest of me has.

After retrieving my black iPhone on the kitchen counter, I frown. Still no signal. Outside, the wind howls. I should get my satellite phone from the truck. But that would mean digging it out of the snow — not something I relish the thought of. I'll catch shit from my brothers for not having it handy. But all that will come later. Now, I've got to focus on *not* ravaging the curvy, black-haired beauty in my bed.

CHAPTER
FIVE
ALEX

That didn't go well.

I watch as he stalks out of the room, taking in his massive shoulders and tapered waist beneath a black t-shirt that accentuates every muscle. I swallow hard against the rising lust in my core.

My lower belly hums with desire and an animal part of me wants to run out to him, wrap myself around him, and beg him to take me. I'm cranky with soreness and fatigue. Sky-high sexual tension isn't helping anything. I shouldn't have accused him of any of that, but at least it kept me from drooling.

The man saved my life and my cello and is letting me stay at his place—no strings attached. He's even feeding me. And that's the problem. None of it computes. Everything comes at a price. Doesn't it? Other than my cello, what could he possibly want from me?

The last thought makes me laugh, considering how hard I'm lusting after him. Maybe he feels it, too.

I shake my head. The man's a total heart-throb, and I'm a plain Jane who'll never fit into single-digit clothing sizes.

The only thing sexy about me is my cello, and he's already made his opinion on that subject abundantly clear.

I snuggle deeper into his soft flannel shirt, relishing in the fact he wears it. This shirt clings to his angular planes and muscles, and it smells like him, too—all pine and soap and mountain man.

Memories of the rescue come in pieces, but the security of his arms stands out. My lower stomach aches, and my panties dampen. *What in the world is this stranger doing to me?*

"Get it together, Alex," I order the way my mother would. I feel disgusted with myself, yet I can't deny I'm obsessed. I've got to get myself under control.

There's no way a hottie like that could want a fat girl like me. He's seen my thick thighs, soft belly, and stretch marks. All the parts of me that scream, "Not a supermodel."

But the thought of him undressing me, his palms and fingers glancing past my flesh as he covered me in his flannel—

"You barely know this guy," I scold myself in a whisper. "You don't fully understand how you got in his house, in his clothes, or in his bed. So, slow down." But, honestly, I don't want to slow down. I want his hands, his lips, his body claiming every inch of me.

Guilt floods me as I hear footsteps heading in my direction. I look down as he enters the room, trying to hide my burning cheeks and lust-filled thoughts.

"Here," he grumbles, setting a steaming stoneware bowl of stew on the nightstand beside the bed, along with a sturdy stainless steel soup spoon. The savory fragrance of meat, garlic, onions, rosemary, and thyme makes my stomach lurch. *How long has it been since I ate?*

"It's hot."

The massive man wears a red half apron, and there's something adorable about him, standing there holding a second bowl of stew and a spoon. He places it next to the first, striding from the room. My eyes linger appreciatively over his khakis and how they outline his muscular thighs and tight ass.

A few minutes later, he returns with a plate of thick, steaming, buttery slices of bread. It looks homemade.

"Do you bake?"

He shrugs, offering the plate to me. I grab a slice, holding my other hand under it to keep the melted butter pooled on top from landing on his comforter. He pulls the apron from his waist in a flash, throwing it between my bread-clutching hand and the bed. I lick butter off my other hand and giggle at his ingenuity.

He groans softly, and I look up, pulling my buttery index finger from my mouth.

His eyes round, and he swallows loudly.

Silence.

"Shit, I forgot to turn off the stove." He nearly runs from the room.

I go back to licking my fingers and diving into some of the best bread I've ever tasted. Perfectly crunchy on the outside and soft on the inside, with a salty, yeasty yumminess not possible from a store loaf.

Now, I'm moaning. My stomach rumbles again, and I take more bites, barely chewing and swallowing before stuffing in more. Ravenous, I finish the slice like a starved bear, licking all ten fingers.

I look up, and the mountain man's standing in the doorway, eyeing me, a chair in one hand and his other hand clenched in a fist at his side.

"I'm sorry," I blurt out, horrified. I've made a royal pig of myself.

He shakes his head slowly, his voice low and strained. "Don't apologize. I'm ... I'm glad you like my bread."

I nod, relieved but still embarrassed.

He enters the room, swinging the chair around with one smooth gesture like it's a toy. He sits with the back to me, straddling it and grabbing his bowl of stew from the nightstand. He's so tall that he easily rests his forearms on the chair's back, dwarfing it. "Hope you like antelope."

"Actually, I'm a vegetarian."

His jaw drops, and now I'm laughing.

"Just getting you back for the cello comment."

"Well played." He smiles before putting a spoonful of stew in his mouth. I stare raptly as he licks the shiny metal utensil clean, sighing with pleasure. Then, his tongue darts slowly over his lips, and I'm a tangle of dark desires. His mouth is the most sensual thing I've ever seen. *He's* the most sensual thing I've ever seen. Prying my eyes away, I squirm, squeezing my legs together beneath the covers.

Following his example, I grab my bowl of stew and take a bite. My mouth explodes with flavors — rich garlic, creamy butter, juicy meat, fresh herbs, tender potatoes, and sweet carrots. I don't know if it's nearly freezing to death or going who knows how long without food, but I feel like I'm eating for the first time.

"Like it?"

I've already got another spoonful in my mouth and am nodding and moaning as I chew, letting the flavors meld in my mouth. A deep rumble comes from his chest, and I don't know if he's laughing at me or with me. But I'm past caring as I take another delectable bite.

CHAPTER
SIX
MAKSIM

Yes, it's damn good stew, but she's killing me here. Between the finger licking and the moaning, I'm wrecked. And then I've got to go and be chivalrous, ripping off the red apron, the only thing hiding the raging hard-on she's given me. I'm trying to be a decent guy but feeling more savage by the minute.

A flood of scenes fills my head as I think of ways I'd like to make her moan ... *and devour her.* Thankfully, the back of the chair covers my cock as we dive into our stew bowls. With each bite, the tension ratchets up until I feel like I'm going to explode.

I watch her pouty lips wrap around the spoon as she licks off another bite, and I imagine those lips wrapped around my cock. Fuck, I never knew dinner could be so damn sexy.

Out of the corner of my eye, I catch her watching me. I swear she's staring at my mouth. But I don't know how I could be so lucky.

Everything about her, from her curly black hair to her ample hips and adorable feet, screams perfection. She's way too good for a loser like me. She's got a $600,000 cello sitting in my living room. All I've got is a sealed juvenile rap sheet a mile long. If she knew the half of it, she'd be climbing out a window to escape.

She finishes before me, sopping up the last of the stew with her second helping of bread, and I lean forward, watching her lick her fingers again. My throat tightens with desire, and my dick presses hard against the crotch of my pants.

"I probably ate that way too fast. But, holy cow, that was amazing!"

I laugh, caught off guard by her sudden wholesomeness. "Holy cow? Who says that?"

She shrugs, her eyes darting curiously around the room and then back to me. "Some habits are hard to break. My parents have a strict no cursing policy."

I can't relate, considering cussing was the least of my foster dad's worries. "Yeah, I was more into blowing shit up and hot-wiring cars. So, the occasional f-bomb usually got overlooked."

"Oh…" She raises her eyebrows.

The room goes silent. *Have I scared her yet?* Considering I'm currently fantasizing about bending her over the bed and filling her with my cum, she probably should be afraid.

We sit in silence for a long time. Well, almost silence. The tick-tock of the grandfather clock, the crackling of the fire, and the roar of wind outside ward off total awkwardness.

Once I've got the party in my pants mostly under control, I get up to put on another album. I'm unsure what she likes, but my CD collection is limited. So, Johnny Cash it is. I hear the opening strains of "Ring of Fire," and it's relatable in new ways. This woman is burning me alive.

"You still use CDs?"

"I've got a record player, too. I'm a big fan of vinyl. Gives a much fuller, better sound. Besides, the internet's too spotty up here for anything else."

She nods, her face lighting up. "You'd love Amoeba Music in the Haight. It's got an amazing collection of vinyl and CDs."

"No offense, but I don't do big cities. Especially *that* city."

"Really? What do you have against it?"

Years of therapy have barely made the subject broachable. I pause, not wanting to sound like a fucking loser. "My parents died in a car accident there."

She looks down, and the room goes silent.

Definitely *not* the vibe I'm going for. The wind howls, and I feign interest in my CDs, kicking myself for introducing a dark rain cloud. My foster brothers would agree that it's one of my hidden talents.

Finally, I clear my throat, venturing, "We've already slept together and eaten together. Don't you think we should know each other's names?"

She giggles, glancing down at my red apron, which she fingers with her right hand. "I'm Aleksandra Petkova, but people call me Alex."

"Russian?"

"Bulgarian."

"I don't know much about Bulgaria, but I'm guessing you're still a Sasha? Or maybe a Sashenka?"

She nods, a smile lighting up her face. "Mostly Sasha. How do you know about those nicknames?"

"My parents were from Russia."

She nods. "So, what's your name?"

"Maksim Borodin."

Her face beams. "Borodin, like the composer?"

I shrug.

"Nice to meet you, Maksim," she nods, her smile softening.

"What else can I get you?" I'm back in the chair, trying to read her expression.

"May I ask you something?"

"Yes."

"How old were you when your parents died?"

The question makes my stomach knot. My throat tightens, but I manage a gruff "Eight."

Her eyes well with moisture, and it's like a gut punch. I never meant to make her sad. *Nice job, dumbass.*

"It was a long time ago."

"Were you with them in the car when it happened?"

I haven't talked about this much outside of therapy, and my throat feels tight. So does my chest. I rub my hand over my heart instinctively, weighing my words. But it's no use. I can't guarantee a steady voice. I nod instead.

A cold sweat and shivers run down my spine as images and sounds flood my brain again. As real and haunting as the moment they happened. *You should be tougher than this.*

"How did you end up here?"

"I know I don't have cable or a TV, but surely there's got to be something more interesting than my life story."

Our eyes meet, and I feel raw, cut open beneath her gaze. I'm still learning to read her, but the look she gives me could make me tell her anything. She's heroin and truth serum rolled into one.

"After the accident, I got passed around to various family members who had also immigrated to the US. Along the way, I got my fill of Russian culture—both good and bad. But I was a hellion, and none of them could handle me, especially with so many kids of their own. I've got a shit-load of cousins—pardon my French—and I was a bad influence. So, I ended up in foster care. I don't blame them, and honestly, I deserved it. I was a big problem."

She's leaning forward, rapt. Curiously, there's no judgment on her face. I'm uneasy with her undivided attention, but I also can't deny her. I feel like a man sinking into quicksand with no hope of rescue.

I clear my throat, continuing, "Eventually, I ended up here with my dad—foster dad. His ranch, Rough & Ready, was the last stop for foster boys before prison or worse. Thankfully, tough love and plenty of manual labor drilled a little sense into my head."

"Your dad sounds like an amazing man."

"The best. His family has lived on this land for generations. He made a promise to each of us foster sons that if we got our shit together and became decent, hardworking men, we'd always have a home here—"

"Seriously?"

"Yep, ten-acre plots apiece as long as we built our own log cabins, made something of ourselves, and kept up the land."

"You built this?"

"With help from my brothers."

She shakes her head, looking around. "Okay, I so can't wrap my city brain around that. Crazy!"

"Not really. My brother Turner's a custom home builder, so these are a piece of cake for him. And I'm the youngest. I helped build plenty of cabins before this one." I leave out the part about my brothers constructing it small with no doors on the rooms. I'm so antisocial they figured I'd never need privacy, let alone to get laid. And, indeed, I'm a total pain in the ass, but she doesn't need to know that.

"How many brothers do you have?"

"Fourteen"

"And they all live up here by you?"

"All but one."

"Where is he?"

"The state pen." I wait for her face to twist with disgust. But all I see is genuine interest. It's a world away from the woman who accused me of wanting to pawn her cello earlier. To say the least, she has me confused.

"I know Dad holds out hope for him, though. I guess we'll see."

"How old are you?"

"Twenty-four. And you?"

"Twenty-one... No offense, but I would've guessed you're at least in your thirties or something. You feel like an old soul."

I shrug, desperate to get out from under the microscope. "We need a change of subject. You've learned everything remotely interesting about me—and I'm using that word liberally. What's your story?"

I've put her on the spot, and her face shows it. She presses her lips together tightly.

After a couple of minutes, I start for her, "You're a musician..."

"That's pretty much it," she replies stubbornly.

Bullshit! I lean forward, getting comfortable in the chair. I'll sit here all night if that's what it takes to get her to talk.

CHAPTER
SEVEN
ALEX

here to start with my boring life? I finger his apron in both hands, feeling oddly turned on by the fact he had this wrapped around his waist not so long ago. When I look up, he's staring intently at me like a hungry wolf on the hunt.

My voice falters. "There's seriously not much to tell. I've played cello since I was six years old and before that, I played violin. But I didn't have enough natural talent. So, my parents switched me."

His eyes probe me, digging soul-deep.

"Umm… I guess you could say I've disappointed my parents. They invested everything in me, in my musical career, certain that I'd be the next Jacqueline du Pré or something—"

"Who's that?"

"A famous cellist from the 1960s."

He shifts in his chair, his eyes dropping to my fingers.

Without him staring directly at my face, it's easier for me to keep going. "I've had some good moments. Like winning a few big-name solo competitions and debuting with the San Francisco Symphony when I was thirteen." My mind wanders back. I feel the precision of my fingers hammering down on the strings as I execute a nearly flawless performance of the Handel Concerto in C. I still remember my cheeks warming and the ear-to-ear grin that left my mouth trembling as I received a standing ovation.

"I guess you could say I've had a decent solo career, but I honestly feel like I'm going through the motions... And I want more out of my life than the dream that my parents imposed on me. Honestly, I don't know if I'd even be a musician if it wasn't for the relentless push I received as a kid. Sometimes, I feel angry and resentful. I feel like they robbed me of my childhood, and I also feel like I haven't had the chance to make any of my own decisions. It's not that I don't love music, but it was never my choice in the first place."

I search his face, looking for a reaction. At this point in the conversation, most people would scold me, tell me I should feel lucky to play music for a living. But scrutinizing Maksim, all I find is genuine curiosity.

"And then, back in July of last year, I read this scathing review of one of my performances by Lawrence Foster, a Bay Area music critic. And it made me question everything. Let's see if I can remember it... umm... 'It's hard to tell if Ms. Petkova or the audience was more fatigued by the performance. There was no passion, no life. The execution was superb, but the emotion behind it was worse than disappointing... It was DOA—*dead on arrival.*'"

I look down, tears flooding my eyes. I wish Maksim would say something, but he's made it clear he's listening. Finally, I manage, "I shouldn't be talking your ear off like this. But for some reason, I feel comfortable around you."

"Even though I'm a creepy, thieving dimwit?" he teases.

"When you put it that way, it sounds so awful." I shrug. "Sorry about that. I'm not going to play this card twice, but I feel like I deserve a pass today, considering I almost died in a blizzard."

"Truce," he replies, holding out his hand to shake. I love the feel of its warmth and strength and how it makes mine look miniature.

His eyes are on me again, soulful, drawing me out.

"Anyway, I've spent my whole life in practice rooms ... practicing six, eight hours a day. Every day. I feel soulless without my cello, yet I know there's more to life than this... Don't you think?"

"You're asking the wrong person..."

"Actually, I think you're the perfect person to ask. You've got no stakes in the game."

His words pierce me, "I've done very little of value with my life. Let alone anything classified as artistic or beautiful, so I don't know what to tell you. But I do know about sacrifice, thanks to my dad, and all I can say is you'll never get paid back for it in this lifetime, but that doesn't make it any less worthwhile."

"See, that's what I'm talking about. Sacrifice. Touching other people's lives. I've never done that. I can list the number of friends I have on one hand."

He shrugs, smiling. "I don't see a problem with that. I could almost say the same thing if I didn't have so many pain-in-the-ass brothers."

"So, that's it? I'm supposed to stay locked up in the practice room forever?"

He's silent for a long moment, and I can tell he's pondering my words. I've never had anyone listen so intently to me before, and it's both an honor and intimidating.

Finally, he clears his throat. "I think you're selling your-self short. Music is your way of touching people. Of connecting with them. I know *this* brings me joy," he finishes, pointing his thumb over his shoulder towards the CD player where Cash continues belting out tunes. "It just sounds like you need more balance in your life. I imagine you're at the point in your career where you can live a little, get out there, and experience life more?"

"That's the problem. I don't even know where to start. And there are so many people I stand to disappoint along the way." I sink my head in my hands, feeling a sob come on.

The bed settles next to me as he sits down, and he's covered the distance so our bodies touch. He wraps his left arm around me, pulling me close and whispering almost inaudibly in my ear, "It's okay."

I turn into him, resting my head on his chest. I can hear his heart pounding. I smell pine and antelope stew and fresh bread and every good thing about him as he pulls me closer. He can claim he hasn't given the world anything of value, but wrapped in his warm embrace, I know better. His beard tickles my cheek as he presses soft kisses on the crown of my head.

"I keep striking out when it comes to winning solo competitions, and when I do perform... Well, I already told you what that critic said about my frigid playing—"

"Fuck him," Maksim grumbles, and I can feel his voice vibrating through my body. "This is why I like dogs more than most people. Take huskies and malamutes, for instance. Both are bred for endurance in cold weather. They're designed for running and sledding, and they love it. They can't get enough of it. Do they need to be in the Iditarod? Nope. Do they have to prove anything to anyone?

No, they just love what they do and do what they love. End of story."

I feel his warm breath on my cheek, and my body aches, longing to feel his lips on mine...

"I don't know shit about music or virtuosos or any of the stuff you just told me. But I do know you're amazing, Alex, and if that critic can't see that, then fuck him. Life's too short not to love what you're doing or who you're doing it with."

The CD player must be on repeat because we've looped back to "Ring of Fire." His mouth hovers over mine, his eyes burning as his lips close the distance between us. I'm breathless, and my chest pounds. Tension builds between my legs, sending excited shivers from the top of my head to the tips of my toes. My hand comes up, stroking his beard, and a hungry growl escapes his lips.

Cash is singing about descending into the flames, and it couldn't be more fitting as a firestorm of unrestrained desire consumes me.

Suddenly, the music stops, and a shroud of darkness and silence descends over the cabin. The flames in the bedroom fireplace become the immediate focal point, subdued crackling gold and blue embers with gray-and-black char flakes.

Maksim lets go of me, standing abruptly and taking a ragged breath. As my eyes adjust to the faint shimmer of light from the hearth, his face looks stiff and unreadable. He shakes his head and rubs a hand over his face, looking like a man trying to wake up from a daze. He mutters, "Power's gone out. Shit, I've got to go check on the dogs and get the generators going."

"Generators?" The way people prepare for life up here boggles my mind.

He ignores my question, turning on his heel and striding from the room. "No telling how long this power outage will last," he mutters more to himself than me. His head pokes back into the room. "I've got a couple of lanterns I can get out for you, and I'll build the fires back up before I go out."

I sink back into the pillows, trying to catch my breath.

EIGHT

MAKSIM

"Good morning, Sasha," I grumble almost to myself.

I hear the creak of floorboards behind me and the padding of soft footfalls. Out of the corner of my eye, I see Alex wearing a pair of my oversized wool socks and swimming in a black hoodie that looks like a dress.

"You make that look good."

This woman, dressed in my clothes, is almost too much to bear. I shift at the table to conceal the immediate dick action she inspires. My thoughts wander into dangerous territory—visions of her here with me, sharing my bed every night and waking up with me every morning. Her hair disheveled and in my hands, her rosy lips full and pouty. To be the man lucky enough to wake up next to her.

Get a fucking hold of yourself, Maksim.

"You don't look like much of a morning person," I laugh, appreciating her glowing makeup-free face and sleepy expression.

"Too early to talk," she protests, her voice squeaky from sleep.

She heads towards the table, and I'm half convinced she's sleepwalking. Her eyes are two slits, and she has her lips pressed firmly together.

"Coffee?"

"Yes, please."

After filling a stoneware mug, I set it on the table with cream. She doesn't take sugar but adds cream until her coffee is a storm of light brown swirls. She nods after the first sip, apparently okay with my coffee-making skills. When your dad's a cowboy, you better know how to make a good cup of coffee.

She yawns. "When did the power come back on?"

I look up to the right. "I think it was about three thirty this morning. All I know is you were fast asleep." *Shit, will she be freaked out that I checked on her in the night?*

Fortunately, she doesn't miss a beat, agreeing, "Down and out for sure." I thought her hair looked sexy before. But I love it wild and ruffled from sleep. This woman is stunning, and I'm pretty damn sure she has no clue what she does to me.

We sit in silence, accompanied solely by the grandfather clock and fire. And it's a good, comfortable silence. The kind you usually only have with someone you've known for years.

Finally, I stand. "I hope the coffee kicks in quickly because it's time for you to meet the dogs who saved your life."

"Really?" Her face lights up.

"I didn't peg you as a dog person."

Grinning from ear to ear, she exclaims, "I love dogs! I would have one in a heartbeat, but the whole nomadic musician thing isn't conducive to pets. I think dogs like a little more stability."

"Kind of like humans?" *I wish she'd consider a change ... one that includes me.*

She frowns.

"Well, you're welcome to get your dog fix here anytime. And I think you owe them some treats."

She nods emphatically. "Just give me a moment to get dressed. Where are my clothes?" Her face goes red, and I wonder if she's thinking about me undressing her. I know I haven't been able to get her curvy body off my mind.

I head towards the dryer in the mud room. "Be sure to wear a pair of my wool socks, like the ones you've got on. Those flimsy ones you were wearing when I found you are useless."

She shakes her head in frustration. "I wasn't planning on a winter camping expedition in March."

"We've had snow on the Fourth of July. The Sierra Nevadas do whatever they want, whenever they want. You've always got to prepare."

"You sound like my dad," she grumbles as I bring her clothes back into the living room.

"You should borrow one of my scarves and hats, too. These clothes are for the Bay Area, *not* the Tahoe Basin—no matter how you layer them."

"Which makes sense, considering I live in the Bay Area," she snaps back.

"But you're here now, and you need to dress like it." I can't help but smile to myself. There's something adorable about her exasperation.

"Double up on the socks while you're at it. You have to wear a pair of my snow boots. Your sneakers are a recipe for black toes."

"Thanks, *tatko*," she remarks as I hand her a pile of

folded clothes. She heads for the bathroom in the bedroom, the only room with anything approaching privacy.

"Did you seriously just call me *tatko*?" I call after her. Silence. I guess she didn't hear me.

Alex emerges from the bathroom minutes later, covered from head to toe. A huge fur-lined aviator hat sits low on her brow, and she's wound a massive black-and-gray scarf around her neck. Scanning her from head to toe, I can't help but laugh at the wool socks pooled at her ankles. One thing's for sure. She won't freeze on my watch.

"It means 'daddy' in Bulgarian," she replies defiantly.

"You know it means the same thing in Russian, right?"

"*Tatko?*"

"Yes, and you're allowed to call me that anytime," I reply.

She shakes her head.

"That reminds me," I say, raising a finger. I cross the room in three strides, grabbing a pair of ridiculously bulky mittens. "Put these on."

She shakes her head.

"Your loss," I shrug. "It'll just make it that much easier for me to kick your ass when we snowball fight."

Without hesitation, she grabs the gloves from me, smirking. "I thought you were too old and grumpy for stuff like that, Maksimka."

Maksimka. No one has called me that in a long time. My heart warms to the endearment, even as painful memories gnarl themselves tightly in my stomach. "We'll see."

She heads towards the door, striding quickly and giggling to herself. Her thoughts are so transparent right now, and I like it. In her devious mind, the little raven-haired elf is already figuring out how she'll clobber me with fresh-packed snowballs when I cross the threshold. But it's a little more complicated than that, thanks to the blizzard.

I hear her gasp as she opens the door, looking out into a wall of white. I've done my best to carve a snowy ramp for her to climb, and climb she must because the snow has piled up to roof level.

"How is this March?" she questions in amazement.

"Welcome to Rough & Ready Country."

CHAPTER

NINE

ALEX

The snow's so deep that Maksim carved a pathway to the surface. I'm wearing his massive boots with a couple layers of woolen socks and snowshoes strapped to my feet, making the effort of walking ridiculous.

But my breath catches in wonder once I'm out of the snowbank around his cabin. Layers of ice and snow trim the trees, and the powdery ground glows like diamonds where rays of sunlight pierce the white atmosphere. Fog and gently swirling powder cushion the air, creating a pristine silence as traces of last night's blizzard evaporate. It's like something out of a picture book or Hallmark card. I didn't know this kind of beauty existed.

My exhales produce great puffs of white. "How can it be foggy and snowy at the same time?"

"Natives call it pogonip," he replies, taking powerful strides in his snowshoes.

"Pogonip?" I shuffle behind him, balancing tentatively. Somewhere across the frozen plains of this surreal world, my shoes remain locked in the trunk of my SUV.

"Frozen fog. It's not good for lungs. So I try not to run the dogs in it."

I look at him with trepidation. "Should we avoid breathing it, too?"

"Dunno. It's mostly the dogs I worry about."

"You talk about dogs the way I talk about cellos."

I wrap his scarf over my mouth to keep out the pogo—*whatever*—falling behind. Now, I struggle to catch up. He pauses for a moment, his face tense. In the distance, I hear barking.

"You may have a point," he concedes.

We head down another snowy tunnel to a door reading Sierra Husky Rescue. The barking and howling intensify as he opens the door, and a flood of memories crashes into me. Cold air on my face. Piled under blankets. A man's low voice calling commands and more dogs than I've ever heard in one place—apart from the Humane Society.

"It's a shame," I call over the canine chorus.

"What is?" Maksim shouts back.

"That I can barely remember the most exciting thing that's ever happened to me."

He turns quickly, "And what's that?"

"Riding on your dog sled and getting saved by you and your dogs, of course!"

He looks flabbergasted, scolding, "You really do need to get out more."

I ignore his tone, continuing, "I was obsessed with Jack London and Gary Paulsen books as a kid. I dreamed of moving to Alaska and going on some big dog sledding adventure. Crazy to think it finally happened—in California, of all places! I just wish I remembered it better..."

He nods, his lips curling up at the corners.

Neatly kept kennels segregate each dog. I can only

imagine how much time he devotes to keeping them clean and dry, especially when they're snowbound like this.

"How many are there?"

"I've got over 50 adults and six puppies. Wish I could take more. It's insane how many huskies get left in shelters —many kill shelters. Same goes for malamutes, which I started taking last year. They demand a lot of work and hours of daily exercise. Most people can't handle it. So, when they end up in a shelter, in a small cage all day, they lose their shit and get aggressive. Many meet a bad end."

"That's so sad."

He grabs my ungloved hand, interlacing his fingers with mine, and I let out an involuntary sigh. A wonderful warmth fills my body as he leads me around to meet each dog.

"How do you do it all alone?"

"I don't. I have a couple of employees and some volunteers. I offer winter dog sledding expeditions to adventurous tourists to help raise money for the shelter, and we do special events throughout the year. My parents left me a decent inheritance, which also helped me get this off the ground."

"How do you exercise them in this weather?"

"Once the fog clears, we'll return to sledding, training, and enjoying the snow. The dogs have been loving this winter."

"Would you take me for a sled ride? When the fog clears?"

Something washes over his face that I can't read. "Maybe." His voice sounds steely, but he grips my hand more tightly.

We walk the entire length of the kennel slowly. He rattles off each dog's name, sled dog role, and any competitions they've been in. I'm especially impressed by the Iditarod racers in the bunch.

Kaya is my absolute favorite. After all, she saved my life, so I shower her in as much jerky as Maksim will let me give her. Besides being a hero, she's also super affectionate and inquisitive. She licks my cheeks, nuzzling into my shoulder with her head when I kneel to pet her. I'd stay with Kaya for the rest of the day, but we still have puppies to meet.

I wrinkle my nose as I squat down, cooing at the husky puppies he mentioned earlier. They waddle around their gray, black, and white mother, wagging their tails and wrestling with each other clumsily. They're tiny fluff balls with squeaky little barks and piercing eyes, and I can't get enough of them. I could spend the entire afternoon playing with them.

"Their eyes are stunning!"

He laughs, "They're the same color as yours, you know."

I take a second look. "You're quite the romantic," I tease over my shoulder. "Telling a girl she's got eyes like a dog."

"Not just any dog. My *favorite* dogs," he corrects.

"So, you breed huskies, too?" I ask, motioning towards the puppies.

Maksim shakes his head. "No, Molly's a rescue from Sacramento. I don't usually deal with puppies, but her situation proved desperate, and fortunately, I had extra room."

Grabbing a couple of metal chairs propped against the building wall, he unfolds one, motioning me to sit. Then, he follows suit, half picking up Molly to pet her vigorously before giving her treats.

He drops a handful of jerky into my cupped palms, and I'm disappointed at the care he takes to avoid touching my skin. *See, Alex, he's just not that into you.*

"They're weaned now, so treats are fine. Just make sure

you break those up into bite-sized chunks so they don't choke."

Molly's got her head resting on his knee as he reaches down to grab one tiny gray-and-white fuzzball speckled with small black spots. He laughs as the little guy squeals and climbs around in his hands. "This one was the runt, if you can believe that. I named him *Kroshechnyy*, but he's gotten so fat and big I probably need to rethink it."

"*Kroshechnyy?* Does that mean 'small' in Russian?"

"It means 'tiny.' How would you say it in Bulgarian?"

"*Munichuk.*"

He nods, petting the pup in his lap and talking to him.

I feel like a voyeur staring into a forbidden world. Who would've guessed puppies could have this kind of effect on a grumpy mountain man?

I bet he'd make a good dad, too. I catch myself, fighting the urge to gasp. Why am I even thinking this way? My face burns. Fortunately, he's busy putting the puppy down and grabbing another nearly all black one.

His voice is warm and affectionate as he talks to each one. And I can't help but chuckle at his long conversations with them.

"Why are you laughing?" he asks, looking up at me as he sets another little one down.

"You're a lot nicer to dogs than people, Maksimka."

He grimaces.

"Should I not call you that?"

"No, it's fine," he replies, rubbing his chest with his right hand. "You must think I'm crazy talking to them like this, but they're smart animals. They pick up on a lot. Honestly, I get along better with them than most people."

I nod.

He side-eyes me, "You might be the exception."

"Must be my dog eyes," I tease.

I don't know how long we play with the puppies. But Maksim has to pull me away, literally. He grabs my hand, squeezing it, and leads me back out of the kennel. He helps me buckle the snowshoes on before I climb the pathway again.

As I follow the tracks we made earlier back towards the cabin, a powdery snowball whooshes into the back of my neck. I turn and take one straight to the face.

"Oh, shit," Maksim exclaims, crossing the distance between us to wipe the powder from my face. "I didn't expect you to turn like that."

But it's game on now. As soon as he finishes brushing my cheeks, I scramble to pack a retaliatory ball of powder.

I launch it in his direction, but he dodges expertly atop his snowshoes. Then, I try another and another. But he's fast and has better balance than I probably ever will. Not to be outdone, I finally land a lucky shot to the side of his face, nearly tumbling backward into the countless feet of powdery snow.

"No falling, Sasha," he warns, gripping my arm to steady me. "Or I'll be digging you out for days."

Maksim's eyes dance with uncharacteristic amusement before going serious again. He removes a glove, reaching forward to tuck a loose strand of hair behind my ear.

I blush as thoughts of last night's near-kiss float through my mind. I'm staring at his lips, and I can't stop myself. I want him so badly.

"Look," he says, pointing towards the horizon.

The frozen fog has dissipated, replaced by a stunning pastel sunset, a study in degrees of vibrant gold and orange, hot pink and rich periwinkle. The Sierra Nevada Mountains stand out in rugged contrast, white and bulging with snow, punctuated by patches of navy blue forest.

"It's beautiful!" I exclaim, keenly aware of the inadequacy of my words.

Maksim stands next to me, his shoulder touching mine. He swallows hard, capturing my eyes with a soulful gaze. "Not as beautiful as you."

I look down, bashfully, not sure how to respond. But it doesn't matter because he doesn't wait for an answer. Instead, he wraps his arms around my waist, pulling me into him. He widens his stance so my snowshoes can fit between his, leaning towards me. I can feel the heat from his body.

He confesses breathlessly, "I can't stop thinking about what might have happened ... if the power hadn't gone out."

Without hesitation, his mouth ravages mine, and his arms pull me against his hard planes, bringing me to my tiptoes. I hope he won't let go because there's no way I'll keep my balance between the snowshoes and his boots. They're so big, I fear he might pick me up and right out of them. I sigh into his warmth, my core tightening with an undefinable ache.

I haven't been picked up much because I'm a curvy girl. But he makes it seem effortless. His lips devour mine, and I let out a sigh as delicious shivers quake through my arms and legs, centering tightly in my lower stomach.

Taking advantage of my relaxed lips, his tongue sweeps into my mouth, claiming me. I have a knot in my throat. My heart thumps against my ribs, and I can no longer catch my breath. I only know one thing: I'm greedy for more of him.

My tongue tentatively explores his in return, and he growls, angling his head to deepen the kiss. My feet are out of the boots and entirely off the ground now, and his hands are on my hips, pulling me into his hard arousal. I wrap my legs around his waist and my arms around his neck, letting my hands run through his thick golden hair. His beard tickles my cheeks.

But as quickly as he starts, Maksim stops. He lets my body drag down him as he gently places me back on the ground and into his boots. I feel his hard rod against my stomach and gasp. Unfazed, he presses me in for a long bear hug. I'm flushed and panting hard, pleased to know his body reacts to me the way mine does to him.

He lets go of me, stepping to the side and interlacing his fingers with mine. Leading me back towards the cabin, he clutches me tightly. My body glows, anticipating the scene to come in the cabin.

But he stops before the shoveled-out tunnel. "You better go inside."

I open my mouth to protest. But he cuts me off. "It wasn't that long ago you almost froze to death. I'm not taking any chances with you. Get inside and warm up. There's more stew and bread in the fridge, so help yourself. And there are some towels in the bathroom if you'd like a shower. I've got to clear the roofs and chimney, but I'll be in shortly."

INSIDE THE CABIN, I'm on cloud nine, reliving the kiss. I'm floating as I slip out of his boots and snowshoes and dance around the living room, feeling deliciously alive and desired. Neither are feelings I'm used to. After returning to Earth, I heat some stew and toast a couple of slices of bread.

I feel unhinged, waiting for him. So, I finally muster the

nerve to examine my cello. My stomach churns as I unbuckle the case, terrified I'll find snapped strings and a fallen soundpost. Thankfully, my imagination errs. I don't see any obvious issues, cracks, or damage. But I hold off playing, wanting a luthier's examination first.

After taking a long, hot shower where I clean everything but dirty thoughts of Maksim from my mind, I sack his bathroom, searching for a razor. A razor in a bearded man's house. Good luck! But I finally find one, still in the packaging, along with a new toothbrush and some toothpaste. Happily, no signs of female life turn up. No tampons or perfume or anything else that would throw me into a jealous spiral. *Do I have a right to feel jealous?* Of course, not. But there's a lot I can't explain about the current situation.

Seven thirty rolls around, and still no Maksim. *Didn't he say he'd be right behind me?* Maybe he didn't find the kiss as earth-shattering as I did. Maybe I did something wrong. I have limited experience with men, after all. Worry twists my stomach, and I'm frantic for his presence, his reassurance.

I finger a black cowboy hat hanging on the hook by the front door, wondering if he wears it during the summer. Below it, I notice a couple of pairs of well-worn, leather-tooled cowboy boots. The thought of Maksim transforming into a summer cowboy makes my body simmer.

I walk around the cabin living room, checking his bookshelves. I find everything from Joseph Conrad to Mark Twain, Ernest Hemingway, and lots of Space Operas. He's also got every book ever written by Jack London and Gary Paulsen. I can't help but giggle as I thumb through a dog-eared copy of *Call of the Wild* with pencil notes in the margin, in the scrawling handwriting of a little boy. Clearly, I wasn't the only kid obsessed with Alaskan adventure.

A thick layer of dust covers the bookshelves, and I run my fingers along one, discovering two photos laid flat. I blow the dust away, staring at an image of a scowling preteen Maksim in a cowboy hat surrounded by fourteen other boys. I take his face in for a long moment. It's strange looking at him without a beard. He's adorable with his strong chin, tousled hair, and glowering eyes. I guess he's always been grumpy. The group looks like the Lost Boys. A second, older black-and-white photo shows a man on an Appaloosa who must be their dad. He's smiling and looks like a kind man.

I decide to dust for Maksim. His place could sure use it. This leads to my discovery of his vinyl collection. I'm shocked to find Tchaikovsky, Shostakovich, Beethoven, Mozart, and more in his stash. Why hasn't he told me he listens to classical music? I'm ready to ambush him with the question the moment he walks through the door. But the tick tock of the clock continues with no sign of him. I finally heat up some supper, resigning myself to eating alone.

By nine, I'm crashing hard. I may have slept in this morning, but I still feel bone tired from the past few days. I might as well take a nap as I wait for Maksim. After all, the cabin's getting colder as the fires die down. I'm unsure where the thermostat is or whether he wants me to feed the fires. He can figure it out when he gets back. Lying down feels fantastic, but not nearly as amazing as Maksim's kiss. I replay it in my mind, touching my fingers to my lips.

CHAPTER
TEN
MAKSIM

I've lied to Alex twice now, and I feel like a low life. First, I claimed I didn't enjoy being in bed with her. Talk about a load of bullshit. And then I said I'd be in as soon as I cleared the roofs and the chimney. I meant it, too. But, as I worked, dark, tangled thoughts filled my head —thoughts I didn't want to bring around her.

Alex is like an addiction. She's in every thought I have, and the more time I spend with her, the less I can imagine life without her. How can this be possible when I barely know her? I have to find a way to stop this before things get any messier. What would a high-class classical musician do with a loser like me, anyway? Eventually, she'd leave. End of story. Only for me, it'd be the beginning of a whole world of hurt.

Alex will leave. She'll go at the first sign of snow melt. You can't do a thing about it. Just like you couldn't save your parents or sister. Talking with Alex about the accident has opened a Pandora's Box of memories. And it sucks.

I didn't tell her everything. Like how I begged my parents to take me ice skating that day. I was a selfish little brat who wouldn't take no for an answer, and that's what got us in the accident. And I couldn't tell her my mother was pregnant with my baby sister. I was going to meet her in a month or so, and we already had her name picked out, Anya. But she died in the crash, too.

Fuck, why does life have to hurt so much?

I should be grateful for what I have—foster brothers and a dad loyal to a fault. But a part of me still questions why I survived the accident. How does it make any sense? Out of everyone in my family, the one who caused the accident made it out with mere bruises and scrapes.

Countless therapists have told me the accident wasn't my fault. And I remember just as many talks with Dad about how shit happens. It doesn't have to make sense and probably never will. As a Vietnam vet, he knows survivor guilt better than anyone. But he also understands how shit can haunt you, despite reason or logic, until you're so mad at the world you have to do something. Lash out, no matter how reckless it looks to others.

The only thing that helps when thoughts like this enter my head is work. So, I clear the roofs and chimney and then spend hours cleaning the kennels and doing minor maintenance jobs that can wait. Except I don't want them to wait because I need to clear my head and regain some perspective.

Eventually, I sit in Kaya's kennel, petting her and talking out loud, "I'm just not cut out for relationships, and there's no denying Alex is a relationship kind of girl. She deserves better than I could ever possibly give her. I can't do this shit. I hurt everything I touch, and hurting her would destroy me." I think huskies understand more than most people realize. Kaya confirms this by burrowing her head between my arms and whining.

THE CABIN IS FREEZING when I finally get back inside, and I throw a couple of logs on the living room fire to bring it back to life. The clock reads nine thirty. No wonder I feel frigid.

I rub my hands together, breathing into my palms as tremors run through my core.

Alex has every blanket my cabin's ever owned, so I sit on the couch, rocking back and forth with my hands under my armpits. Despite the flames licking over the new logs, my teeth chatter. I head into the bedroom to grab a sweater. I should be quieter, but I feel irked about sneaking around my own cabin. I've got to get this woman out of my life and fast.

"Are you okay, Maksim?"

"Yes. Go back to sleep, Aleksandra."

I hear the blankets shift, and I can feel her looking in my direction even though the bedroom fireplace has died down to burnished cinders, and I can't see her face.

"Are you angry?" she asks.

"No, are you?"

"No, but I did get worried when you didn't make it in for dinner. Your soup's in a bowl in the fridge."

"I'm not hungry."

"Okay, it'll be there for you tomorrow, then. You must be freezing. Come get in bed," she orders.

My pulse spikes despite the cold still gripping my core. "No, I'll be fine. I just need a sweater."

"Come get in bed. It's the fastest way to warm up, and it's not like you wouldn't do the same for me."

She doesn't know what she's asking. I shift my weight

thoughtfully, trying to assess how long I can lie next to her before I incinerate.

"Come on," she repeats, and all the second thoughts and doubts ricocheting through my head vanish in the allure of her sexy voice. I need her more than I've ever needed anyone. Pain and loss feel distant, irrelevant in her presence.

I clamor out of my freezing clothes, shivering against the frosty bedroom air. I should build the bedroom fire back up or adjust the thermostat. But all I can think about is getting her curvy body under my hands.

I climb into bed beside her, wearing nothing more than boxer briefs. Grabbing onto her ample hips, I press her into me with a satisfied groan.

Fuck me! She's wearing nothing but her lacy bra and panties. I'm a goner now.

"Geez!" she cries.

I wrap my arms around her, keeping her from flying out of bed.

"You're freezing!"

"I know," I growl, teeth chattering in her ear. "Remember, I'm returning the favor."

After a few tense minutes, she quits arching away from me. I hear her let out a ragged sigh as she settles into me, surrendering to the process. Instantly, my arteries and veins burn with lust for her.

"How long were you out there?" she asks, tensing as I wrap my cold leg over her hip, drawing her ass against me. My cold feet nearly send her scrambling away again.

"Dunno," I reply, snuggling into her soft, curvy body. She's hot in every imaginable way, and I'm warming up a whole helluva lot faster than she did a couple of days ago.

That also means my cock has a mind of its own, and before I know it, it's rock hard and pressed into her back.

"Sorry," I whisper.

She swallows hard. "Don't apologize." Lacing her fingers through mine, she pulls me closer as my heart thumps. My knuckles graze over her chest, and my breath catches in my throat as my fingertips brush over her pearled nipples. I feel like my heart will explode along with my self-control.

"Sasha?" I pant.

"Yes," she replies softly.

I want to tell her how much she already means to me. Forbid her from leaving me ... *ever*. But I'm nervous I'll scare her. Instead, I relish the silence ... the feel of her warm flesh on mine, as I listen to her breathing relax.

Finally, I start, "I need to tell you something."

"Okay." Her voice is relaxed and sexy as hell.

I swallow the lump in my throat, trying to concentrate. "You remember yesterday when I told you I didn't like lying next to you? Well, that wasn't exactly true. Honestly, it was fucking fantastic. I didn't mean to lie, but I didn't want to come off as a creep."

She sighs softly, snuggling back into me. "While we're on the subject of confessions, I have to admit I snooped around your cabin tonight."

"That's fine. I have nothing to hide."

Yawning, she asks, "The vinyl collection. It's yours, right?"

I nod.

"Why didn't you tell me you listen to classical music?"

"You didn't ask," I reply with a shrug. "With a last name like Borodin, how could I not?"

"Then, you are related to the composer?" She cranes her neck in my direction.

"Only very distantly. I'm not even exactly sure how because I can't ask my parents. But I do remember my family mentioning it."

"Why didn't you say yes when I asked you about it before?"

I feel uncomfortable talking about my family and my last name. How do I make her understand that? Finally, I reply, "Because I see family differently than most people. It's not sealed by blood. It's made through love and loyalty. Wyatt's the closest thing I have to a dad, and I lost contact with my bio family a long time ago. I feel no connection to them, although I do miss my parents. Honestly, does my relationship to some stuffy old composer really matter?"

Her reply, if there is one, is inaudible. She's silent for a long time. I feel her body relaxing, and I'm torn about saying anything else. But I have to get this off my chest. "There's one more thing..."

"Yes?"

"After the kiss ... I had to clear my head. That's why I didn't come in. I can't trust myself around you."

She says something I can't make out, and I realize she's falling asleep.

Despite the racing pulse and hard cock, I finally manage to pass out.

MORNING WOOD AWAKENS me in agony. I've got to get out of here. Between the lack of sleep and temptation overload, my self-control hangs by one tattered thread.

But her grip tightens on me. "Where are you going?"

I run my hands through her silky black locks, shuddering. "I can't take this anymore," I explain huskily. "I've got to get out of here."

Her left arm comes up, palming my chest, and her elbow brushes against my hard dick in the process, sending throbbing waves of desire through me. I need a release so badly I grit my teeth together.

"Stay here with me."

"You don't know what you're asking for."

"I may be a virgin, but I'm not a nun," she replies.

Suddenly, she squints her eyes shut.

"What?"

She opens one eye. "You must think I'm such a loser. A twenty-one-year-old virgin. See, I told you I've never been outside a practice room."

The confession crashes into me. I have to claim her. I have to make her mine and then find a way to keep her. No matter what it takes.

She fills an emptiness in me I didn't even know existed. She breathes life into my world and makes me want to be a better man. The kind of man that deserves her.

A foster kid delinquent and a virtuoso cellist may not make sense on any rational level. But I'm not feeling especially rational right now. I must have her. No matter how selfish it makes me. I have little to offer, but I can guarantee one thing. I'll stop at nothing to make her happy.

I bring my hand up to her cheek, taking her beautiful face in for a long moment before confessing, "As a twenty-four-year-old virgin, I don't have much room to talk."

"Seriously?" her eyes round, and I swallow loudly, trying to gauge her reaction. Her hand finishes its molten path up my body, coming to rest on my bearded cheek.

"How is that possible? I mean, you're so hot. I bet the girls throw themselves at you."

I laugh at how wrong she's got it. "It's a small town, Alex. Hard to get away from my past, and most people here know every gory detail. How do I put this? I was the guy who pulled fire alarms and put stink bombs in the bathroom. *Not exactly boyfriend material.*"

"Well, they better continue leaving you alone," she replies, and I swear she sounds jealous.

I wrap my hand in her hair, drawing her possessively towards me for a kiss. She returns it passionately, and my cock tents even harder in my shorts. I close my eyes, concentrating hard on not coming. Between clenched teeth, I say, "Either let me go or let me have you—*all of you*. I can't take this in-between shit a second longer."

CHAPTER
ELEVEN
ALEX

My breath catches in my throat. "I want you, Maksim. More than I've ever wanted anyone."

With one efficient move, he pulls me on top of him, and I feel his hardness on my stomach. I exhale in shock. He's huge.

"What's wrong?" he demands, his lips tracing sparks down my neck. His hands rove across my body, squeezing my ass as he grinds into me. I gasp, and he lets out a frantic groan.

I prop myself up on my arm, stealing a look down at his tented boxer briefs. "How is *that* going to work?"

"We'll figure it out." He sighs, pulling me back down into him. His tongue and lips tease my collarbone until my whole body shivers. Flames lick my neck and shoulders where he tastes me.

I shudder, arching back, and he closes the space between us. His mouth takes in my breast, and he teases the nipple with his tongue and teeth through the satin and lace. I gasp, savoring the exquisite feel of his hot, wet mouth.

He fumbles with my bra, his large hands clumsily fighting the clasp. Finally, he laughs, giving up. "It's like a chastity belt or something. How do you make *that* work?"

My left hand comes up, unfastening the black satin with one astute move, and his eyes darken as my bra sinks between us. "You're so beautiful, Alex."

His large hands cover me, passing hot palms over my flesh, and his mouth takes in the other nipple, flooding my body with white-hot, burning need. I'm moaning and bucking under his mouth, and he turns so he's on top now and in complete control, holding me in place as he covers my body with kisses. "You taste so fucking good."

Another moan rips through me as the pressure in my wet panties continues to build. Maksim's hands come down to my waist, squeezing my hips as I arch against his mouth, still teasing my breasts. The world feels hazy and far away. The only thing clear is the bliss he's filling me with.

He smiles a boyish grin, asking, "You like that?"

"Yes!"

His head bows towards my nipples again, and his hands sink into the waistband of my underwear as he growls into me.

"I need more of you," he exclaims, frustration etched in his face. "I need to taste all of you."

The spot at the top of my thighs tightens, surging with heat. He crawls down my body, kissing every inch of me until flames radiate from my core. I've never had anybody touch me this way, and I'm afraid my body won't please him, that I won't please him. I've been told my whole life I'm too fat, too curvy.

But my fear melts away in the devilish look on his face. He brings his hand to the waistband of my panties, pulling

them down to my ankles and onto the floor with one efficient sweep of his arm. "Much easier than the bra," he
teases.

My heart pounds as I focus on the contrasting sensations of cold air and fire hot hands on my inner thighs,
claiming places no one has ever touched. When his hands
reach the dampness between my legs, I moan.

So does he. "Fuck, you're so ready for me, baby."

He parts my legs with his large shoulders, draping my
right leg over his body. Tracing kisses up my left thigh
towards my aroused core, he ratchets the tension in my
lower body until I'm gasping for air. Desperate for release, I
plead, "I want you inside of me, Maksim."

Exhaling raggedly, he whispers, "I know, baby. But I've
got to get you ready first. Pleasing you will always come
first."

His lips hover over my pussy, and I can feel his hot
breath teasing me. My hips dart towards him reflexively,
and he scolds, "Patience." Then, he turns to my right thigh,
torturing me with every brush of his lips and swipe of his
tongue. I'm out of my mind with arousal as his fingers find
their way to my pussy lips.

More beast than man, he grinds his hips into the
mattress. "Sasha, I need you so bad. So fucking bad."

His fingers slide through my wet folds, making my hips
move erratically back and forth. I need some kind of release,
but I don't know how or what. His hot tongue covers my
clit, and I let out a visceral sigh. My hips push up towards
him, and he responds with a hungry growl, licking and
sucking and nipping at me.

"There's no way you're a virgin," I pant, pulling myself
onto my elbows and looking towards him.

He laughs between my legs, his low voice vibrating

ENGRID EAVES

through my core. "I am a virgin. But that doesn't mean I haven't done my research. Am I doing okay?"

"Yes!" I scream as he goes back to teasing my pearl. His finger crashes in and out of me, and he adds a second, causing me to squirm. His other arm wraps around my waist, and he holds me down as the intensity of his touch leads me nearly over the edge. I'm climbing higher and higher as his fiery tongue traces circles on my clit. I can't take anymore.

"Come for me, baby, please," he implores, and I skitter over the top of whatever this feeling is, my hips crashing and shuddering into his hand as he alternates between sucking and flicking me with his tongue.

CHAPTER

TWELVE

MAKSIM

The light of early morning dances over her sexy curves and her ebony hair feathered out on my pillows as I scramble out of my boxers.

I know I'm repeating myself, but I can't help it. "You're the most beautiful thing I've ever seen," I whisper, barely hiding the emotion in my voice.

I feel like I could fucking cry just looking at her. "I don't know how we're going to make San Francisco and Rough & Ready work yet, but I'm never letting you leave me. You understand?"

I expect to see fear or concern in her face, but she smiles, reaching towards me with her arms. Her legs are still parted and wet with arousal. I hesitate, wrapping my fingers around the base of my rod and closing my eyes in concentration.

I'm about to spill my load, and I don't want to do that to her. I also don't want to hurt her by taking her too quickly. Thinking better of it, I change positions lying back into the mound of blankets behind us.

"As much as I'd like to be in charge of this next part—"

Stretching out my legs, I bid her climb onto me with the hand not holding my cock. "It might be better if I let you take me at your own pace. But promise me you won't stop until we're one."

Her hooded eyes cloud with worry. She swallows hard, and I encourage her to straddle me.

"I'm not on the pill," she says quietly. "Do you have a condom?"

Shit. "No, I don't." I let out a heavy sigh. "I wasn't expecting this, you know."

Her face looks torn as she hovers her wet pink center over me, teasing my cock with her juicy opening. I'm still clutching the base of my rod, trying to slow my progress, moments away from spilling everything.

Why do we need a condom anyway? We're both clean, obviously, and didn't she hear what I said?

Between gritted teeth, I say, "I'm fucking serious when I say you're staying with me, Sasha. Whatever it takes. And you're having my babies, so don't worry about that shit. Now quit teasing me, and make love to me."

"Do you mean it, Maksim? Are you sure about me—about us?"

"I've never been more sure about anything in my life. I want you with me forever, Sasha. I know we've only known each other for a few days, but I can't imagine my life without you. And I'll do whatever it takes to make sure you feel the same way."

"I already do," she replies softly.

Letting out a heavy sigh, she leans forward resting her forehead on mine. My hands come up masterfully grabbing her hips.

"Are you ready?"

She nods confidently, and I slowly guide her down over

me. I shudder at the tightness and wetness of her hot body, and it takes everything not to explode instantly.

But it's not time yet. I grasp her hips tightly, getting a slow rhythm going and ignoring the scowl she gives me each time I push a little deeper.

"You promised you'd give me everything," I remind her as I put more pressure on her hips, and she bites her lower lip, wincing.

Her breasts dance as her hips roll over me, perfect pink-tipped ivory globes. I lean forward taking her nipple in my mouth to distract her as I crash deeper into her.

She's resisting now, and I know it's going to hurt, but I need to be inside her ... *all the way.* She feels like warm velvet, and I'm losing myself in her heat. I can't think straight. All I know is I have to make her mine forever. I won't settle for anything less.

She moans, relaxing slightly as my tongue flicks her rosy nipple before sucking it into my mouth. I use the moment to pull deeper into her. She gasps.

"Look at me," I growl. Our eyes lock, and I'm so close to coming inside her, I can't hold on much longer. With another thrust and pull of her hips, I'm buried completely inside her, feeling her pussy grip me to the point of pain.

Her fingernails scratch into my back as she orgasms again. I relish the marks she leaves on me, ready to wear them with pride. I plunge again and again, her hot walls spasming around me. Unable to hold back any longer, I fill her with a visceral shout.

We collapse onto the bed together, and I wrap my large frame around her as our breaths slow and sync. I stroke her silky black hair, marveling at its lustrous glow in the dim light and hoping our babies will have her beautiful curls.

It might freak her out since we've only just met, but I'd

give anything for my seed to find its mark right now, filling her belly with our first baby. I want everything with this woman—*without hesitation*. I want the family that got taken away from me as a kid, and to add to the family I found later with my dad and brothers.

"This may be too soon to say, but I love you, Sasha."

She pulls my arms more tightly around her, and I kiss her neck and cheek never wanting this moment to end. "I love you, too, Maksimka."

THIRTEEN

Boom! I nearly jump out of bed hearing my cabin door crash open. My brothers Christian and Logan talk loudly as they stomp into the living room.

"Oh, Maxie," Logan calls out in his annoying older brother voice. "Somebody hasn't been answering their satellite phone."

If ever there was a time I wish my bedroom had a door, it's now. Before I can say a thing, they burst into the room, their jaws dropping to the floor.

"Have you ever heard of a thing called privacy?" I ask darkly. Alex is sitting up in bed next to me, trembling and hanging her head as she covers her breasts with a blanket.

Christian is the first to speak. "No way, Max! You finally managed to get laid."

"Fuck!" I exhale, feeling angrier by the second.

Alex looks up at me, her face beet red and filled with countless questions.

Logan exclaims, pointing his finger at her, "I've been looking for you!"

Christian's and Logan's eyes burn a hole through Alex as she asks in a shaky voice, "Looking for me?"

I frown, rubbing my hand over my heart. *I knew this was too good to last.*

"Yes, missy, we've been looking for you for more than twenty-four hours now. There's a CLEAR Alert out on you. People were starting to fear the worst," Logan replies, running his hands through his hair and eyeballing me fiercely.

Christian shakes his head. "Fuck, Maksim, you've got yourself in quite a predicament here."

"What do you mean? I haven't done anything wrong."

"Well, you'll have to explain that to Sheriff Colletti and quite possibly the FBI. This went from a missing person's case to a possible kidnapping last night after we found Ms. Petkova's car."

"Kidnapping?" Alex gasps. "You've got it all wrong. Maksim saved my life!"

"Well, what else were we going to conclude with a broken driver side window, missing cello, and no trace of you?" Christian counters.

I let my head fall back in frustration, sighing loudly. I knew the damn window would come back to haunt me. Never thought the cello would, too, though. No good deed goes unpunished. "I had to break the window to get Alex out. She locked herself inside during the blizzard and was hypothermic."

Alex nods and starts to speak, but Logan cuts her off, exploding back at me, "And your next logical step was to bring her back to your place and fuck?"

If I wasn't naked, I'd be out of bed with my brother by the shirt collar for calling what Alex and I did earlier "fucking." Next to me, Alex buries her head.

Logan looks down, shaking his head. "And why haven't you been answering your sat phone? Or using it to call for help? We've torn Rough & Ready apart looking for her."

I growl, "I left it in my truck and didn't want to dig it out. There's a good ten feet of snow out there!"

"So, instead you let us launch a multi-county missing person's search on the taxpayer's dime?" Christian's face has gone from calm to agitated.

"We didn't know anyone was searching for me," Alex interjects in a breathy tone. But then she looks at me confused, "Why didn't you tell me you had a satellite phone? We could've called people to let them know I was okay."

I shrug, kicking myself for my foolishness. "I had other things on my mind," I grumble, my cheeks burning. That's what I get for days spent thinking with my cock instead of my brain.

Logan stares at the ground, his face unreadable and his fists clenched at his sides.

Alex continues, "I had no idea people would start searching for me so soon. All I knew is Maksim couldn't get a signal because of the blizzard, and my cell phone is still somewhere in my car. I'm sorry."

Christian retorts, "Ms. Petkova, what do you think happens when a person goes missing in a blizzard? And a famous one, to boot!"

I glance sideways at Alex, and she shakes her head. "I wouldn't say famous but, yes, well-known in the classical music world."

My stomach knots.

"You should've checked your fucking sat phone," Logan declares, shaking his fist at me. "Me and my search and rescue crew haven't slept in more than a day trying to find

Ms. Petkova. We've covered dangerous terrain and risked our necks for what? So, you could play lover boy uninterrupted?"

Alex argues, "It's all my fault—"

But Logan cuts her off, turning to me. "There's something I'm not understanding. Why couldn't you retrieve Ms. Petkova's cell phone when you got her and her cello out of the car?"

I reply angrily, "I kind of had my hands full when I found her, and I was racing against another storm. We barely made it back to the cabin. It was a total white-out. I couldn't see shit. I had to leave navigating to the dogs."

"The dogs?" Logan asks.

Nodding, I fill in, "Yeah, I was out training the dogs when I found her. It was actually Kaya that stopped and started digging for her car."

"Really?" For one moment, Logan's face shifts from angry to vindicated. "I told you she'd make a good avalanche rescue dog."

"Yeah, but you've fucking ruined her as a lead dog," I mumble.

Christian butts in. "Can we get back to the matter at hand? While Logan has a good point about Ms. Petkova's cell phone, it wouldn't have mattered anyway. The cell phone tower's been out for days, thanks to this weather. But the sat phone? Either you were being lazy, Max, or you had pussy on your mind."

Fuck all. I glower, crossing my arms.

"I think we know the answer to that," Logan says, glaring at me, and the room goes silent.

Finally, Christian orders, "Ms. Petkova, I hope you're ready to straighten this whole mess out because there are a lot of people at the Sheriff's Department wanting answers.

And anything else you need to say, Maksim, should be said under the advice of legal counsel. Now, both of you hurry up and get dressed. We'll be outside making phone calls."

Christian, clean cut with dark blond hair and a crisp tan-and-black sheriff's uniform, strides out of the room. Logan follows behind, stroking his well-trimmed black beard pensively.

Alex's face is still the color of one of my burgundy blankets, and we dress in silence. I'm too pissed to talk, and I think she's too mortified. I glance over at her, disappointed she's back to wearing her own clothes. I liked seeing her in my oversized hoodies and shirts. Her eyes search my face, and I don't begin to know what to say. She looks like she could burst into tears, and I feel like I could punch a wall.

Finally, I say softly, "Well, you just got to meet two of my foster brothers."

She nods, looking pleadingly at me. She wants me to say something, but I don't know what.

The front door squeals open again, and Logan calls inside, "You two ready?"

I grab one of my hoodies and hand it to Alex. "Wear this. It's freezing outside." She nods, staring at me breathlessly.

She opens her mouth to speak—

At the same instant, Logan stomps back into the room, and she presses her lips into a thin line. He orders, "Come on, you two. Let's go get this handled." He's carrying her cello in the white case. "Ms. Petkova, do you have any other belongings we need to grab?"

I'm ready to put my foot down. Let him know she's staying with me. But to my surprise, she replies, "I need a bag for the rest of my clothes." She's referring to the many layers of clothes I had to peel off her when I found her.

Logan looks at me. "Get her a bag."

Now it's me giving Sasha the pleading look. Is she going to leave me like this? After what we just did? After what I just told her? The sting of it all makes it hard to breathe. I head into my closet, find a tote bag, and start putting her clothes in it. She says nothing, looking away.

FOURTEEN

MAKSIM

H ours of sitting in a sparsely furnished room in the Sheriff's Department, refusing to talk to Sheriff Colletti, have given me plenty of time to think. I'm not especially worried about the baseless kidnapping allegations against me. I don't even care about the mess of reporters outside, salivating for a sensational story.

What's got me bothered is how little I got to speak to Alex after our rude awakening. I don't know what she's thinking or feeling, which worries me.

The past couple of days have shown me a glimmer of the life that I want. A radically different life with the woman I love. And that verb "love" is so fresh and new to me that a stupid smile keeps plastering itself on my face every time I think about it.

Of course, my smiling gives Colletti more reason to berate me, accusing me of not taking things seriously. And I guess he's right. But, fuck all. It's hard to keep a straight face with the charges he's trying to pin on me. The man's known me since I was eight years old. If I was some creepy kidnapper, any sheriff worth his salt would know that by now.

I still can't fully wrap my head around the fact that Alex and I are in love. But I'll do whatever it takes to make her mine forever. I can already hear what everyone's going to say. Since I'm twenty-four and Alex is twenty-one, we can't possibly have it all figured out. Marriage is too big a commitment. We need to wait. But I think we've got it more figured out than they do, and I need to find a way to make her see that.

As things currently stand, I don't have her phone number, and I haven't had the chance to make my intentions clear. If I don't handle this right, I could lose her before ever making her mine. I'm not about to let that happen.

I know what Christian or Logan would tell me. Play it safe. Let things cool off. Act casual. *Fuck that*. Advice like that is what has both of them single in their mid-thirties. What Alex and I have is insane and unpredictable and fucking beautiful. I'm not going to throw a wet blanket on it by trying to act cool. And I'm not about to let life seep in to try to explain away the miracle, quantify it, measure it, dissect it until the wonder evaporates.

Sheriff Colletti's still yammering, and it makes me laugh because he won't get me to talk, no matter what. He can keep me here all day if he wants, but it's a waste of both of our times.

I don't know how or why, but I've got this incredible peace that everything will work out between Alex and me. There's something I need to do, though. But I'm still not decided on exactly what that is.

So, I think about the one person who's taught me more about love than anybody I know: my foster dad Wyatt. The old cowboy and widower who took a chance on me when everyone else gave up. I didn't make it easy on him, but once that man loves, nothing'll change his mind. Not social workers or other parents or principals. None of them could convince him I was a bad kid, even though I tried him sorely. What would he tell me about love?

I know it would have to do with Ruby Jean, the love of his life, whom I never met. Those two were crazy in love, the kind of love most people can't wrap their heads around. So, instead, they label it foolishness.

I remember what he told me about how they met. He was just back from Vietnam and making his way home to Rough & Ready by bus. He saw her waiting at the bus station in Denver, Colorado, and instantly knew he had to marry her. So, he walked up to her and told her as much. She laughed and blushed and questioned his intentions. But he made sure they sat on the bus together. By the time they reached Salt Lake City, where she was supposed to catch a connection to Phoenix, they were engaged. He made it official by buying her a bus ticket to Sierra Country.

My face scrunched up when he told me that story as a kid. I think he read my mind because he explained, "Folks said all sorts of things about Ruby Jean and me. That we were stupid and foolish, dumb and reckless. But you know what I found out being married to that amazing woman? The best kind of love is stupid and foolish. It's dumb and reckless and makes no sense to other people. *Because it's not for them.*"

My brother Flynn bursts into the room, making Colletti and I jump. He's a lawyer and my ticket out of here.

"Can I see Alex?" I ask.

Flynn shakes his head emphatically. "Please do me a favor and avoid Ms. Petkova on our way out. The last thing we need is to add flames to the media firestorm brewing outside. You should draw the blinds, Colletti. I don't know how you can stand working here with all those faces staring through the glass. Makes me feel like I'm in an aquarium—on the fish side of things."

I level my gaze at my brother. What I want to say is, "I can't make any promises." But I don't want to give Colletti a chance to stop me, either. Instead, I nod once in acknowledgment.

My heart pounds in my chest as we pass through the doorway, and I know I'm about to see Alex again. "Hold up," I tell Flynn as we walk past Cricket's desk. She's the dispatcher, and I've known her since I was a kid.

"Hey, Cricket, I need a pen and something to write on."

She looks up at me, her gray eyes round and confused, I suppose by the current allegations against me. But her face relaxes when I smile, and she hands me what I'm asking for. It's one of the Sheriff's Department business cards. I flip it over and scratch my number on the back. "Thank you."

"Sure thing," she says in her tiny, smoky voice.

"What's that for?" Flynn asks, his eyes narrowing.

I shrug.

Alex is in the waiting room, still wearing my hoodie, and she's standing with an exhausted, older-looking couple, who I assume are her parents, and a blonde with green eyes. The man has silver hair, a clean-shaven face, and a large rounded nose, and the woman has graying, curly black hair and wears a sour expression. Alex's gaze meets mine, and emotion floods her face. Then, I hear the word *pokhititel* come out of the man's mouth. "Kidnapper" in Russian. I can't imagine the definition's much different in Bulgarian.

Alex protests, "Dad, haven't you listened to anything I've said?"

But he ignores her, glaring at me, his nostrils flaring.

Turning towards him, I reply in fluent Russian, "You need to understand what I'm about to tell you." Over the past couple of days with Alex, I've learned that Russian and Bulgarian share many common words and phrases, but the pronunciations are very different. So, I'm unsure if he'll get what I have to say. But he needs to.

He looks taken aback and replies testily, "I speak some Russian."

"Good," I reply, continuing in my parents' native tongue. It feels strange to use these words again, both on my lips and in my mind. It's been a long time, but the past few days with Sasha have brought up many memories, which she's helped me reconcile without even knowing it. Leveling my gaze at him, I say, "I wish we were meeting under better circumstances. Know this: I didn't kidnap your daughter, but I am going to marry her." He stares blankly, his eyebrows shooting up, and I wonder how much, if any of that, Alex understood. All I know is her face beams at me, and I'm done talking to her dad.

Striding past him, I head straight for Alex despite the verbal protests of Flynn and Sheriff Colletti. Without hesitation, I pull her into my arms, claiming her mouth ravenously. In response, she clings to my neck, kissing me just as wildly. The office goes crazy around us, but I don't care because I know this will all work out somehow.

I step back and say firmly but breathlessly, "Don't forget about me." I put the card with my phone number in her hand, turning without looking back to walk out of the Sheriff's Department.

Annoyed, Flynn shakes his head, asking, "Do I even want to know what you and the old man were going on about?"

"I was just filling him in on the facts."

Christian and Logan rush up behind us, following us into the media frenzy. I'm sure the reporters got some nice pictures of Alex and me making out for their news stories, and I hope they use them because I'm ready for the whole damn world to know how much I love her.

"Little bro's got some new moves," Christian teases, and all I can do is give him a warning growl.

Logan's got his hand on my shoulder, and I try to shake it off, but he won't let me. He says, without even missing a beat, "I'm still pissed at you, bro. Will be for a while. But who's the hot blonde with Alex?"

I shake my head. Some things never change.

FIFTEEN

MAKSIM

Back at the cabin, I see Alex everywhere. She's tangled in the blankets of my unmade bed, lazy and sated from lovemaking. She's sexy and sudsy in my shower. Of course, that's a sight I can only imagine since I was being such an ass last night—refusing to come inside to face her and my feelings. She's at my dining room table drinking coffee. It's hard to fathom how much she already means to me even though there's so much we still don't know about each other.

I take care of the dogs, making sure everyone's got plenty of food and their fill of belly rubs. Every day, the puppies are getting bigger, making more noise, and finding more trouble.

Next, I spend a good stretch of time just sitting outside and taking in the majesty of this incredible place. That's the hard part about living in the Sierra Nevada Mountains—it's too easy to take for granted.

My breath comes out in big white puffs as I think back to the snowball fight with Alex and how I let her clobber me in the face. I could've easily dodged that snowball. But I knew it would make her happy. I remember how she almost fell, throwing that white missile, and I had to steady her. Then, the sunset we watched together. Thank God, I finally got up the nerve to kiss her. I wasn't sure how that was going to go. It certainly wasn't my first kiss, but it was the first time I felt so unhinged and crazy over someone.

When my teeth start chattering, I head inside. I know I shouldn't expect anything. At least, not for a while, but I can't deny how much I need to hear her voice. *She'll call. I just need to be patient.* I heat up some of the antelope stew, and I can't help but reminisce over watching her eat it. I don't think I've ever enjoyed anyone enjoying my cooking or baking that much.

I hear a snowcat engine outside. Two visits in one day from Logan is unusual. But then, what hasn't been unusual about today?

Within minutes of the engine cutting, a loud banging rattles my door. Now, he decides to knock.

"I'm coming," I holler, getting up slowly. What a fucking night and day it's been. Fatigue is finally starting to catch up with me. A thick knot lodges in my throat as I realize less than twenty-four hours ago, Alex and I were in my bed.

There's another impatient round of banging. "Hold your horses, Logan."

I can hear the wind howling outside. I wonder if another storm's on the way.

I open the door, staring at Logan's ugly mug for a moment. He says, "I've got a special delivery for you," turning to the side. I see Alex standing behind him, her eyes large and her brows knitted together. She's holding the bag of clothes I helped her pack earlier, although the cello's nowhere in sight.

"She wouldn't give me a break until I brought her back here," he explains.

An instant smile stretches across my face, from ear to ear, and her forehead smooths as her face relaxes. Stepping forward, she whispers, fighting a sob, "Maksim, I'm so sorry about everything that happened today. The way my parents treated you—"

I cut her off with a kiss, pulling her into my arms with a relieved growl. She drops the tote, her arms encircling my neck, and her fingers threading through my hair. I moan hungrily against the taste of her sweet mouth as her vanilla smell envelopes me. Her tongue is in my mouth, claiming me just like I've claimed her, and Logan takes his cue, mumbling to himself, "You two are fucking crazy."

Yes, we are. The best kind of crazy. I pull her through the doorway into my cabin, shutting the door behind me, and her hands are already fumbling with my shirt.

"One second," I say breathlessly, opening the door and yelling after Logan, "Thank you for bringing her back to me."

A smile dances in his eyes, and wistfulness colors his expression. "You might want to take this inside," he observes, handing me the tote.

I grab it with a nod, asking, "Are you good? You need to warm up or anything before heading home?"

"No, I'm okay, Maksim. Just jonesing for some shut-eye. You have a good night." I don't wait to see him walk away. Instead, I slam the door shut with too much vigor, turning to find Alex waiting for me. I throw the tote to the side. Her cheeks are flushed, and her lips are still swollen from all the making out we've done over the past day. I wrap my arms around her as she frantically starts pulling at my clothes.

"Aren't your parents going to be worried about you?" I

question as she unbuttons my flannel, letting her hand trace a trail of fire down my chest to the front of my pants.

"No, I had a long talk with them today. It took hours, but they finally understand what happened. What you did to save me."

"And did you understand what I told your father in Russian, Sasha?"

Her eyes flood with joy. "Parts of it. He filled me in on the rest."

I shrug out of my shirt. Then, she grabs me impatiently by the front of my jeans, pulling me closer to her.

"And what do you think, Sasha? Will you stay here with me—no matter how stupid other people think we're being, how crazy we might seem?"

"Yes, Maksim, this is where I want to be. With you always." She drops to her knees on the carpet in front of me, and my cock goes instantly hard.

"What are you doing?" I ask, my voice dark and heavy with desire.

"Now, it's my turn to taste you."

She unzips my Wranglers slowly, and my heart's racing out of my chest. I've often wondered what this would feel like, and I let out a sharp exhale when she takes me in her mouth. "Wow," I exclaim shakily.

She replies in a sexy, low tone, "I don't know if I'm doing this right."

"Oh, you're doing fine ... whatever you're doing ... yes." I feel like my whole body's melting into the silky warmth of her mouth. When she moans, it sends delicious sound vibrations through my body.

"You're so big, Maksimka. I can barely fit you in my mouth."

Fuck. "I'm glad you—" I can't even talk. She licks and

sucks me until I'm so close to the edge that I have to stop her.

Frowning, she asks, "Am I doing something wrong?"

"Not at all," I reply slowly, my eyes in danger of rolling back in my head. "But I'm a greedy man, Sasha, and I need to be inside your pussy again."

She starts to stand, and I command, "No, stay on the rug in front of the fireplace. That's right where I want you. I pull off my jeans and boxers impatiently, my hands clumsy and shaking. Dropping down next to her on the rug, I take in her gorgeous, love-filled face in the golden light of the fire. With clumsy urgency, I rip off her yoga pants and lacy panties, spreading her legs. I let out a contented moan as I sink into her. A thousand shivers run through me, and she wraps her legs around my waist, drawing me into her. I feel her hot body tight around me.

"I could stay like this forever," I say gruffly, stroking her ebony curls feathered out around her head like a raven-hued mane. She's still so tight, and I have to move gently. But we find a slow, sizzling rhythm. The constraint breeds an exquisite pain, heightening my senses as I dive headlong into perfect bliss with the only woman I want to love for the rest of my life.

Afterward, she lies in my arms as we stare into the fire. There's never been a more perfect moment, but something nags at the back of my mind. "Where's your cello?"

She must be close to sleep because she jerks a little at my words. "Oh, my parents have it with them. They're heading back to San Francisco tomorrow and want to get it to the luthier as soon as possible."

"And when are you going back to San Francisco? Or are you staying with me?" I ask, my chest tightening.

"My friend, Jess, the blonde with me earlier at the Sheriff's Department, is driving back in a couple of days. So, I'll go with her, unless my SUV's ready. I'm sorry I didn't introduce you two. But so much happened today."

"There's plenty of time," I reply, the uneasy feeling continuing to grow inside of me. "Anything wrong with your SUV apart from the window?"

"It may need a new front driver's seat."

"You took it to RJ's?"

"Yes. Is there another mechanic in Hollister?"

I shake my head.

She continues, "If I head back with Jess, I'm hoping you can pick it up for me and keep it here until I get back?"

"Of course. I'll settle up with RJ for any repairs, too."

"No, Maksim, my insurance will cover it."

"Okay, but if it doesn't, I'm paying. I did the damage, after all. And besides, you're my woman. So, I'll take care of you from now on."

"You already saved my life."

"That was just the beginning. I promise you." I feel my throat tighten at the thought of her leaving me. God help me if she wants to do a long-distance relationship. It won't work for me. I need to wake up with her every morning and fall asleep beside her at night. I roll onto my back, pulling away from her.

"Maksim, what's wrong?"

"You don't sound like you're planning on staying."

"I am," she replies softly. "But I have a lot to sort out in San Francisco." She looks around the cabin. "I have stuff to pack and bring. I hope you don't mind your cabin getting a girly makeover."

"Not at all," I reply, turning back towards her and palming her cheek. "But can we promise to keep being apart to a minimum? I need you with me. I don't want to do any of that long-distance shit."

"I don't want to do it, either. But I have a lot to sort out. I'll need your help with it. And then, before you know it, I'll be here with you all the time, and you'll probably wish you could get rid of me."

"Never," I reply, capturing her mouth with mine.

EPILOGUE

MAKSIM

THREE MONTHS LATER

I stand outside Davies Symphony Hall in San Francisco talking to my brother, Christian, on the phone. He's currently parked by the side of a country road waiting on potential speeders or DUIs. To say the least, he's got time to talk.

"I'm fucking out of my element," I breathe into the phone, reeling from what I just saw. I wanted to surprise Alex by driving to San Francisco to attend one of her concerts. But now my nerve is evaporating.

"I've heard her practicing, but to see her play live with a full orchestra. She was amazing, bro. I don't understand why she'd ever want to settle down with a guy like me."

Her triumphant face flashes through my mind as she stands before the orchestra, her arms filled with flowers, receiving a standing ovation. I thought for sure she'd cry. Hell, I was tearing up. But she stood there matter-of-factly like the stage was the most comfortable place in the world. "Who am I kidding, Chris?"

Christian laughs that knowing older brother laugh. It annoys the hell out of me. "Remember what Dad always says, 'Fish or cut bait.'"

"Very deep, bro."

"Seriously, Max. The girl's head over heels for you. Everyone can see it. She's going to say yes. I promise. Dammit, I'll grow a beard if she doesn't."

I let out a gruff sigh, eyeing a man in a black trench coat smoking near me. A tux bow tie and shirt peek out from the coat, and it's obvious he's eavesdropping on me. Between the crowds, sirens, and honking horns, I'm ready for a fight if that's what he wants. He throws his cigarette to the ground, grinding it out with his heel, and walks toward me.

This should be good.

"Chris, let me call you back." I put my cell phone in my back pocket, clenching my fists at my sides as the man stops in front of me.

I still hate big cities, and coming to San Francisco, where I have so many traumatic memories, is like visiting hell. But I'd do that and more for Alex. I hope she feels the same about me.

The man looks me up and down for a long moment, asking, "Are you Alex's cowboy mountain man?"

I'm taken aback by the question but nod. I've dressed up in a suit with my black Stetson and best boots, but it's not lost on me that I stand out in this place. Along with my beard, I must be a dead giveaway.

"I'm Frederick." He offers his hand, and we shake. I can't help but notice the weak grip and clammy palm. He wouldn't last a week in Rough & Ready. "I'm a violist with the orchestra, and I've heard *all* about you from Alex."

My fists clench at my sides again, and he smiles, raising his eyebrows. "You really are a mountain man, aren't you?"

93

"I'm Maksim, and I own Sierra Husky Rescue."

He nods knowingly. "Yeah, Alex told me about that, too. I've known her since we were both kids. We started in the same studio, but then she switched to cello. Anyway, I couldn't help but overhear the conversation, and I think I need to help you get backstage before intermission ends." He turns, waving me over his shoulder to follow.

I have red roses and a box of Belgian chocolates for her in my truck. But the ushers wouldn't let me bring them in. I hesitate for a second about going to get them. Considering how far away I'm parked, it's not an option. And I'm not sure how long these intermissions go anyway, so I follow after Frederick, my heart pounding.

At the backstage entrance, Frederick has to do some fancy talking to get the guard to let me in. I remove my hat, holding it with my right hand over my chest as we head down a long hallway filled with photos of special guests and past performances. I spy an image of a younger version of Alex playing her cello. This woman's way more famous than she lets on, and my stomach knots tighter.

Musicians mill around in black clothes and tuxes, and Frederick greets a couple of people curtly while walking past. His step is brisk as he takes me down another long hallway. People are lined up in front of a door that says "Dressing Room," and it's there that I see Alex's shiny dark curls and beaming face. She's talking to someone and signing a program with a black felt pen.

I realize the line is for her and see people holding flowers and small gifts. Now I'm sweating about the presents still in my truck. *Dammit.*

I'm about to get in line when Frederick turns and gives me an impatient nod in Alex's direction. "It's your turn," he says as Alex looks up and our eyes meet.

Her eyes pool, and I've got a lump in my throat. She's a goddess in her sparkly green evening gown, and I almost feel uneasy approaching her. But the desperate need to officially claim her drives me on.

I wrap my hands around her waist, holding my hat brim with my fingertips so that it balances against her curvy hip. I touch my forehead to hers, asking, "Is this okay?"

Tears stream down her cheeks. "I can't believe you came for me. You hate San Francisco."

"Baby, I keep telling you. There's nothing I wouldn't do for you."

"He's out of line," an oblivious patron complains behind me.

Before I can say a thing, Frederick is on it. "Be patient. I promise this'll be worth it."

"I have roses and chocolates for you in the truck," I explain. "But the ushers wouldn't let me bring them in. I guess they thought I'd rush the stage after your solo."

Alex giggles, and then she covers her mouth with both hands as I kneel down on one knee, pulling a small box from my coat pocket.

"Sasha, you're the best thing that's ever happened to me. I know you think I saved your life the day I found you. But honestly it's you who saved mine. I can't imagine living without you. Would you please do me the honor of becoming Mrs. Borodin?"

Before I can protest, she kneels down in front of me, cupping my face in her hands. She whispers, "Yes, Maksimka. There's nothing I want more than you." My lips capture hers for a long, deep kiss. I don't care who the hell is watching. She's mine now.

Hoots, hollers, and cheers go up around us, as musicians gather by the line of patrons in the hallway to see what's going on. I stand up, pulling my wife-to-be beside me, and putting a possessive arm around her waist.

"Let me be the first to congratulate you both," Frederick says, stepping forward to hug Alex and shake my hand.

I place a hand on his shoulder as he turns to go. "I owe you one, Fred."

He nods, breaking the first smile I've seen since meeting him. "Make her happy."

"That's what I plan on doing for the rest of my life," I reply, beaming down at my gorgeous fiancée.

BONUS SCENE
ALEX

SEVEN MONTHS LATER

BUNDLED BENEATH BLANKETS and furs, I watch the world fly by in a blur of white. Maksim promises he'll teach me how to drive the sled. But for now, he wants me to get the full effect of the Sierra backcountry. It's beyond exhilarating—especially thinking about how he saved my life less than a year ago.

We stop in a beautiful clearing, the icy sun high and distant overhead. Maksim stakes out the dogs and gives them water before diving under the blankets to cuddle with me.

Before I know it, his hands are at the waistband of my pants, his thick cock pressed against my thigh.

"I need you, Sasha," he growls in my ear.

"I need you more," I breathe as he dips his head beneath the covers.

"Maksim, what are you doing?" My voice rises as I feel him crawl down my body, tugging at my pants. It takes effort—he's a big man, and the sled isn't made for two. I pull up the blankets and peer beneath them to find his arms locked around my hips. He presses a brazen kiss where my legs meet.

"You know what I'm doing," he grumbles, finally working free the button and zipper. Triumphantly, he drags my pants down to my knees, growling deep in his throat as he buries his mouth against my panties. What was already wet turns into a drenched invitation as a painful throb twists me in knots.

"But out here?" I whisper. "In the middle of everything?"

"Out here, in the middle of nowhere, Sasha," he replies, pulling my panties down enough so that he can sink his mouth into my heat. "You're not in San Francisco anymore."

He dives in, kissing me until a low moan escapes me.

"But what if someone comes along?" I gasp. "What if one of your brothers—"

"I'll shoot anyone who wanders onto my land or gawks at me making love to my woman. Brothers included."

"You're a madman," I moan as his fingers part me and his tongue finds my clit. I jerk reflexively, crying out again. "You're really doing this out here?"

His tongue is buried deep, and I cover my mouth with a hand, stifling an appreciative whimper. My core tightens as he relentlessly plays with my pearl, alternating between sucking, circling, and flicking.

Suddenly, he throws back the covers, glaring up at me.

"What?" he growls.

My last question evaporates as I scramble for the blankets, but he stops me.

"I need room for what I'm doing, Sasha. And I know

you're going to like this." He pins me to the sled, indigo eyes wicked. "Stop worrying so much."

"You're crazy," I murmur before he sinks a thick finger into me, quivering at his skilled touch. I tighten around him, shameless, ravenous for more.

"Maybe for you," he snarls. "Now, quit worrying so much. Just enjoy. Before this is over, I swear, you'll be the crazy one." He finally breaks into an ear-to-ear grin as I let out an exasperated sigh, and he dips his head to devour me some more.

I cover my mouth, barely able to stifle my screams as my hips crash up towards him, begging for release. "These pants have to go," he groans, fumbling with my snowboots and clothes until they lie next to us in the snow. "And these, too," he orders, removing my scarlet lace panties and tossing them into the snow.

"Maksim," I scold between pleasurable moans. "I don't want my panties covered in snow. What am I going to wear on the ride back home?"

Maksim grabs my legs, parting them and putting them over his shoulders. I sit up on my elbows, scowling at him. "You're shameless."

"Sashenka, you're killing me here. You and I are the only two people on this entire mountain, and I'm not stopping until you're fully satisfied. So, relax."

He sinks his finger back into me slowly, finding the rough bundle of nerves near the front that he knows sets me on fire. His hot mouth and soft beard graze over my pussy again, teasing me until I melt into a molten pool of desire.

"That's right, baby," he encourages. "Let me please you." He looks up between my legs with that boyish grin of his and adds, "And then, I'm going to make you come again."

I give up fighting my husband. I ride his hand and his face, mewling into the wilderness. Even after I shatter around his fingers, he doesn't stop.

"Maksim," I plead. "I need your cock."

"Patience," he murmurs darkly. "You'll have me soon." He swipes his tongue through me again. "You taste so good, baby. Can't get enough."

His fingers and tongue please me until I beg and scream through another climax, lost in a dizzy haze of bliss.

When I'm completely spent, I stare up at the winter sky, hot breath floating in white puffs toward periwinkle heights. Every part of me melts, completely sated, into the sled's bed. Maksim pulls back, unzipping his pants.

I have no muscles left, but I still tilt my head up, taking in my blond husband's gorgeous face as he kneels over me.

"Now, I want everything, wife. Total surrender. Without complaint. Do you understand?"

I snort weakly, still caught in the afterglow. "With a firebrand like me? Never, husband."

"One of the many things I love about my little bobcat," he says, like he's assigning me yet another nickname. "Her sharp claws."

"What I like about you is entirely different," I reply in sultry tones, my eyes jumping to his thick girth.

"Then, why fight me so, Sashenka?"

"Because you love it."

"I love you. Can you fault me for wanting to prove it?"

"Yes, when it involves public nudity—"

He brings a finger to his lips, shushing me and smiling seductively.

"You are so infuriating sometimes."

He grabs my hips, pulling me toward him and sinking into me, savoring every inch.

"Infuriating," he groans. "And what else?"

"Dimwitted."

He thrusts. "Yes?"

"And a thief."

"Not anymore. Not since I was a kid," he replies, breathing hard and driving into me again. He changes the angle to deepen his stroke, and I hear my voice echoing through the trees.

I pant, "You stole my virginity."

"Oh no," he chuckles. "You gave me that."

I try to let out a frustrated sigh, but it sounds more like a moan of pleasure. I manage a scowl, instead.

"Nothing else?" he grasps my hips tighter, his rhythm more urgent, his face dark and dangerous. "What about a creep?"

"You're no creep," I cry, arching into him as I unravel all over again. He crashes into me, letting out a throaty scream and spilling himself inside. Scooping me up into his arms, he holds me. I wrap myself around him, breathing hard against his ear.

"No creep?" he murmurs against my mouth.

"No, you're my Maksimka." I cup his bearded cheeks, watching emotion swim in his eyes.

"That's right, Sasha. I'll always be all yours. Forever."

Wrapped together beneath the blankets, listening to the dogs and the quiet of the mountain, I whisper, "Tatko."

"Yes, baby?"

"That's it."

"That's what?" he grumbles groggily.

"You're going to be a tatko."

His body stills. "I'm going to be a dad?"

Maksim says the words slowly and emphatically, like he can't quite catch his breath.

"We have our first doctor's appointment in two weeks to hear the baby's heartbeat."

"Are you serious?"

"Yes, are you happy, husband?"

He pulls me close, hands splayed protectively over my belly. "I've never stopped being happy since the day I dug you out of the snow. Thank you for making me a tatko," he whispers, claiming my mouth hungrily as we sink back into each other's love.

LOVE AT FIRST CAMPFIRE

AN AGE-GAP MOUNTAIN
MAN / CURVY GIRL ROMANCE

PROLOGUE

JESS

"Craven's out."

I don't know how long I stare at the text from my editor at the *Chronicle*. I'm parked on the street near verdant, tree-lined Golden Gate Park, enjoying one of those sunny lunch breaks you can't pass up in San Francisco. But now my appetite evaporates.

As a true crime reporter, I rarely see people at their best. But Craven is a special kind of monster. Unfortunately, making a monster your business risks gaining their attention. Something the tight knot in my stomach attests to.

But I had to do it.

I had to know what happened to the string of girls and women missing in the Bay Area over the past decade. Most in national parks, filling female hikers across the state with dread.

One name kept popping up as I dug into the case, pouring over files and reading through mountains of evidence. *Ted Wesley Craven.* By all accounts, an upstanding citizen and acclaimed high school teacher, the cops never counted him a serious suspect.

But after diving into his website viewing history, social media posts, past cell phone locations, incongruent testimony, and anything else I could get my hands on, another picture emerged. My articles soon revealed him as the only suspect that mattered. Obsessive work led to breakthroughs in the case and award-winning bylines. It also landed me in his cross-hairs.

While he sat behind bars, I shrugged off the occasional threatening missive he sent to the *Chronicle's* office or my home address. Information comes so cheap on the internet, and I can only guess what he knows about me.

None of it mattered until procedural errors with the evidence chain of custody came to light. Then, a mistrial and now me staring at my cell phone, hands shaking.

I'll never forget how he looked at me across the courtroom during his murder trial. His black, remorseless eyes, unblinking and emboldened by rage, chilled my blood.

"Thanks for the heads up," I text back.

"Why not take a few extra days away from the office while all this blows over? Where did you say you were going for the wedding again? Tahoe?"

"Rough & Ready Ranch."

"And that's where?"

"Sierra Nevada backcountry."

"Sounds like the perfect place to lay low for a bit."

"Agreed," I reply.

"Have fun and enjoy a much-needed vacay."

I reply with a thumbs-up emoji, setting my phone on the passenger seat next to my purse. The news confirms a feeling I've had all day—a feeling I can't shake. Like someone's watching me. Even now, the hair on the back of my neck stands up. Yet, checking my rearview mirror, I don't see anyone.

I can't let my imagination run away with me. Or start living in fear. Maybe the stress of being a maid of honor is getting to me. I don't know.

My phone vibrates, startling me. I have a text from my bestie, Alex. She's getting married this weekend, and there's still plenty to do.

I open her message, immediately deluged in catering drama.

"How about I come in a few days early? Take some of the planning burden off your shoulders?" I text.

Next thing I know, my screen lights up with her Face-Time call. I deny the video. The last thing she needs right now is to see me upset.

"Hi, sweetie," I greet her.

"He's out, isn't he?"

She's too perceptive. I sigh, "Yep."

"Do you think he's following you or anything?"

I look around, still feeling oddly nervous. "No, everything's fine...and you know I can take care of myself. Anyway, enough about me. You're about to tie the knot! How can I help you feel less stressed?"

"Just promise me you'll be extra careful. When are you getting in?"

I look down at my car's dashboard, realizing my lunch break is nearly over. I don't have to go back into the office. But traffic will be miserable leaving the Bay Area this afternoon. Between packing and picking up my maid of honor dress from the seamstress, there's still plenty to do, and I can probably miss a jam if I head out after six.

"Maybe ten or so."

"Will you stay here?" she asks hopefully.

I can't stifle a laugh.

She and her hot mountain man fiancé can't keep their

hands off each other, and their cabin is relatively spare in the privacy department.

"What?" she asks a little defensively.

"No offense, but you and Maksim need your privacy."

She giggles.

Looking at the dashboard clock again, I press my fingers to my temple. I wasn't planning on leaving for a few more days, and I still have so much to do. But getting away from the City right now sounds undeniably appealing.

"Thank you for the offer, but I'd prefer my own place."

"Hollister Bed and Breakfast?"

"If I can extend my reservation, yes."

"Alright. Well, drive safely, and be careful. I won't stop worrying until you get here."

"I'll text you. I promise."

By the time I extend my reservation at the hotel, pick up my gown, finish packing, and eat dinner, I'm behind schedule. It'll be midnight before I get in. Hollister's a small town, with something like 2,000 people, and the owner of the bed and breakfast, Mrs. Chatterton, sounds elderly. The last thing I want to do is make her wait up.

I call her again, arranging to pick up my hotel room key nearby at the gas station. Apparently, her grandson owns it, and it's open twenty-four seven. My head's on a swivel in the parking lot on the way to my red Camry. I don't want to indulge paranoia. But having my face plastered on the missing persons board at Walmart is unthinkable.

My shoulders and neck finally relax about two hours into the drive, when I break free of the congestion at the Bay Bridge and again in Vallejo. The radio blares rock hits from the 90s and early 2000s. I no longer shoot constant glances in my rearview mirror, settling into singing along with the satellite radio—"Glycerine" by Bush. I feel liberated, escaping the City, my job, and Craven.

CHAPTER
ONE

*S*eriously? Of all the women in the room jonesing for love, how did I end up with the bouquet? It's not like I caught it.

Honestly, it clobbered me. The bundle of pastel roses, freesias, and lisianthus mixed with deep purple anemones and verdant rosemary nearly took my head off. I put my hands up to avoid a scratched face or bloody nose. But the crowd gathering around me doesn't care about that. Instead, they clap and cheer at the strange irony of the situation.

The self-avowed single girl singled out by fate. Bah! I force a stiff smile as my fellow bridesmaids shoot me dirty looks.

But the garter toss takes the cake. My best friend Alex's crazy, beautiful wedding has thirteen groomsmen, twelve of whom mill around the dance floor as Alex takes a seat. Maksim dives eagerly into the fluffy layers of her skirt as Christian, the sheriff, and Fletcher, the doctor, talk trash about their catching abilities.

Hawk, the pilot, and Rock, the tattoo artist, hem and

haw, looking resigned. And others, like Zane, the cowboy of few words, put on a polite face. Only Logan, the swaggering mountain man with smoldering good looks, hangs back, leaning against the barn wall. Even in his tux, the definition of his athletic frame puts a tight knot in my throat. He's got a folded twenty-dollar bill in his hand, and I watch him pay off Alex's adorable, ten-year-old cousin to stand in for him.

"Are you serious right now?" I ask, leaning back against the wall next to him.

"What?" he replies, raising an eyebrow and grinning. My heart flutters.

This guy's a walking red flag. Apparently, he's the player in the family. But he shares my dry sense of humor, which I've counted a huge bonus in the midst of so much crazy wedding drama. Wedding drama not so much from my girl, Alex, but from her over-the-top Bulgarian mom and aunts. I don't understand half of what's been said this week, but it has involved many melodramatic hand gestures and percussive monologues.

Logan's sarcasm provides a nice counterpoint, even though everyone's warned me to stay away. "Bribing a child to save you from the specter of domesticity?"

He shrugs. "Just a little insurance in case my luck's as bad as yours—"

The curly, auburn-haired boy shrieks as he dives for the garter. Jumping to his feet, he holds it aloft, cheering and doing a victory dance.

Logan's shoulders drop, and his face relaxes. Then, things go haywire.

"Here you go!" The mischievous boy tosses the garter over the heads of the other groomsmen and straight towards my face. Only Logan's quick reflexes save me.

Holding the lacy white loop of fabric where he catches

it, inches from my face, he frowns, asking drily, "Let me guess. You were that girl on the school playground with a ball magnet for a head?"

I laugh, nodding. "Yep, soccer balls, tetherballs, a baseball once, too."

He flinches, closing his eyes. "Ouch!"

Immediately, Logan's brothers raise a ruckus.

"It still counts," Christian declares, pointing Logan's way. "Even if you made the kid catch it for you."

"Buddy, what happened?" Logan calls back towards the little boy.

"I got it for you."

The mountain man shakes his head. "That's not what I meant. You were supposed to keep it. Now, give me back my money."

"No!" the little boy screams, running away as the DJ throws in his two cents.

Logan lets out a deep-chested laugh, shaking his head as he looks down at the floor. "Not quite how I saw that going down." The dark-haired mountain man with mahogany-colored eyes and a neatly trimmed beard glances my way, flashing a broad smile and tucking the garter into his pocket. "Not sure what to do with that."

"By that, are you referring to the garter or the little boy running away with your money?" I quip.

He shakes his head, clarifying, "Both."

"You want this?" I reply, offering him the bouquet still in my hand.

"Nooooo," he says, shaking his head vigorously.

I look up, and all eyes are on Logan and me. Alex and Maksim motion towards the dance floor, both grinning ear to ear. I've never seen my bestie so happy, which warms my heart towards Maksim. Whatever he does for her, he does right. But I'm not about to be the center of attention, even though I know I can't say no to Alex. I shake my head, hoping beyond hope Logan will put a stop to this.

"Come up," Alex orders, looking gorgeous in her lacy white strapless ballroom gown and gorgeous upswept black curls, and my stomach sinks. Alex's wedding has had a laidback vibe up to this point. She and Maksim even opted for a first look before the wedding, which surprised me since she's usually pretty old-fashioned about things. And so I was hoping—*really* hoping— I'd manage to escape this next part.

Why did I have to catch the bouquet?

Alex motions me to the chair she sat in, and Maksim has his hand on his brother's arm, leading him over. Logan's face is a visible apology as he bends to the will of the crowd, taking a knee before me with a begrudging, albeit good-natured, smile. The DJ announces the all-time stupidest tradition in wedding history, and I want to bury my head in my hands. But if I'm going to get objectified, it might as well be for my bestie. So, I plaster on a fake smile and mentally count each second until it's over.

My pink maid of honor gown has a slit up the side, and I unceremoniously stick out my leg to get the show on the road. Up to this point, I've never touched the burly mountain man. I've never had any reason to, and I just want this done. He gazes at my leg for one long moment, and I swear his face fills with appreciation. But it's probably my imagination.

Then, his left hand comes up, grasping the back of my calf to steady it as his right hand slides the garter over my ankle. The moment his warm flesh touches mine is pure combustion. I catch my breath. He hesitates, his nostrils flaring as he lets out a sharp exhale, and his eyes lock with mine. *Does he feel it, too?* Guiding the garter up my leg, his touch leaves a trail of fire, and he moves slowly, until my whole body feels hot and needy.

I'm stunned. No man's touch has ever done this to me. I stare wide-eyed in his direction, my mouth hanging open. It's probably not my best look, but I can't help myself—the feel of his skin against mine sends delicious shivers of desire coursing up and down my leg, creating an unexpected tightness in my core.

Logan's eyes are still on my face, and I know I should look away, but I have to gauge his reaction. I have to know if there's any part of him that feels what I'm feeling. His eyes have gone from the color of dark chocolate to nearly black, and he swallows hard, clenching his jaw until a muscle shows.

Squeezing my leg with both hands, he slides the garter just above my knee, letting his fingertips linger there for one moment as he straightens the lace. Applause breaks out, and Logan sets my leg down gently, looking away to stand by Maksim. Alex pulls my gaze from the muscular mountain man, offering a hand to help me up. We face the crowd as everyone claps, and I take in large gulps of air.

CHAPTER
TWO

JESS

What *was that?* The pounding of the music starts again as the lights drop, and I feel dizzy although all I've drunk tonight is Pellegrino. My leg still sizzles where Logan's hands touched me, and my pulse pounds in my temples as his eyes meet mine momentarily. The surprise has left his face, and now his expression looks guarded, unreadable. I let out a puff of air, shaking my head and trying to get a grasp on the last handful of minutes.

"Nice, you two," Alex congratulates, leaning in to kiss my cheek.

I grumble, "For the record, there is no 'us two.'" But my heart races out of my chest.

My eyes search for Logan again, and I find the broad-shouldered man standing with Maksim, Alex's blonde, bearded groom. Maksim leans in, winking at Logan, and I hear him tease, "I guess this means you're next, bro."

Logan grumbles, putting up his fists for a quick round of shadow boxing with Maksim. The way his thick neck and muscular shoulders and arms ripple with the movement takes my breath away—even though his tux jacket hides most of the action.

Alex catches me staring at him, and her right eyebrow shoots up. I deflect the question on her face with distraction, reassuring, "The wedding couldn't have gone more perfectly."

"Really? You think so?" Her head bobbles from Logan towards me, and I really need to change the direction of the conversation. If I can't explain what just happened to myself, how am I going to put it into words for her?

I nod defiantly, "It was perfect."

She gives me a sideways glance and half-smile, but I can tell her mind's going a mile a minute.

Logan and Maksim head back to Alex and me, and my pulse quickens. Logan shrugs nonchalantly, ordering Alex, "You better get him out on the dance floor while you can. Knowing my brother, he's about to throw you over his shoulder and drag you back to his cabin."

"There will be no dragging," Alex laughs, her cheeks flushing.

"Wait, I can do that?" Maksim teases, throwing a possessive arm around her waist. "He's right, Sasha. I can't stand being away from you much longer."

They're in each other's arms! How is this *being away from each other?* I laugh under my breath at their saccharine PDA. Both are relationship people, something I have trouble wrapping my head around. Kind of like I'm struggling with what just happened with Logan. I press my fingers to my temple. Obviously, my imagination is in overdrive.

Maksim and Alex beeline for the dance floor, and the DJ turns up the music and drops the lights. The bride-grooms and bridesmaids (except Logan and I) assemble on the dance floor, and there's plenty of jockeying for partners, thanks to the uneven spread of men and women.

Logan faces me, and I can't escape his soulful glance. The music booms in my chest and through the barn's floorboards, and he has to scream into my ear so I can hear him.

"Wanna get out of here?"

The feel of his warm breath on my neck and cheek sends delicious shivers down my spine, converging in my lower stomach. I should say no. Besides, as Alex's best friend and maid of honor, I've got to stick this out.

"I can't," I yell back, "Although I'd love to."

"Just for a few minutes?"

A slow song begins, and a quick scan of the dance floor reveals groomsmen still looking for partners. A couple of pairs of male eyes drift my way. Coupled with the loud music and steadily rising temperatures, Logan's offer proves too good to resist.

I nod, and he grabs my arm, leading me around the outer edges of the barn and out into the chill of the fall night. By the time we reach the fire pit, his hand has covered the distance from my upper arm to my hand, and our fingers intertwine. My body feels like a live wire, and I'm gasping for breath like I've been jogging. *What is this man doing to me?*

It's more than the warmth and security of his touch, although I savor both. There's a connection between us. A crazy chemistry that I can't define. I've felt it since the day I met him, although I chalked it up to his insane good looks, a shared sense of humor, and similar outlooks on life. But then the garter happened.

Why does he have to be a player? Worse yet, why does he have to be my bestie's new brother-in-law?

I need to drop his hand. I need to put up clear boundaries, but I don't. I can't.

Why not?

I could chalk it up to feeling on edge about Craven. Throughout this week at Rough & Ready Ranch, I've looked over my shoulder more times than I care to admit. It's stupid. After all, I'm in the middle of nowhere. *What will going back to San Francisco feel like?* I close my eyes, shaking my head against the thought.

"You okay?" Logan asks, his brows furrowing.

For one awkward moment, I weigh telling him about Craven. But the last thing I want to do is ruin an otherwise beautiful night, especially by mentioning that name. Instead, I go for a white lie, "I'm fine." Before he can press me further, I change the subject, pointing toward the fire and saying, "This is great. I've never been around a campfire. Or been camping, for that matter."

"Seriously?" his face scrunches, and he looks down laughing. "You really are a city girl." Stealing a glance his way, I appreciate how the warm illumination of the flames accentuate his tan skin and hard, angular planes.

"Well, that and my parents were alcoholics. So, we didn't get out much. They couldn't get it together for stuff like family vacations." *Why am I telling him this?* I look away, embarrassed.

"I understand," he replies, staring into the flames, and I feel bad complaining about my life. Yes, I may have had it shitty, but I emancipated at sixteen, never looking back. I know many kids had it worse.

Alex told me that Maksim, Logan, and the other groomsmen here are all foster brothers. They came together under the same roof at Rough & Ready Ranch, with Wyatt as the patriarch. But I can only guess what their lives were like before. What I do know is that Maksim, Logan, and all but one of the foster brothers live in cabins on large parcels carved out of the original homestead.

He glances towards me out of the corner of his eye, a frown forming on his kiss-worthy lips. As if reading the countless questions in my mind about his past, he takes a deep breath, saying, "My bio father didn't have a problem with alcohol, per se. Just domestic violence...and guns."

Pausing for a long moment, Logan looks down, and I can see the muscles tensing in his neck and jaw. Gruffly, he finishes, "My mother didn't make it out, and neither did that bastard. Serves him right. Fortunately, he fucked up killing me."

I suck in a breath, and he drops my hand. But he does it half-heartedly, making me instinctively grab it tighter.

He rubs the scar I've noticed on his neck, and I wonder how that fits into the picture. I want to ask but don't want to make him uncomfortable. As an investigative journalist, I'm good at getting people to confide in me—sometimes more than they mean to. It's how I win awards. But it's not fair play outside of work.

He looks down at our joined hands for a long moment and then at me. "I've never told anybody that. I mean, apart from Pop." I know he's referring to Wyatt, his foster dad, and I can see the mixture of pain and shame on his face.

"I like your dad," I state, trying to lighten the mood.

"Yeah, he's a good man."

"Like you."

He stiffens, momentarily. Then, turning to face me, he grabs my other hand. With a formal smile, he says, "Jess, I feel honored you enjoyed your first campfire with me. It's been nice getting to know you."

He's saying goodbye for the night—*maybe forever*. But,

despite his words, his feet don't move. And his hands don't leave mine. Staring into his warm eyes, I wait breathlessly, hoping he won't walk away, although it makes no rational sense.

"You know, I'm nothing like my bio father. I would never hurt a woman...or a child."

"I know," I reply. "Just like I'm nothing like my parents."

He nods, his face relaxing. "I knew you'd understand."

I smile. I've only known him for a week, but I've noticed how attentive and sweet he acts with Wyatt. Alex told me he's a search and rescue unit lead. I don't know what that entails—apart from risking his life regularly to save others—but I know he's one of the best men I've ever met. Player or not.

The silence has gotten heavy, awkward. I break it, suggesting, "Maybe we should go back inside?"

He hesitates for a long moment, looking down at our hands. *How I wish I could read his thoughts!* Finally, he says, "Not yet. I have something I want to show you."

I raise an eyebrow curiously before looking back inside the barn where the dancing continues. I have to admit that I want nothing to do with it.

"Okay, only for a few more minutes."

"Deal."

THREE

As soon as our feet hit the grass of the meadow, I undo my bow tie and unbutton my tux shirt a couple of notches. I want to pull off my coat, too, but that would mean letting go of her hand.

I don't know why I just confessed all that to Jess. What astounds me even more is that she hasn't run away in terror. But then it sounds like her childhood was no rose garden, either.

Jess's eyes round as she surveys my unbuttoned shirt, and she swallows hard. It's nice knowing my attraction for her isn't one-sided. I remind myself it can't go anywhere, though.

Of course, that begs the question: Why am I holding her hand? I shake my head. I don't feel like thinking right now.

Instead, I say, "The wedding was great, but that other stuff is not my thing."

"I get it," she replies. I knew she would.

I loosely thread my arm around her waist, leading her toward the game trail that runs down to the creek. A full harvest moon hangs overhead, large and golden. As beautiful as it is, I'd prefer a night with a new moon, the better for stargazing. But this country sky will still outdo Frisco by a long shot.

I wasn't sure how Jess would respond to me putting an arm around her, but if she notices, she doesn't react. I like being close to her like this—smelling her lilac, honey scent and feeling her soft warmth.

"The other night at the rehearsal dinner, I remember you talking about how much you wanted to try stargazing out here. Now, don't get your hopes up too high because the moon is full and putting off a lot of light. But if we get away from the barn a ways, we should get some decent views."

"This is so exciting! A campfire and stars in the same night!" she exclaims, wide-eyed.

It's the most unguarded I've seen her this week.

Bathed in ethereal light, the path is easy to follow. As we dip down towards the embankment, the sounds coming from the reception in the barn fade. A steady chorus of crickets take their place, chirping to the moon for a chance at a mate. But the threat of frost in the air has turned their song raucous, frantic.

"Hard to imagine snow will bury this place in a month or less, and the creek will freeze," I muse. All the more reason I've got to get this situation with Pop straightened out. He needs a live-in nurse to help him. I can't stand the thought of him out here alone, even though we all live nearby and visit often.

The bubbling of the creek is framed by thick tufts of grass around its marshy bank. The water has shrunk to half its size since the spring thaw. I jump it with ease, turning to offer my hand to Jess.

She hesitates, and I feel awkward. Ignoring my hand,

she hikes up her dress with both hands and leaps from one bank to the other. Hitting an extra mushy patch, she stumbles, and I grab her arms to keep her from falling. I don't want this night ruined by wet, muddy clothes. Although the thought of getting her out of them makes my cock twinge.

"Thank you," she says, looking down and shaking free from my grasp.

"You don't like taking help from others, do you?" I observe with a chuckle.

"What makes you say that?" she asks, straightening her back and smoothing her skirt.

I've tried to figure her out all week, coming no closer in the process. When we talk, I feel like she's reading my mind. She's just as sarcastic as I am and funny as hell. Based on looks alone, she's a blonde bombshell with golden, shoulder-length hair and the curvaceous body of a 1950s pinup—*definitely my kinda girl*. But there's nothing weak or vulnerable about her. It makes me feel a bit uncomfortable since I've staked my bread and butter on rescuing people, attracting many damsels in distress along the way.

I don't risk putting my arm around her again. Instead, I fist my hands at my sides. The moonlight washes over her, stealing my breath. She looks like an angel. All soft curves and golden tresses, and that cupid's bow mouth I long to taste. But after shaking off my help by the creek, I'm unsure how she'd handle another move from me.

So, I call out directions. "Head towards those two big boulders over there. It'll be a good spot to scope out the stars."

She hugs herself with her arms, and I imagine pulling up behind her and enveloping her in my arms. But as pretty as she is, she's also a cactus with sharp spines. So, I hesitate.

Nevertheless, Pop raised me to be a gentleman. Changing my mind as quickly as I make it, I offer her my tux jacket.

"Oh, I'm fine," she refuses.

"The hell, you're fine. I can see goosebumps on your arms. Take it."

She shakes her head stubbornly.

Okay, if she wants to play that way... I turn on my heel, striding back towards the bank we just descended.

"Wait, where are you going?"

"Woman, either put on this coat, or we're heading back inside. I'm not about to stand here watching you freeze."

"But what about you? Won't you be cold?"

With three long strides, I close the distance between us, wrapping the black jacket around her shoulders and laughing. "Are you always this stubborn?"

She nods, and I swear her cheeks have darkened. This small success gives me courage, and I grab her hand again, lacing my fingers through hers. I've never felt a softer palm or set of fingers, and I like how her hand fits snuggly in my larger one. As we near the boulders, she slows behind me, and I glance over my shoulder.

She's cheating.

"Don't look up yet," I scold. "We're almost there."

"Okay," she replies in a breathy whisper.

Her hand is soft, but it's also icy from the night air, and I can't help but feel pissed she didn't tell me she was cold sooner.

I motion for her to lean against one boulder because I plan on taking the other. But I think better of it last minute, standing next to her with our shoulders touching and hands still interlocked.

Why I do this, I can't say for sure. Maybe it's her addictive smell. Or her pouty lower lip, which sets me on fire, filling my head with indecent desires. Maybe it's my need to see her face light up when she sees the Milky Way here for the first time.

"Alright, you can look up now."

Her lovely face darts heavenward, and she exhales loudly. My heart races in my chest as she squeezes my hand. "Logan...this is...this is... There are no words for this!"

I feel vindicated. Making a journalist speechless isn't an everyday occurrence, after all.

Her mouth parts, and her eyes widen as if she's trying to take in the whole universe in one long gaze. I fight the urge to kiss her. Would she taste as good as she looks?

She finally manages to speak. "It's breathtaking!"

Actually, *she's* breathtaking. But she's not ready to hear that. And I sure as hell am not ready to deliver those words. Nothing about me is relationship material. *Nothing*.

FOUR

I don't know how long we lean against the boulder, her neck craned towards the stars. But her hand never leaves mine, and my eyes never leave her face. When she gets out of her own head, feeling instead of being so cerebral, it's a total turn-on. I wish she'd do it more. A lump rises in my throat, and a strange part of me wants to protect her...to care for her.

Her gaze turns from the universe towards me, and she catches me staring. Her eyes meet mine confidently, and a surge of blood rushes to my cock.

Fuck, I'd love to have her in my bed. But she's my sister-in-law's best friend, which means she's off-limits. If we got together and then fucked it up, it could prove awkward... even miserable for all involved.

And I'm pretty sure I'd fuck it up. *Something I'm not about to do to Maksim or Alex.*

But I'd be lying if I said I didn't want her.

Her eyes are on my mouth as she asks, "What are you waiting for?"

"Come again?"

"Are you going to kiss me or what?"

I tip my head back, looking at the stars. "I don't know if that's a good idea. If things didn't work out between us, it would be hard on everyone."

"Oh, I already know they won't work out."

My eyes dart to hers. "And how do you know that?"

"Well, bribing Alex's cousin pretty much says it all. You're not interested in relationships."

I counter, "And neither are you."

She nods. "And then there's the constant stream of women throwing themselves at you..."

I laugh. "You sound jealous, Jess."

She exhales sharply. "Absolutely not."

I ask again, "So, why wouldn't we work? I'm just curious."

Laughing, she replies, "Does it really matter?"

I kick the dirt in front of me, letting go of her hand and stepping forward. "Considering you're preemptively dumping me...and asking me to kiss you at the same time, maybe."

"I'm just being logical." Her voice trails off.

"I've scared you, haven't I?" I glance back over my shoulder towards her. "What I told you earlier about my family... I shouldn't have. It would freak anybody out."

She steps forward, grabbing my arm, and looking up at me, her face grave. "The fact you're a survivor? That you overcame extraordinary odds as a kid to grow up and make a living saving people's lives? How could that freak me out?"

"I'm not talking about that. I'm talking about what my father did. Forget I mentioned it."

But looking down into her wide pale green eyes, I know she won't.

So, I continue, "I just need you to know I'm a good guy, despite my bio family and history."

"Good guy? You're a hero, Logan. You save people for a living."

The way she's staring up at me, breathless and unguarded, quickens my pulse. She wants me as much as I want her. It's obvious, overwhelming.

Why should I care if she doesn't think we could work out? After all, isn't that usually my line when relationship talk happens?

Resolving to enjoy the moment and quit worrying about shit I can't change, I cover her adorable mouth with my own. Something I've fought hard against all week. Her lips relax, and my tongue sweeps into her warm invitation, sending flames trailing through my veins and arteries. She tastes like sugar and flowers, and I can't hold back a hungry growl. My heart races as I put my hands on her waist, fitting her soft body against my hard planes.

She melts into me, trembling, and the feel of her full breasts on my chest makes my cock throb, sending urgent waves of desire to my core. Her hands pull my shirt from my tux pants. I shudder at the touch of her feather-light fingertips as they trace the muscles of my back, sending shivers of desire up and down my spine. *Why didn't we try this sooner?* We've wasted a whole week, and I'm determined to make up for it.

The urgency in her touch makes my heart pound out of my chest, and I feel savage, out of control. I can't get enough of her...her taste, her feel, the way her tongue returns the sensual dance. Letting out a ragged sigh, I step back, rubbing my hands over my face and shaking my head to get my bearings. "Damn, woman, you're dangerous."

She laughs, and I catch her cheek in my hand, turning her face up towards mine.

Flirting, she asks, "Is it really so dangerous to want to get to know you better?"

"It is, if this is going to fuck up Maksim and Alex's world in any way. If that's the case, I'm putting an end to it now."

She shrugs. "You're getting ahead of yourself. What I want comes with no strings attached."

"Are you sure about that?"

"I'm sure," she replies firmly. "I don't want any complications tonight, just great sex."

"Where have you been all my life?" Leaning in, I take her mouth again, moaning against the way her tongue mates with mine. She's an amazing kisser, and I can't get enough of her soft, candy-flavored lips. My hands slide down over her curvy ass, and I squeeze, pulling her possessively into my hard arousal. She gasps, molding her soft body to mine, as her hands palm my back, drawing me closer.

My right hand drops to the slit in her dress, caressing her soft, smooth leg, a desire I haven't been able to erase from my mind since the garter. I slide my hand up, playfully pulling and releasing the small scrap of lace so that it snaps against her leg. She shudders, and I drop to my knees tracing hot kisses from her knee slowly up her thigh, savoring the taste of her soft skin with every swipe of my tongue. The way she angles her hips towards my head tells me everything I need to know.

Letting out a ragged breath, she places her hands on my head, guiding me toward her precious core until her invitation turns into a barrier. Breathlessly, she stops my head from traveling any further up her thigh. I know she wants me as desperately as I want her, the way she threads her fingers in my hair. But she's stubborn as always. I let out a growl of frustration, trying to turn my brain back on.

Panting, she whispers, "Okay, rain check."

I shake my head reluctantly. "Rain check?"

She nods, before resting her head back against the boulder and gulping for air. "We have to," but her resolve sounds as shaky as her voice.

"You don't want me to stop," I mumble sensually, my lips returning to her skin, and she nods in agreement. But she pushes my head away for a second time, and I know she's made up her mind.

"No, I don't want you to stop, but you have to stop. We have to. I'm being a terrible maid of honor right now. I mean, beyond terrible. Awful. The worst."

She's right, but it's not what I want to hear. My cock's rock hard, and I'm desperate for release. I haven't had blue balls like this since high school. I sit back on my heels looking up at Jess. She's a fucking goddess in the moonlight, every inch curvy pastel and soft femininity, from her platinum locks to the pink-tipped toes peeking out of her high heels.

"Rain check," she says again, still panting, and I wrap my arms around her hips, drawing her close and planting a kiss on her dress in the spot between her thighs.

I look up. "Fuck, Jess, You're killing me here. How long a raincheck are we talking?" *Please don't say the next time you visit from San Francisco.*

"Just until the wedding's over."

"So, tonight, then?"

"Yes, after the wedding's officially over."

I rub my hands over my face, taking a couple of deep breaths before I jump to my feet and adjust my pants so I can walk mostly pain-free.

Once the blood starts returning to my brain, I can think more clearly. I don't know what it is about this girl, but she suspends all reason, all logic. Despite a deep attraction to her since day one, I had things under control. I had it figured out until that damn garter incident. Fuck! I took one look at her leg, and I knew I was a goner. By the first touch of her skin, I had to claim her. No matter how off-limits she might be.

Shaking my head, I try to sound reasonable again. "I've got to check on Pop and get him settled in for the night, anyway. I should also make sure everyone has a safe way home from the ranch. Hopefully, nobody got hammered tonight."

Jess smiles, taking my hand, and it takes everything in me not to stride back to the boulder, pin her against it, and show her how turned on she's got me. Thankfully, we walk in silence back towards the barn, giving me extra time to clear the cloud of lust from my head. I take a couple of deep breaths to get myself pulled together, and she laughs at my efforts.

"This is your fault, you know," I say giving her a fake glare.

"I take full responsibility."

"And you'll take the consequences, too."

Her face reddens, and I can't help but laugh. Considering what we were just up to, I can't imagine a few words making her blush. I find it irresistible, all the same.

Soon, far off sounds of clinking plates and glasses, music, and people chatting greet my ears. My cock's still ready for action, but at least I can hide it with the tux jacket.

Jess's next words catch me off guard, as if she's mid-thought and suddenly talking out loud. "That's another thing I like about you."

"Are we making a list?"

She hesitates, looking down. "Well, I guess we could."

"What's that?"

"You're not a drinker."

"Don't get me wrong. I like an occasional beer but never to get drunk. It doesn't fit with the whole search and rescue MO. I never know when I'm gonna get the next notice that a search party is forming."

"That's got to be disruptive."

"Yeah, but I guarantee the people who are lost or injured feel even more disrupted. So do their families. I'm just happy to be a part of recovering them...hopefully safe and sound."

"You're a true hero," she replies, making my heart expand.

I steal another of her honey kisses. It puts a lump in my throat.

"Whatever it takes to get you in my bed. I'll wear a damn cape, if you like."

Her eyes rove over me before she replies, "Nope, I think naked will work just fine."

I kiss her again, and her tongue flicks flirtatiously into my mouth, making my cock an instant ramrod. "Fuck, Jess. You want to go back in or not? You're giving me real mixed signals here."

She laughs and winks.

I'm out of breath, and so is she as we climb the embankment, veering toward the barn. But it's not from walking.

I'm careful to drop her hand before going inside, and she returns my jacket. Instead of entering together, I hang back a few steps, tucking my shirt in and putting on my jacket before entering the tealight-illuminated barn.

Jess's lips look a little puffy, and her cheeks are flushed. Hopefully, no one will notice.

CHAPTER
FIVE
JESS

"You need to be careful," Alex whispers, concerned. I hate seeing her like this, but I don't need a mother.

"Careful of what?" I reply, trying to ignore her furrowed brow and frown.

"Logan is nice and all. But he has quite a reputation."

"Sweetie, this is your wedding night. The last thing you need to worry about is me. Besides, I can take care of myself."

She hugs me, and I can see Maksim eyeing her over my shoulder. The moody mountain man wants her alone. "I know you can take care of yourself, but I don't want you getting hurt. Besides, he's a lot older than you."

"Really?" I reply defiantly, "I forgot to card him."

Maksim comes up behind her, wrapping his arms around her and kissing her neck. I don't think conjoined twins spend as much time together. But such is love, I guess.

"You ready yet, wife?"

Alex's eyes narrow, and she whispers, "Do you have a ride back to the bed and breakfast?"

I left my car in Hollister, carpooling earlier with the other bridesmaids out to Rough & Ready Ranch. Her head darts around, looking for them now. "They didn't leave without you, did they?"

"It's fine," I reply, waving her off. "There are plenty of people to give me a ride back to Hollister."

Her eyes dart towards Logan. Mine follow. He's on the other side of the barn, kneeling beside his dad.

"Sasha, you're killing me here," Maksim pleads.

"Get out of here, you two," I order.

Without hesitation, Maksim picks Alex up in his arms as she protests. "You heard Jess. She's got this covered."

"Maksimka, put me down!" she orders, but the hulk of a mountain man lets out a roar of laughter instead. "Keep it up, baby, and I really will throw you over my shoulder and drag you home."

She giggles, and I wave goodbye as the happy couple leaves.

My eyes stray back towards Logan, now helping the elderly cowboy to his feet. Wyatt, the foster dad of this manly crew of foster brothers, looks tired as he shuffles beside Logan. The gorgeous bearded mountain man searches the crowd for a moment before his eyes find me with a satisfied grin and wink.

Shaking my head to clear my thoughts, I dive into completing my maid of honor duties. I ensure the caterer has everything she needs, including a check for the night's festivities. Then, I do the same with the DJ.

"Hey, Frederick," I say, catching the attention of Alex's musician friend, who played the ceremony and cocktail hour with his quartet.

The gaunt, fine-boned man nods curtly in reply, grabbing

his trench coat and instrument case. I can't remember if he plays the violin or viola because classical music isn't my thing. But I do know one thing. "You guys sounded amazing tonight." I try to hand him a check Alex's parents made out earlier, but he refuses it, rolling his eyes. "Consider this my gift to Alex."

"Then, consider this a travel reimbursement."

"Nope," he replies stubbornly, and despite my urgings, he continues to refuse until I finally give up. We shake hands, and he leaves. Watching him walk away, I know I could ride back to Hollister's bed and breakfast with him. It would probably be smarter than spending the night with Logan. But I say nothing.

I find Alex's parents and hand the check back to her father, Gregor. "Frederick wouldn't accept it." Olga, her mother, clicks her tongue angrily as she eyeballs the check, saying something in Bulgarian. Gregor shrugs his shoulders resigned. Growing up next door to Alex, you'd think I'd know Bulgarian by now. But the language never clicked with me. The food sure did, though!

"I've put all of the wedding gifts on one table," I tell Olga, "Is there anything else you need from me tonight?"

"No, thank you, Jess," she replies, and they start towards the barn doors.

Gregor stops, turning to ask me, "Do you need a ride back to Hollister?"

I shrug. "No, I'm good. Have a great night, you two."

Olga gives me a suspicious look before Gregor scolds her, and they turn to leave.

I see why when I look over my shoulder.

"Hey, sexy," Logan growls into my ear, grabbing me around the waist and pulling me back into his firm body. I let out a soft sigh before swiveling my head guiltily around the room. Fortunately, only the catering staff are still here and nearly finished packing.

"Don't you think it's time we get you out of those heels and that dress?"

I lean back against him, feeling my heart start thumping again.

Still, I want to make sure I haven't forgotten anything. I survey the room one more time.

As if reading my mind, he replies, "They've got it covered. Now it's time for me to cover you."

CHAPTER
SIX
JESS

Outside, the cool air of the night sends goosebumps up and down my arms, and Logan is fast to wrap his jacket around me for the second time. He leads me towards a silver Chevy dually. I should ask him to take me to my hotel room. But the words never come out.

He opens the passenger door to his truck and grabs me around the waist, effortlessly boosting me into the seat. The handsome ebony-haired mountain man leans into the cab to fasten my seatbelt, and I can't believe my eyes. It's like he's from another century. Clicking it into place, he turns, his face inches from mine.

Leaning in for another ravenous kiss, he claims me unrepentantly. I let out a soft moan as his lips and tongue ratchet the tension deep in my core.

Reluctantly, he pulls away, exhaling and grabbing my hand. He puts it on the bulge between his legs, confessing, "This is what you do to me, Jess."

The words put a lump in my throat. So does the massive girth under my palm. I'm no longer thinking about anything but getting back to his cabin. The ache between my legs has turned into a throb. Only one thing will satisfy me...

He closes the passenger door, jogs around to the driver's side, and hops into the cab. Starting up the truck engine, the Foo Fighters' "Everlong" blares through the speakers, and I steal glances at him out of the corner of my eye.

What would it be like if he and I were together? If we were like Maksim and Alex? But I banish the stupid questions, reminding myself of Alex's warning. *Logan's only in this for the sex. And isn't that all I want, too?*

To stop the thoughts in my head, I ask, "So, how old are you, Logan?"

He shoots a wary look my way, and I apologize feeling immediately stupid. "If that's too personal, you don't have to answer."

"No offense, but we're about to get real personal, Jess. Are you having second thoughts?"

"Nope." I don't know if I'm lying or telling the truth.

"I can take you back to the bed and breakfast, if you prefer. There's no pressure...really."

"No, I want this," I reply.

"No strings attached?"

"No complications."

"Kinda like friends with benefits?" he asks.

I one-up him. "Acquaintances with benefits."

He laughs, "Acquaintances? Not after tonight."

I eye him suspiciously. For all the no-strings-attached talk, he's giving off mixed vibes.

"Remember, we can't catch feelings for each other."

He holds up his hand, "Scout's honor."

I start playing with the radio, and the conversation

stalls. There are no streetlights out here. The night presses in on us, growing darker and colder by the minute.

"Thirty-five." He gives me a sideways glance.

I nod, not especially surprised by the answer.

"And you?"

"Twenty-four."

"Shit."

"What?"

"You're eleven years younger than me."

"I can do the math. Is that a problem?"

He grimaces, letting out a sigh. "Only if we let it be."

"Couldn't agree more." I reach across the truck console, putting my hand on the iron-firm rod behind his zipper.

He lets out a groan as I massage him. "Shit, girl, you're gonna make me drive off the road."

"Don't get distracted, then."

He lets out another groan. "Easier said than done."

I knead into his hard cock more confidently.

"You keep that up, and I will stop this truck, bend you over the tailgate, and fill you with my cum."

I apply a little more pressure.

"Fuck!" he bellows.

I try to loosen the belt of his tux pants and unzip the zipper, but his dick is pressed so hard against it, I can't budge the button.

He pulls my hand away, putting it back in my lap.

"You know, two can play at this game." Reaching over, he sticks his hand beneath my skirt. Catching my breath, I close my eyes focusing on his hot touch.

When his fingers hit my wet panties, I moan, and he lets out a low rumble. "You're ready for me, aren't you?" He slides the fabric to the side, and I groan as his fingertips glide through my folds. How he drives stick with his hand in my panties, I don't know. And I don't care. Instead, I bite my lower lip, focusing on his rough fingers working in and out of me and his thumb circling my clit.

"Wait 'til I put my tongue on you," he says with a naughty smile, bringing his fingers to his mouth and licking them clean. "You taste so fucking good." He's got a pained expression on his face now, and he shifts in his seat.

CHAPTER
SEVEN
LOGAN

The wheels of my truck squeal up the dirt road to my cabin, and my breath comes fast now. One taste of Jess, and I'm ravenous. I park the truck with a jerk, hustling around to the passenger side. If we don't get in the house soon, I'll rut with her in the damn dark.

I pull her out of the truck, and her body slides down mine until her feet touch the ground. I can't help myself. I pin her against the truck with my hips, crashing into her as I ravage her lips. My hands come up to the top of her dress, palming her breasts, and I can feel her heart pounding in her chest. My thumbs go to her pearled nipples, teasing them, and she arches back as my head dips down to tease her through the fabric with my teeth.

Every cell in my body wants to lift her skirt and have her right here. But we've got to be more responsible than that. I grab her hand, leading her towards the door. We're breathing like we're at the top of Mount Everest.

Inside, Max barks ferociously.

"I didn't know you had a dog," she says.

I look back, and she's got a worried expression on her face. "Don't worry. His bark's worse than his bite."

"That's good because it sounds like Cujo in there."

"I know, right? But he wouldn't hurt a fly."

The door opens, and I muscle in first, holding the furry brown-and-tan canine back with my knee. But the move only slows Max momentarily. Before I know it, he frantically sniffs at Jess. "Back off!" I command.

Jess puts her hand out. He comes right to it, covering her in slobbery kisses and rubbing his head against her palm.

"You better watch out. Once you start showing him attention, he'll never let you stop."

She looks up, laughing. "What's his name?"

"Max."

"You named your dog after your brother?"

She's not the first person who's asked me this.

"I didn't give him his name. Max was a service dog in Afghanistan, where he got wounded. A Marine buddy up in Idaho connected me with him, and I couldn't say no. Since nursing him back to health, he's been the best service dog I've ever owned."

"Better than Kaya?" she teases, referring to Maksim's lead sled dog. A while ago, I trained her for avalanche rescue, and next thing we know the husky helped Maksim pull Alex out of a snowbound car during a freak storm. That's how they ended up hitched.

Max's ears perk up at the name Kaya, and I laugh. "Kaya's Max's girlfriend. Isn't that right, boy?"

"I never would've guessed."

I continue, "In answer to your question, he's better than Kaya. Although she's definitely won major brownie points in the family. If it wasn't for her finding Alex, I'm pretty sure Maksim would've turned into a grumbly old monk. He was already halfway there."

She laughs. "Setting aside the fact Kaya and Maksim saved Alex's life, I'm also amazed about how happy he's made her. I thought she'd never find anyone she wanted to hold hands with, let alone kiss. She was the girl who said 'ew' when we played spin the bottle... The one time her parents let her go without practicing."

"No wonder they're perfect for each other."

The room grows quiet momentarily before she asks, "Is Max a German shepherd?"

"Nope, a Belgian Malinois."

"He's beautiful."

I nod in thanks, saying, "Have a seat if you like," with a sweep of the hand. The sexy blonde heads to the couch with Max trailing behind. The fuzzball jockeys for a place on her lap as soon as she sits. She lets out a surprised, "Oh!"

"Max, down."

He's not listening, and it irks me. I head towards the door, whistling for him to follow, and he does so begrudgingly, looking back over his shoulder at Jess. I know how he feels as I look at the adorable woman in my living room. I want her undivided attention, too.

After letting him out to the bathroom, I turn back to Jess, rubbing my hand over my heart. "Can I get you anything? A beer? Wait, you said you don't drink. Juice or water?"

"I'm fine," she replies, smiling and looking around curiously. Over the past few days, I've noticed how observant and detail-oriented she is. It's easy to see why she's such a great journalist.

Outside, Max goes crazy, barking and growling.

Jess looks up, her eyebrows knitting together. "Is he always like this?"

"Only when he sees a bear or mountain lion."

"A bear or mountain lion?" she exclaims, her voice raised.

I shrug. "Yeah, there are plenty around here. Excuse me while I see what's going on with him."

Her face looks skeptical , and she calls after me, "Don't get eaten by a bear."

I've got the door open and am halfway out before hearing what she says. I peek back in teasing, "Don't worry. I won't go *Revenant* on you or anything."

She giggles nervously.

Outside, I stand on the porch ordering, "Come, Max!" He ignores me, staring into the woods with his hackles raised. The last thing I need right now is him getting in a fight with a predator. Talk about a cock block. "Come!" I order impatiently. He's still not listening, and it takes me a good five minutes to get him to respond. I don't know if it's Jess's company, but he's a mess tonight. It'll be back to the drawing board with obedience training come Monday morning.

Back inside, I lock the front door while Max transforms from vicious guard dog into a teddy bear, inching his way into Jess's lap again. I can't blame him. "He thinks he's a lap dog."

She laughs, "He's a big baby, isn't he?"

"Your crate," I command, and he heads over to his bed in the corner. I latch him in for the night, giving him a Greenie.

"Now, where were we?" I ask, offering her my hand.

EIGHT

In my bedroom, I kneel in front of the hearth getting a fire going while Jess uses the bathroom. The chill in the air gives me the excuse I need, but there's more to it than that. I can't get the picture of her bathed in the coppery tones of the campfire out of my head. Knowing I only have this one night with her makes me greedy, and I need to see her that way one more time.

She walks back into the room, standing by the side of the bed, and my breath catches in my throat. I run my hand through my hair, taking her in for a long moment. She's breathtaking, and I want to remember her standing here in my bedroom, just like this, for a long time.

"Why are you staring at me?" she asks, her eyes widening.

"Because you're gorgeous," I respond unabashedly.

She frowns, and I realize I've overstepped one of the boundaries we spoke of earlier. Don't catch feelings, as she put it.

"You should quit talking," she says, her voice low and seductive as her hands go to my chest.

I pull her into my arms, kissing her until she moans under my lips. My dick's rock hard, and I feel like I'll explode. "Fuck, Jess, I need inside you now."

She pulls back. "Just so you know, I'm clean and on birth control."

I nod. "I'm clean, too, and I've got condoms," I reply, covering her mouth with mine.

"Yes," she sighs into my mouth.

I push her gently back into my bed, crawling beside her to reach into my nightstand drawer. I pocket the first condom I find, returning my focus to her.

"I can't stop thinking about how you taste. I need to taste more of you."

She lies back, and I pull the multi-layered skirt of her gown up, finding a dark pink lace G-string at the apex of her thighs. I cover it with my mouth, nipping and teasing her through the lace. Her fingers thread into my hair, pulling me down. Her panties are dripping wet, and I bury my nose in their intoxicating scent. Removing them with my teeth, I throw them to the side. She lets out a giggle, and then I part her creamy thighs with my shoulders, diving into her silky folds.

Her pussy's swollen from the truck foreplay. I push a finger into her, moaning and grinding into the bed beneath me at how tight she feels. She's slick as wet silk and hot beneath my hands. My cock wants in so bad, but I won't stop until she's fully satisfied. I dive knuckle-deep into her, creating a steady rhythm before putting my tongue on her pearl. Her hips lift towards me, and I love how responsive she is to my every touch.

I find her G-spot, and she thrusts into my hand. "There it is."

"Yes," she pants.

I work the spot with increasing pressure, ratcheting up her pleasure until she's begging me to keep going. I flick her clit between my teeth and tongue, devouring her sweet honey, and she shudders wildly as my finger crashes into her. Finally, she can't take anymore. Writhing on my bed, she comes into my hand, and I feel like I could conquer the world. Fuck, I've never seen anything so lovely. She falls back, and I climb her body until we're face to face.

"You seemed to like that," I observe quietly, and she wraps her hand around my neck, pulling me in for a kiss. My mouth devours her, my tongue showing her with a slow, steady rhythm how I'll work her pussy. Her hand slides to my rod, taking hold of it, and I shiver as she tugs it back and forth. I can still feel her legs shaking.

"How do you want it?" My voice sounds strained, pushed past the brink of control.

"Doggy style?"

I nod. "But first, I want you naked."

She hesitates.

"Now," I command. I can tell by the way her eyes dilate and her lips part that she likes me in control. Sitting up, I unbutton my tux shirt and throw it on the floor beside the bed. Next, my undershirt comes off, and then I stand, scrambling out of my pants and boxer briefs while she wiggles out of her dress. I let out a moan, taking in her matching dark pink bra, which she unclasps. It falls to the floor, revealing generous breasts I can't wait to devour. But we're past the point of foreplay now. They'll have to take a raincheck, as she puts it.

"Get on the bed, on your knees," I command as I reach down to pick up my pants, searching the pocket for my condom. I open the package and slide it down over my long girth, and she looks over her shoulder, watching, her eyes molten with desire.

Coming up behind her, I smack her ass. She lets out the most adorable cry, and I grab onto her hips. Fuck, I love this view of her wide ass with her legs spread for me.

Teasing her opening with my tip, she shudders again, and then I plow into her. She lets out a gasp, followed by a sexy moan. I should take it slow. But she's got me so worked up, I can't stop. The tight heat of her body clamps around me, and I find the perfect rhythm, making her writhe under me again.

"Yes, baby, cover that cock with your cream."

As she spasms around me, I release into her, giving everything I've got. We fall onto the bed next to each other. Both shaken and catching our breaths. I pull the condom off carefully, knotting it and throwing it into the waste basket by the nightstand.

"That was so, so good," she says, still breathing hard.

I tuck a stray hair behind her ear, smiling. I've never come so hard in my life. But I doubt she wants to know that.

"You taste amazing. You feel amazing. Fuck, Jess." I stare up at the ceiling, letting it all sink in.

Licking her flavor off my fingers, my cock jumps back to life. I'm already addicted to her. I won't rest until she's on my tongue again.

She wraps her fingers around my cock, and I let out a happy groan.

I've never allowed myself to have a woman twice in one night. Usually, I'd be cleaning myself up and urging her home. But something's different with Jess. I want her again. I shouldn't, but I can't help myself.

"We should do it again," I pant, looking in her direction.

I hope my eyes aren't too pleading. But I don't know what I'll do if she says no.

"Seriously?"

I look down at my already hard cock in her hand. "I'm pretty sure you know what you're doing."

Her eyes follow mine, giggling. All she manages is, "Wow."

"Wow, as in yes?"

"Yes."

I reach for the side table, pulling out another condom, and I take her again. This time, at a slower pace where I can savor everything about her, face to face. Yeah, I know this is a one-night thing. But I'm determined to make it a night she'll never forget.

When she's about to orgasm again, she closes her eyes. I want to command her, "Look at me." But that would definitely break her rules. Besides, she may be thinking about somebody else. The thought guts me, and I try to push it from my mind.

Pumping my release into her, I squeeze her hips so tightly I'm afraid I'll bruise her. The last thing I want to do is hurt her...*ever*. But she fills me with an animal desire I struggle to control.

NINE

JESS

I startle awake, disoriented and peering around the dark bedroom. It takes a moment for me to remember where I'm at.

Logan's cabin.

Shit.

I've never slept over at a guy's house before. Doing so breaks one of my cardinal rules, and I realize with a panic I need to get out of here...before things get any weirder.

In the kitchen, I hear pots banging and Logan whistling. I shut my eyes in a panic. *Please don't tell me he's cooking for me.*

What was I thinking last night when I let him bring me back here without my car? I guess that he'd give me a lift back to the bed and breakfast afterward. But what happened between us last night was no one-night stand.

I've only had sex a couple of times in my life, and they were all one-night stands. There's no other way to enjoy the gratification of sex without a relationship. And I've never been interested in a relationship. But what's going on now feels increasingly complicated. The room shrinks in around me as I put my head in my hands. I need an escape plan.

Sitting up, my muscles ache in places I didn't know I had them. My mind wanders back over the night, and I know why.

Logan took me not once, not twice, but three times, leading me over the precipice of countless mind-bending, earth-shattering orgasms. I close my eyes, remembering the feel of his rock-hard body moving over mine, his hot breath on my face as we climax together. And I'm instantly dripping.

I'm in trouble.

Never in my life have I spent time with a man that makes me feel the way Logan does. I could get used to this, and it scares the hell out of me. I'm not a relationship kind of girl, and I never have been. My journalism career has always come first, and it's alway been enough. Who needs a personal life when your bylines are syndicated, and *Dateline* is begging you for interviews?

Besides, what would I have to offer in a relationship anyway? I grew up in a dysfunctional household with parents who alternated between vicious fights and blackout drinking. I wouldn't know the first thing about how to act in a relationship. I'd make a huge mess of it. And I can't make a mess of anything that could negatively impact Alex.

Hands shaking, I'm about to scramble out of bed and back into my gown when the door opens. The dark, bearded mountain man pads into the room casually, followed by Max.

"Morning," he says in a low rumble, and his smile and shirtless body undo me. All he has on is a pair of flannel pajama pants that cling to his muscles in all the right places.

"How do you take your coffee?"

"Black."

"I guessed right then." He closes the distance between us, sitting on the edge of the bed next to me. He hands me a sturdy ceramic mug, and I take it gratefully, wrapping my hands around its warmth.

Cocking his head to the side with a sheepish grin, he says, "I'm sorry I didn't let you sleep much last night. But I couldn't get enough of you." His soulful eyes search my face. I squirm under his gaze, uncomfortable receiving his total focus.

Staring into my coffee mug, I take a deep breath, steeling my nerves. *This has to stop now...before it spirals out of control.*

"Are you okay?" he asks, his brows knitting together. "I didn't hurt you or anything?"

I look up with a smile, and my cheeks heat. *What is this guy doing to me?* "Not at all. I had a fantastic night."

"Any way you'd consider giving me today, too?"

He's staring into my eyes, willing me to say yes.

"Wouldn't that break the terms of our agreement?"

"That," he says, exhaling. "No strings. No complications. Yeah, I remember. But we never agreed to no hiking. I've got the day off for once, and I was thinking you might like to see more of Rough & Ready Country. The trail up to Wild Horse Falls is pretty popular and has nice views. Maybe you could write a travel article about it or something—"

"I'm a true crime writer, not a travel writer. And I didn't exactly wear clothes suitable for hiking," I reply, looking across the room to where my gown fell last night.

"I've already got that figured out. We'll swing by Hollister on the way so you can get changed at the bed and breakfast. And we can get lunch at The Human Being to pack along. That is, if you think you'll be hungry after the mound of food I cooked for breakfast."

"What are you doing, Logan?" I don't know how else to ask but point blank.

His eyebrows raise a little, and he looks away. "What do you mean?"

"Breakfast, hiking, lunch. This all feels a bit complicated."

He shrugs. "Can't help it if I'm old fashioned when it comes to hospitality. Don't worry, I won't get attached." But his face looks conflicted.

I relax slightly, even as the words put a pit in the bottom of my stomach.

I should say no to hiking. I can feel the word on the tip of my tongue. But I can't spit it out.

Max whines, looking up at me, and what comes out of my mouth shocks me. "Can we bring Max with us?"

"I wouldn't do it any other way."

He flashes an ear-to-ear smile, and I return it like a fool. *What am I thinking?* I have to head back to San Francisco today. But before I can change my mind, he leans in for a tender kiss.

Definitely not a one-night-stand kiss.

"Alright, get your ass out of bed, lazy head. Time to get moving."

I watch him swagger from the room with Max at his heels, admiring the taper of his muscular back down to the waistband of his flannel pants, which showcases his tight ass and powerful thighs. The door closes, and I get up, stretching as the coolness of the air hits my naked body.

The door opens again, and he pokes his head back in. "If you'd like to borrow some of my clothes, they're... Hello." His eyes snap towards me, and my cheeks burn. I reflexively wrap my arms around my waist as his eyebrows shoot up.

"Don't do that," he scolds, striding into the room and closing the door swiftly so Max can't follow.

My arms fall to my sides, and my fists ball. Standing here makes me feel incredibly vulnerable, but I'm not about to let him know that. He lets out an appreciative sigh. "Fuck, you're even more beautiful in the morning light."

My eyes drop to the ground. "You don't have to flatter me—"

"Flatter you? Is that what you think this is?"

I push my chin forward, trying to act more confident than I feel. "I'm no typical beauty."

"No, you're not," he replies, closing the distance between us, and taking me in hungrily with his eyes. "You're fucking gorgeous. I think there's something we need to do before breakfast and hiking. If you're not too sore?"

I've messed up every part of this one-night stand, but it's too late now. So, why hold back? Especially when my pussy's aching for him again. I wrap my arms around his waist, fitting my soft curves against his muscular core. Taking a deep breath, I savor his musky masculine smell as I kiss his chest.

He grabs my ass, pulling me into him. "This is what you do to me. Flattery or not." I can feel his rock-hard arousal, and it makes me smile as I step back towards the bed, tugging on the front of his flannel pants. He lets out a low growl.

"You said you made a big breakfast, but I'm not hungry yet. Think you can help me work up an appetite?"

"Fuck, yeah, baby."

I've never willingly let a man call me "baby" before. But it sounds good on his lips. Then, again, no man has ever made me orgasm before, let alone multiple times. Honestly, I believed that kind of pleasure only came from a vibrator. Logan proved me wrong over and over last night. And I must say what he gave me was a whole lot more satisfying than anything I've ever received from personal gratification.

I know I'm treading on dangerous ground. But as he claims my mouth, I don't care. My heart pounds in anticipation, and I embrace the craziness of it all as he pushes me back onto the bed, devouring me.

TEN

LOGAN

I doubted we'd ever make it up here, especially after our torrid morning. And that's not to mention the steamy early afternoon shower we shared before I realized I needed to put my foot down and get us out the door.

What it is about this woman, I can't say. But she's got me nursing a constant hard-on. We cut out the trip to the cafe since we got such a late start. Besides, it felt pointless after the big breakfast. She fussed about me cooking for her. I don't think she's used to people taking care of her, but I'm hooked on the idea. Besides, considering how many calories we've both burned in the last twelve hours, neither of us would have moved without some bacon and eggs.

I watch her snap pictures of the falls, exclaiming how stunning they are. I rub my hand instinctively over my heart. As I share more pieces of my world with her, she can't get enough. Kind of like how I can't get enough of her.

"You want me to take a picture of you with the falls?"

She nods enthusiastically, and I jump up, striding over

to her. She hands me her rose gold phone case and walks toward the edge, calling Max to her.

"Watch your footing," I warn yet again. As a search and rescue unit lead, I can't count how many times I've rescued or recovered someone who slipped on the wet rocks here. The aftermath is never pretty. But then, I know better than most people just how unforgiving nature can be.

She frowns, and I realize I'm acting more like a dad than a boyfriend. *Okay, wait a second. Not a boyfriend—a one-night stand.*

One night.

Those two words make my chest ache. During the two-hour hike to the falls, I wracked my brain for excuses to get her back to my place tonight. She checked out when we stopped by the bed and breakfast to get her luggage. It gave me hope. But then she declared San Francisco her final stop of the day.

If I keep her out here long enough, maybe she won't want to drive back in the dark. But knowing her, she'll do it anyway. Just to prove a point. And then I'll worry about her getting home safely. Hell, whether it's light or dark, I'm going to worry about her.

Would it be too much to ask her to call me when she gets home? Just to let me know she made it safely? I shake my head. Yeah, it would. She's made it clear she doesn't want me getting possessive.

Fuck, if I'd known how hard this was going to be last night, maybe I would've said no to kissing her in the first place. But would I really have done that? I know better. Jess has just given me the best night and day of my life, and if that's all I get, it's still worth it. Even though tomorrow will hurt like hell.

I keep clicking photos of her and thinking. I even take a

video of her, asking what she thinks of the falls. Covertly, I text myself a copy. *What the hell am I doing?* I haven't been able to honestly answer that question since standing in front of the campfire last night holding her hand. Sure, it really started with the garter, and even before that. But I still had some self-control. Then, I started talking about my past, telling her things nobody knows about me. I started thinking thoughts I shouldn't think—possessive thoughts that overrode my normal rules. And now here I am. *Fuck.*

Behind me, a voice asks, "Can I take a picture of you two?"

You two. I wish. I turn, and there's a middle-aged brunette, reaching her hand out towards me with an off-leash collie. I'm about to say no because I'm sure this crosses a line in Jess's rulebook.

But then I hear the curvy blonde's voice override me. "Thank you!"

I stalk towards her, smiling. Her surprise move has given me hope, even though I know it shouldn't. She beams up at me, fisting the back of my t-shirt in her hand to draw me closer. I don't know if I could ever get close enough to her to feel truly satisfied. *Is this why Maksim is such an idiot around Alex?*

I shake my head. The woman snapping photos scolds me to hold still, and I do so begrudgingly. I can't let myself think thoughts like this. Jess has made it clear what she wants, and it isn't me.

Jess leans forward, grabbing the phone from the woman, and we both thank her again.

"We should probably start back," Jess says, looking down. Her words gut me. I have to remind myself that we barely know each other. I'm not the settling down kind of guy. Where would it get me? A ball and chain and a brood of kids? That thought has always repulsed me. But now I must admit, Jess would make a mighty fine ball and chain. And the thought of her belly rounded with one of my kids—

Stop fucking thinking like this, Logan!

I rub a hand over my face, stealing a glance her way. Jess is more than a one-night stand, and she has been since the day I met her. Maybe that's why I fought so hard all week to keep things platonic. Concern about messing things up for Alex and Maksim was really just an excuse for deeper fears—like the fear of finding someone I could never let go.

Jess is strong and resilient with a wicked sense of humor to match my own. She understands me in ways nobody ever has, and she doesn't judge me for my past. Hell, she thinks I'm a hero, and it's a total turn on to her. Yet, she doesn't *actually* need saving, and there's something wildly sexy about that in my book. She's independent and witty and makes me smile until my cheeks hurt. I want her in my life. It's that simple. I know my job doesn't allow for relationship drama and distractions, but she's also highly career driven. We could make it work—no matter what she said last night.

"You sure you can't stay a little longer in Rough & Ready? We could go back to my place and have dinner. I could build a campfire, and we could check out the stars again?" I'm grasping at straws and feeling more pathetic by the second.

Her eyes round and her brows crease, but she shakes her head, looking away.

Well, that hurt. "We better get you on the road before dark." No matter how much I want her to stay, I agreed to her rules, and I'm a man of my word.

She looks over her shoulder at me, and I swear reluctance or disappointment flickers across her face. I want so badly for her to say something. To stop me in my tracks, to tell me maybe a few strings are allowed. I've already tried to make a move. Now, it's up to her.

Instead, she presses her lips together, her face unreadable. And the path darkens as we head back into the thickness of the woods.

Jess grabs my hand again, lacing her fingers through mine, and I swallow the lump in my throat. I don't squeeze her hand anymore, but I try to memorize how it feels.

My cell phone vibrates in my pocket. I don't want to stop, and I don't want to let go of her hand. But I know I've got to see what's going on. I open the notification from Connect Rocket: "Search party forming in one hour. Meet at the warehouse. Bring dogs."

"Hold on," I say, stopping to text back. "I'm at the Falls. 90 minutes out. Be there ASAP." It took us two hours to get up here, but the trail back is downhill, so we'll be done in half the time. I'd anticipated walking slowly, making it last. But with someone missing, I no longer have that luxury. And why draw this out any longer when she's made her feelings toward me clear?

"What's wrong?" Jess asks, breathlessly.

"Time to get back to work."

"Is somebody missing?"

I nod. "I'm sorry to do this, but we'll need to pick up the pace."

"Of course," she replies, worry shadowing her face.

Now that the adrenaline's going and someone needs help, I can't make casual conversation. On the way up, I learned about Jess's past. How she emancipated at sixteen and then earned a 4.0 GPA in high school, garnering enough scholarships to pay her way through journalism

162

school. No wonder she's tough as nails and unwilling to take help from anyone.

I confided more in her, too. Things I haven't even discussed with my brothers. Like how I'm worried about Pop these days. He's gotten frail, and I don't like him living alone at the ranch.

But I'm careful not to spill my guts about anything else...like I did last night. After all, what's the point? In her book, I'm just a good fuck.

At the trailhead, I see my silver Chevy parked alongside her red Camry. We're the last two cars in the parking lot as dusk falls. She's breathing heavily, and I realize I pushed her too hard. But for her part, she never complained.

"Shit, Jess, I didn't realize how tired you were getting. Why didn't you say something?"

She smiles thinly. "It's okay, You need to go. I need to go, too."

I stare at her for what feels like a fleeting eternity before bringing my hand up to palm her cheek. Words fail me, so I lean down, planting the softest kiss on her lips. I meant to end on a note of passion, but tenderness won out. I don't think I've ever kissed a woman like that before. I want to tell her how much I need her, that she needs to stay. That I want her to stay. Instead, I flash her a fake-ass smile so she won't feel sorry for me.

Her face looks sad, although her mouth turns up slightly at the ends.

I can't help myself. "You probably don't want to hear this, but I'm going to miss you."

"I will miss you, too, Logan."

My heart jumps in my chest, and I hold up a hand, "Wait, I have something for you."

Her eyes widen, and I turn, clicking the key fob to

163

unlock my truck. I open the glove compartment and run my hand along the bottom until I find what I'm looking for. I turn around, handing her a single key on an orange whistle keychain. "That's a spare key to my place. If you ever need anything. If you want a break from true crime, or you're looking for a vacation, or whatever, use it." I want to say more but don't.

She shakes her head firmly. "I can't take this. I mean, won't this put a cramp in your player style?"

Leveling my gaze at her, I keep it simple but emphatic, "That's the point." *Why would I want another woman in my bed when I could have you?* I almost say it, but stop short. If she felt the way I do, she wouldn't need to ask that question. She'd already know the answer.

She opens her mouth, and I know I don't want to hear what she has to say. Instead, I hoist her into my arms, kissing her until she's breathless and speechless. Then, I let her go, walking away without looking back.

CHAPTER
ELEVEN

JESS

As I drive through a blur of tears, Logan's truck is in my rearview mirror. I wipe my eyes with the backs of my hands, trying to get a hold of myself. What's wrong with me? Is it the lack of sleep? Hormones? I don't know.

I take a deep breath, trying to pull myself together. I know how dangerous it is to drive emotionally, but I can't pull over. He's following behind me, and I know he'll pull over if I do. I can't keep him from his job any longer.

I feel relieved and devastated when I see his truck turn left toward Hollister. I'm headed for the freeway, and I know I need to put distance between us. Serious distance. But the thing is, I don't want to.

Oh, how I've made a mess of this! But then so has he. I don't even have his number, although it'd be easy enough to get from Alex. That is if she'd quit mothering me.

The house key Logan gave me burns a hole in my pocket. He shouldn't have given it to me. But I know why he did. The past twenty-four hours have been unlike anything I've ever experienced. I'd be an idiot not to want more. By the look on his face when we said goodbye, I'm pretty convinced he feels the same way.

But that'll change with time. Give the tall, muscular mountain man a few weeks away from me, local chicks throwing themselves at him, and I guarantee he'll forget me. It's a certainty, whether I like it or not. And the last thing I'd want to do is use his key and walk in on that. It would destroy me.

Up ahead, I see construction cones in the road and a man in an orange vest and hat holding a "SLOW" sign. I shift down, approaching cautiously, and the bearded man glances over his shoulder, turning the sign to read "STOP." *This is the last thing I need right now.*

I look down at my phone and back up at the construction worker, drumming my fingers impatiently on the steering wheel. Who knows how long I'll have to wait for the pilot vehicle to take me around. Letting out an exasperated breath, I let my head fall back on the headrest, staring at the ceiling.

To kill time, I flip up the screen of my phone, and it goes straight to my texts. I see where a video text of Max and I in front of the waterfall went to a new number. My heart jumps. Apparently, I have Logan's number, after all. And maybe he feels just as torn about me leaving as I do about going. That's definitely what his last kiss felt like.

I take a deep breath, letting it sink in. Maybe I should turn around. Head back to his house. I have a key, after all. I don't know how long he'll be out working, but I could be there when he returns. We could have dinner and make a fire and talk and laugh and have amazing sex. Or we could just sleep in each other's arms. That would feel amazing, too.

My cellphone screen flashes with Alex's name and number.

"Hey, sweetie, why in the world are you calling me on your honeymoon?"

She giggles into the phone, "Our flight leaves tonight. I just finished packing and have probably twice as many clothes as I need. But you know how that goes."

"Sure do. I hope you and Maksim have an amazing time. Every time I meet him. I like him more because he makes you so happy."

"You sound like you've been crying. Are you okay?"

I pause longer than I should.

"Jess, what's wrong?"

I hear a loud knock on the window and gasp audibly, jumping in my seat. The construction worker's at my window. "Alex, can I give you a call right back? I've got somebody at the window."

"At the window? Where are you?"

"Four eighty-eight. Stuck in a construction zone. I'll call you right back."

I roll down my window, annoyed a stranger has caught me crying. But honestly it's none of his business anyway.

"Yes?" I ask, hesitantly looking up.

My eyes narrow as I take in the face, a strange face with oddly familiar eyes—

Ted Wesley Craven.

Gasping, I try to shift from park into drive, but the cold metal of a pistol barrel pressed into my temple stops me. "Try it, and you're dead, bitch."

I put my hands up reflexively, and he yells, "Move over," shoving the gun into my forehead and forcing my head to the right. "Now!"

I'm trembling so hard I can barely get over the console. He fumbles with the door before reaching in to unlock it from the inside. I look in the passenger side mirror, hoping that someone's behind me. But the two-lane country road is desolate.

I reach for my cell phone, but he snatches it out of my hand, twisting my wrist and nearly breaking it in the process. He shoves the phone in his orange vest pocket, climbing into the driver's seat.

"You've been a naughty girl," he says, pulling a fake beard from his face. I can't stop shaking as he shifts from park into drive. Driving through the cones, I watch them scatter in the mirror, my stomach dropping. "Fucking Logan Caples, Rough & Ready's search and rescue lead." He clucks his tongue against his teeth, shaking his head.

Fear paralyzes me, but I manage to choke out, "Don't say his name."

"Who's holding the gun, Ms. Steele? I'll say whatever the hell I want!"

"So, you've been following me all this time? All the way from San Francisco?"

"Yes, Jessica, I did my research. Just like you did your research about me."

He smells so strongly of body odor that I gag, moving to get further away from him. "But I had no clue what a little slut you are. I thought for sure you'd head home last night, and I'd finally be able to finish this. But you're making me work overtime." I look into the passenger side mirror again, and he continues, "Your Search and Rescue boyfriend isn't coming for you, Jess. He's looong gone. On a call clear across the valley. He'll never hear you scream."

Horrified, I realize Craven made the search and rescue call.

My hand reaches for the passenger door handle, and he

locks it from his side, fumbling with the child lock. But we both know it won't work in the front seat. Exasperated, he screams, "Don't even think about jumping out!"

But that's precisely what I'll do. Years of reporting true crime have taught me it's my best chance at survival. No matter how grim the odds. And certainly better than being at this monster's mercy.

I fling the door open, staring at the dizzying blur of pavement below. He speeds up, slamming a hand into my chest to hold me back. I grab my cell phone in his pocket, and he pulls it away, launching it out the window. Between juggling the cell phone and holding me in the passenger seat, the pistol topples to the passenger side floorboard. I try to dive for it, but his arm holds me back.

He slams on the brakes, and my body crashes into the dashboard as I try again for the gun. The car swerves, losing control. Tires squeal sickeningly. We free-fall through the air, spinning away from gravity for one dreadful moment, before slamming back to the ground.

Blood gushes from Craven's forehead as he cradles his head in his hands, his body crumpled in the driver's seat

"You, dumb bitch!" he screams. And as much as I need to find the gun, I need to get away from him even more.

CHAPTER
TWELVE

JESS

S haking gives way to adrenaline, and I scramble through the still-open passenger door, frantic to put distance between us. He grabs my ankle, digging his nails into my flesh, but I use my other foot to kick him until he lets go. Craven appears dazed by the crash, and I've got to take advantage of it.

In the car, he rages, "You fucking bitch!"

I remember the reports about his notorious anger—anger that allowed one woman to escape. I know I need to exploit it now. I sprint into the woods and away from his blood-curdling shrieks. It won't be long before he's after me again. I have to find a place to hide, a way to get away from him. A sharp pain stabs into my stomach, and my heart pounds so fast that I feel like I'm having a heart attack.

Behind me, a gunshot rings out, and my whole body jerks in response to the sound. I don't have my phone. I don't know where I'm going. And Logan thinks I'm headed back to San Francisco, never to talk to him again. Alex is on her honeymoon, and no one will suspect anything's wrong until the weekend ends and I'm not at work. There are countless ways he could torture and kill me over the course of a weekend. I know his style better than anyone, and my stomach churns.

He's screaming behind me, and I'm running so fast my stomach feels as heavy as lead. But I can't stop—no matter what. I know with one hundred percent certainty it'd be better to die in a struggle than to let this man take me alive. I suppress a sob at the thought of Logan finding my body in the woods. Is *this* really what my entire life's been leading up to?

Jumping over boulders and across logs, I speed faster than I ever thought possible. But I can hear the fiend behind me, blasting through brush and tree branches. Soon, I listen to his breathing, too. "Please, Lord. Please don't let me die here," I plead internally. I can see Logan's body crouched over mine, holding me lifeless. I can't do that to him. I can't do that to *us*.

"I'll chase you all night if I have to, you little cunt!" The convicted murderer closes in on me, and my legs start to give out.

A large body crashes into the back of me, pushing me to the ground and knocking the wind out of me. I try to scramble for purchase beneath him, but he's too strong and heavy.

"You're going to pay for this!" he rages in my ear, and I gag at the smell of his putrid breath, gasping for air.

Grabbing me by the back of my hair, he pulls me to my knees, and my hand dives into my pocket. Reflexively, I seize Logan's key in my fist like a weapon. Between the swing of my arm and the momentum of him pulling me backward by my hair, I sink the key deep into his neck.

The whites of his eyes grow huge, and he lets out a startled rattle, dropping my hair. I fall to my knees, searching his hand and the ground for the gun. I lunge towards the spot where he dropped it, falling short.

Then, he's on top of me again, smashing my face into the forest floor until my mouth tastes of gritty dirt and rotten leaves. We're both reaching for the gun, and I realize there's no way my shorter arms can outmaneuver him. He's crawling forward now, closing the distance to the firearm.

His weight shifts with the effort, and I free my pinned right arm, punching him again in the neck and then the face with the key. His hands shield his face, letting the gun drop, and I run for it.

I know I can't win the weapon wrestling match, and I don't have the stomach to punch him again.

Running uphill, my pace slows, and my pulse pounds in my temples. The forest is dark, and the sun is setting, making it hard to see. "Lord, show me a way," I whisper.

The hairs prick up on the back of my neck, and I suddenly halt. My toes slide forward, and I swing my arms to catch my balance. Thousands of feet below, I see the last traces of Gold Run River disappearing into the night. I stand on the edge of a sheer cliff, and the drop is dizzying. I've never been afraid of heights, but now my head spins.

I think Logan said it's called Good Luck Gulch, but I'm not sure. There doesn't seem to be anything lucky about it now.

Behind me, I hear Craven's fevered screams, and I know there's only one thing I can do. Scanning the precipice below, I try to work out a way down. But it's no use. You'd have to be a professional mountain climber to pull this off. And even then, I'm guessing it'd be a nail-biter. As thoughts of Craven's past victims fill my head, though, I realize I'd rather take my chances with the cliff.

My legs tremble beneath me as I scan the edge, looking

for a way down. Anything. I see a dip in the ground to one side and rush in that direction, nearly sliding off the top. The dirt gives way beneath me as I slide forward, rolling onto my belly and grabbing frantically onto bushes as gravity shoves me forward and down. My legs shake, and I scramble for a footfall. I hear the sickening sound of stems snapping and roots pulling up where I've grabbed the foliage with my hands.

Looking up, I see Craven emerge from the trees, searching frantically for me and holding the gun. It doesn't occur to him to look down, where only my head and arms remain. Maybe the bushes I hold finally give way or my hands slip. Either way, I plummet into darkness.

CHAPTER
THIRTEEN
LOGAN

"Something feels off," I state numbly into the satellite phone.

"Roger that," Christian replies.

"So nobody showed up to file a report?"

"Still waiting," my sheriff brother grumbles into the phone.

"And you said Cricket had an odd feeling about it, too?"

Christian grunts. He usually does that when I mention the dispatch girl. Everyone knows he's got the hots for her, but he won't do anything about it.

"Alright, we'll get back to it."

I rub my hands over my face, trying to focus. Max whines, nuzzling my hand when I drop it back to my side. This is exactly why I don't do what I just did with Jess. Now, I can't fucking think straight. My mind wanders back to the last twenty-four hours. I feel her lips on mine, her soft and yielding body beneath me—

Pull it together, Logan. A life could be on the line!

We're two hours into a search for a missing hunter. It's a typical case this time of year. The details of the call reporting the hunter missing don't add up, though. First, the caller claimed to have been on the same hunt, saying he got separated from his buddy. But then he couldn't answer basic questions about what roads they used to access the game management unit associated with the tag or where he and his friend got separated. You could chalk it up to stupidity or lack of knowledge about the area, but my gut says otherwise, and in the world of search and rescue that's what you often end up relying on.

My phone rings, and I stare at the screen. Christian again. "Yes?"

"Dispatch just got confirmation from 9-1-1. The call came from a cell phone on four eighty-eight, five miles past the Wild Horse Falls trailhead."

"What?" *That's right where Jess and I were a couple hours ago.*

"And ShotSpotter just picked up gunfire about three miles into the woods near Dead Man's Drop." *Again, mere miles away from where we hiked earlier. And only minutes away from where I last saw Jess's red Camry driving away.*

"That's more than a half hour away."

"Yep."

"Are you sending deputies?"

"Of course. Wonder if that's your lost hunter?"

"If so, the game warden'll need to follow up with him." We can't have shooters discharging firearms in an area closed to hunting, especially right next to one of Rough & Ready's most popular hiking trails.

Grabbing the walkie-talkie, I say, "Louis, you find anything? Over."

"Nada. Over."

"Chris thinks we need to regroup back near Wild Horse Falls."

"Wild Horse Falls?"

"Roger that. I'll explain on the way. Over."

Louis and I meet back at the truck and load up.

"How did Wild Horse Falls get brought into this?"

"Looks like whoever reported the missing hiker may have been turned around."

None of this makes sense, though. Four eighty-eight is well marked, and so is the Wild Horse Falls Trailhead. And both are closed to hunting.

My phone rings, and I answer it from my steering wheel. "Chris, you're on speaker."

"I'm sending the GPS coordinates for the call and the gunfire. I've got three deputies en route."

"Three? What aren't you telling me, Chris?"

"Nothing. Hollister's rolled up the sidewalks for the night, and we haven't gotten any other calls. Might as well send in a little extra manpower. You can never be too safe."

Those are rare words for my brother. But I'm glad for the extra help because I sure as hell don't feel on top of my game right now. Chris texts the coordinates, and I click the highlighted text, sending it to my GPS.

The radio is low, and I turn it off. Louis and I drive in silence until my cell phone rings. It's Maksim. "Hey, bro, you're on speaker. Aren't you supposed to be on your honeymoon or something?"

"We fly out in a couple of hours. But Alex is ready to postpone everything."

"Already tired of your shit? Can't say I blame her."

Maksim grumbles something inaudible, a common response for my grumpy little brother. "No, she's freaking out because Jess won't call her back and—" I hear Alex's voice saying something and then him handing her the phone.

"Hi, Logan."

"Hey, my new little sis, what's wrong?"

"I'm worried about Jess. I was on the phone with her a couple hours ago, and she said she was waiting in a construction zone on four eighty-eight and someone was at her window. She said she would call me right back only she never did. And then I started wondering, who does road construction on a Sunday around here? It just doesn't feel right."

Doesn't feel right. That's what everyone keeps saying about tonight. "I'd have to call the DOT to double check on that. If it's an emergency, I could see weekend construction. You know, the roads are still a mess after last year's hard winter."

"Mmhmm." She doesn't sound convinced.

I pause unsure of what to say next. "May I ask why you're calling me?"

"Because I called over to the Hollister Bed and Breakfast, and Mrs. Chatterton seems to think you were the last one with Jess. And she said Jess didn't sleep there last night." She says the last sentence in a lowered voice with a smattering of recrimination. *Man, I wish I wasn't on speaker phone right now.*

Wearing a face-splitting grin, Louis tries to give me a fist bump. I wave him off with a warning glare.

Turning back to the phone, I swallow. "That's right."

"Hmm." After an awkward pause, she continues, "I was wondering if you knew where she could be. Or if you could try calling her. Maybe she'll pick up for you. I just need to know she's okay before I fly out."

I reply, "Last time I saw her, she was headed towards the freeway and San Francisco. I'm sure she's fine."

"I don't know. It's not like her to not answer her phone.

Especially on a long drive. She calls me while commuting all the time."

Alex stops, but I have a sneaking suspicion she's leaving something out. "Level with me, Alex. What aren't you telling me?"

She lets out a heavy sigh, speaking so fast I have to concentrate on her next words, "I don't know if Jess told you this, but she's been worried about this guy she helped put behind bars for murder. He just got released from prison on a technicality, and her editor warned her to lay low for a while. The thing is, he's written the newspaper and Jess some threatening messages. But I don't know how big a threat he really is because, obviously, she doesn't tell me everything that's going on in her life." By the disappointed tone in her voice, I know that last part is directed at me. "Anyway, that's why she came up early this week. She's tried to act like everything's fine for the sake of the wedding. I know this has been bothering her, though."

Her words feel like a slap in the face. *Why didn't Jess tell me about any of this?* I guess because I was just a good fuck.

"What the hell?" Louis exclaims, pointing through the windshield.

Thick rubber tracks are burned into the roadway ahead. I veer to the side of the road to park because this is where the GPS directions end.

"What is it?" Alex asks breathlessly.

"Nothing. I'm at work. Anyway, I'll try to give your friend a call and tell her to call you. Now, stop dilly-dallying and get ready for your honeymoon. You're freaking your husband out."

"Thank you, Logan." She doesn't sound very grateful, though.

"You're welcome. Bye." *Thank God that call's over.*

FOURTEEN

LOGAN

Louis steps out of the truck for a smoke, muttering, "You dirty dog, Logan. Banging your new sister-in-law's friend."

"Shut the fuck up," I reply begrudgingly as I go into my texts, locating Jess's number thanks to my earlier video text. "It isn't like that."

"Don't tell me you're getting soft in your old age," he jokes.

I shake my head. Maybe I am, but either way, it's none of his damn business. I select her number, and the phone rings five times before going to voicemail. I didn't think she'd pick up for me. But I still feel like an idiot.

"Did you hear that?" Louis asks.

"Hear what?"

"When you were making the call. Try again."

I scowl at him.

"No, seriously, boss. Dial the phone again."

That's all I need is Jess thinking I'm stalking her, too. Talk about looking needy. Especially considering how things ended. But Louis won't let it go, and I sure as hell don't want to call Alex back without any news. So, I try again, frowning.

A faint chiming punctuates the night, and my heart drops into my stomach.

Redialing for a third time, Louis and I cross the road, following the ringtone. My pulse is going a mile a minute as my mind races through possible explanations. I press the call button again, and with a few more steps, I'm staring down at the illuminated, cracked screen of her rose gold cell phone case.

Louis lights up the ground with his flashlight. "No footprints. No signs of a struggle. Nothing."

I don't need him telling me what my eyes can already see. But I know he's trying to help. I run a hand through my hair, standing there in disbelief. "It doesn't make sense. She would never be this careless with her phone. How the hell did it end up on the opposite side of the road?"

"The tire tracks!" Louis exclaims.

I grab the cell phone, and we sprint back across four eighty-eight.

"Aren't you messing with a potential crime scene there, Logan?"

My throat thickens at the word *crime*. I shake my head. "There's no fucking way."

"Yeah, but you heard what Alex said."

I feel like I'm in some kind of nightmare that doesn't make sense. It's surreal. My sister-in-law's words run through my head. But how could this be? Did somebody follow Jess all the way to Rough & Ready?

"Are we still looking for a middle-aged hunter, or what's the deal?" Louis asks.

"I don't know," I answer, my voice catching in my throat.

"Well, what's Alex's friend look like?"

"Her name's Jess...Jessica Steele. Twenty-four. Blonde hair, green eyes. I'm guessing five-foot-five inches and something like one hundred forty pounds."

Pavement gives way to the forest floor, thick with pine needles and telltale signs where tires tore up the ground. Racing down the embankment, I see her red Camry, wrapped backward around a tree. *I need to wake up from this fucking nightmare.*

Both the front doors hang open, but there's no one inside.

Pulling the flashlight off my belt, I shine it into the car, squatting down. Louis follows suit. A trail of blood greets us, and I let out a strangled sigh. For a moment, I'm six years old again, hiding behind a couch during my parents' last fight. I couldn't help my mother. I was too young. But I'll be damned if I let *this—whatever this is—*take another woman that I care about away from me.

Louis leans in for a closer look, and his flashlight darts around the car.

Kneeling next to him, I try to keep it together. To think twenty-four hours ago, I knelt on a dance floor sliding a garter over Jess's shapely leg. *How the hell can this be happening?*

Louis's eyes widen. "Shit, man, this doesn't look good."

I grab him by the collar of his SAR vest, throwing him off balance and shaking him. "Can you just shut the fuck up for a moment, and let me think?"

He raises his hands, sinking back into the forest floor, and I let him go. I'm never like this, and I can see the shocked look in his rounded eyes.

"Sorry, man," I apologize, my voice going brittle. I sit back on my heels, my hands fisted in my lap.

In the distance, sirens signal the arrival of the deputies. I think about the gunfire again, feeling hollowed out.

Louis stands up, motioning for me to follow. "We should get the dogs."

I nod, jumping to my feet, and we head towards the truck, where three officers wait. I open the extended cab, sliding the latch on Max's crate to open the door, and he jumps down, wagging his tail. I don't bother with a leash because he's an air-scenting dog. I let him scent Jess from her phone. He wags his tail, instantly recognizing her. "That's it, boy. Help me find Jess."

I look over my shoulder where Louis stands with his dog, Sherlock, on leash. He's talking to the deputies. Glancing up at me, he says, "We'll be right behind you."

Max puts his nose to the ground, sniffing furiously. Slowly, painstakingly, he heads for the car, zig-zagging back and forth as he narrows in. I hold my breath, and every sense is alive as I strain to detect any signs of her. A cry, a broken twig, a footprint. Anything that might tell me where she is.

Louis and the deputies follow close behind, but they're moving more slowly because Sherlock's a trailing dog and works on leash. He takes his scent from the car. I swallow the bile rising in my throat as the image of blood flashes through my mind again. "You have to hold on, baby. I'm coming."

Two distinct sets of footprints catch my eye, one small and the other large. Based on the distance between steps, both were running. Max stops for a long time in one spot. I shine my flashlight in that direction. The ground's torn up, indicative of a struggle, and I see droplets of blood. Alex's words run through my head again. Why didn't either woman tell me Jess was "kind of being stalked"?

Max gets worked up now. His tail's waving frantically, and he's doing zoomies back and forth between me and what I can only presume is her. "Jess! Jess!"

Nothing. I can't hear a thing. I move forward, my legs numb beneath me. The dog streaks back and forth. He leads me to the edge of Dead Man's Drop, and I let out a frustrated "Fuck!" That echoes down the gulch.

Moments later, I feel a hand on my shoulder. "Logan, you're too close to this. I'm not sure you should be here." Louis's voice sounds hushed, and I know he's coming to the same conclusion I am.

"Seriously, man, you should—"

I put my hand up to silence him. We stand there for a long, tense moment. Through clenched teeth, I say, "I'm not leaving until I bring her home."

The three deputies stand beside us now, looking down into Good Luck Gulch. It's at least a five hundred foot drop. I bury my head in my hands, not caring what anyone else thinks. *How the fuck could something like this happen?* The last time I saw her, she was driving down four eighty-eight as I turned left towards Hollister.

My mind races back over what we know about the case. Her phone chucked to the other side of the road. Her car crashed in the forest. Her scent leading here, to the fucking edge of a notoriously dangerous cliff. I look at Max. He has to be wrong.

"Louis, what'd Sherlock give you?"

He runs a hand through his hair, his face solemn. "Same thing as Max."

I look down at the brown-and-tan dog, pacing back and forth between me and the cliff. I head to the very edge, shining my flashlight into the blackness of night, and he barks relentlessly. He's giving his trained alert—that he's found Jess.

FIFTEEN

I'm staring into the wide hazel eyes of a hyper-curious and mischievous dark-haired five-year-old boy missing both front teeth. I don't know his name, but I know he's my son, and I've got a towheaded sixteen-month-old girl on my hip, chewing a teething cracker. My heart warms as a man walks into the room, holding a newspaper. "Another amazing article, baby," he says, stooping to kiss me. His dark beard tickles my cheek, and I've never felt happier or safer, surrounded by my family...until I hear a desperate scream.

My eyes flutter open, and I raise my head tentatively. I think I hit it in the fall because I've got a pounding headache at the base of my skull. And I'm having the most vivid dreams. My cheeks feel frozen where tears stream, but I don't dare wipe them away or move an inch.

Why did it take falling off a cliff to realize what matters most? I've been selfish my entire life, only thinking about myself, my career, my accolades, my long list of awards. To prove I was better than my loser parents. I never once stopped and thought about the potential of a husband or a family. How I could make another person happy...even bring new life into this world.

The temperature has bottomed out, and goosebumps cover my body. My teeth chatter, and I long to hug my arms around me for warmth. But I'm afraid to move.

I don't want to start sliding again and this time, cascade over the clump of windswept evergreens that narrowly broke my fall. I won't get so lucky a second time.

Night shrouds the gorge in a thick veil, making it easier to pretend the cliff doesn't exist. But it's never far from my mind.

Logan's key and a clump of roots remain clutched tightly in my right hand. How I managed not to drop it on the cliff's edge, I don't know. But then, I don't think a bear could pry it out of my grasp.

The thought of how I used the key on Craven sickens me. But it's also my only tangible connection to Logan. And I need one right now, especially if I'm going to get through this freezing night and survive.

My head sinks back onto the cold ground, and I close my eyes, thinking about what a difference twenty-four hours can make. Last night, about this time, Logan and I leaned against a boulder by the creek, stargazing and making out.

Tears sting my cheeks anew as I realize how idiotic I was. How could I say goodbye to a guy like that? And all because I'm afraid of commitment? Stupid.

Yes, I know he said he wasn't relationship material, either. But I'd give anything to feel his warm arms around me now. To hear his voice chuckling as we crack jokes and flirt.

I've never met a man more attuned to my sense of humor, my outlook on life, my sexual needs. If I'm being honest, I know he didn't want me to go. He practically begged me to stay, yet I remained hellbent on leaving.

And for what?

To keep my heart from being broken? To be the perfect career girl who doesn't have to rely on anyone for anything?

To prove I didn't need him? Well, there's no two ways about it—I need him. I need him more than I've ever needed anyone.

This realization makes my heart feel surprisingly light and happy, in spite of my current situation. Yet, I remind myself it won't matter unless I survive tonight, and then I have to see if he's willing to give us a shot.

I close my eyes, and the tangible image of the little boy and baby girl reassure me. *"You can do this, Mommy,"* the boy *says with an adorable lisp from the lack of teeth.*

I can hear Logan's voice now, too. Distant yet unmistakable, and my ears strain against the night. I must be hallucinating because it's different than the little boy's voice. Instead of being in my head, it's in my ears.

I hear a dog barking, too. A dog that sounds like Max.

My heart jumps. Could it be? Could Logan be out here, doing search and rescue work?

After what Craven told me, there's no way. But I hear Logan's voice all the same. Mixed with others. I strain, listening. Who is he talking to?

Irrational fear grips me as I realize he could be up there with Craven. He could be in danger, and I have to find a way to warn him.

I try to call out, but my voice won't cooperate. "Logan! Logan!" The barking increases, but I'm not convinced he heard me. "Logan!"

Still nothing.

I close my eyes, frantically deciding what to do. I know

he's more than capable of taking care of himself. But Craven has a gun, and he's a monster. I have to find a way to warn Logan.

The whistle!

I gasp as I remember the keychain whistle Logan gave me. I have to use it. But first, it means loosening my hand's death grip. My fingers feel frozen in place. I don't know if it's a trauma response or what, but I can't make them move.

I let out a frustrated sigh, trying again, and this time they cooperate. Carefully, I move the keychain around in my hand, nearly dropping it three times. Each time, my heart falls, and my breathing increases. *Don't fuck this up, Jess.* Finally, I'm holding onto the whistle.

Next, I must bring my hand up to my face. My arm feels paralyzed, but slowly, I work the whistle up to my mouth. *Don't drop it!* I latch onto it with my teeth, trying to blow through it, only managing a wan little sound.

I have to try again. I wrap my lips around it this time, tasting Craven's salty, metallic blood. I gag, nearly dropping the whistle again. But I have to do this. Trembling all over, I suck in a deep breath, blowing as hard as I can. I do better. Empowered by the success, I try for a third, getting a clean, clear, high-pitched sound off.

Now, two dogs are barking, and the voices of the men above me sound strained, even excited. "Jess!" Logan screams, and I let out a triumphant laugh. Tears flow down my cheeks, and I blow the whistle again.

"It sounds like it's coming from underneath us," says a voice I don't recognize.

I swallow hard, trying to wet my dry mouth and vocal cords enough to make them work. "Logan! Can you hear me?"

The male voices hush, and then I hear, "Yes, baby, I can hear you. Where are you?"

My whole body relaxes, and I let out a stifled cry, sobbing joyfully.

"Baby, you've got to let me know where you are." His voice is the most beautiful thing I've ever heard. I love him, I love his voice, I love everything about him. Now, the tears pour, and I can't speak.

After a few minutes, I hear, "Jess, tell me where you are!" His words come out as an order, pulsing with frustration.

"I'm in the trees." It sounds so preposterous that I start giggling hysterically. Is this more of a trauma response? Maybe shock? I don't know.

I hear the male voices above me, their tone questioning. I still haven't warned Logan about Craven.

"Logan, there's a man with a gun. His name is Ted Wesley Craven. He's a convicted killer, and he could be anywhere out there. Please be careful."

"Babe, I'm only getting part of what you're saying. I'm coming down."

"No, no, Logan." I can't let him risk his life on account of me. The dwarf tree stand is precarious. There's not enough room for two people on it.

The men discuss something in low tones.

Calling up, I scream, "I'm fine. I promise—just a little cold. But don't come down here. There's not enough room for both of us."

Can they hear me? Am I talking to myself?

I see flashlight beams over the edge now. The men argue above me. I clamp my eyes shut. This is the most awake and alert I've felt since the fall, and accompanying it is keen awareness of the dull throbbing in the back of my head and neck and the sharper pain in my leg. It feels pinned or stuck to something—one of the tress, I guess.

My breath comes in faster gulps, and I stir, my limbs trembling uncontrollably. Dirt and pebbles fall beneath me as the tree limbs rattle, settling lower. I take in a sharp breath, and vertigo engulfs me as I stare down into the blackness of night, knowing the rugged mouth of the gulch waits to gobble me from my perch. A pit forms in my stomach as I chew my lower lip, my heart racing frantically out of my chest. *How could Logan possibly save me without risking his own life?*

CHAPTER
SIXTEEN
LOGAN

The deputies think I'm crazy. They don't want me night rappelling down Dead Man's Drop, and under any other circumstances, I might agree with them. But what they don't understand is I can't live without Jess. This realization slammed into me at her car, when I saw the blood. I don't have time to think about what it means, but it animates everything I now do.

Louis has worked with me long enough to know which fights to pick and which to leave alone. He's also a seasoned mountain climber, and I've seen him do plenty of sketchy climbing stuff over the years. So, he has no room to protest. Putting his arm on my shoulder, he asks, "What's the plan, boss?"

I'm checking my headlamp, so I look away while talking to him to keep it from flashing in his eyes. "I'll rappel down far enough to ascertain her location and any injuries. If all goes well, we may be able to buddy rappel her. Get Hawk and the helo on standby."

He nods matter-of-factly, turning to one of the deputies

and barking orders. I pack what I can from my first-aid kit, including a hypothermia blanket and water.

"How's that tree anchor?" I ask.

He shrugs, "It'll do." That's Lou for you.

Without hesitation, I start my drop over the cliff's face. Far from my most graceful descent, the lack of light and distinct undercut of the wall prove tricky. I push all thoughts from my mind as I lean back into it before maneuvering—okay, smashing—into the undercut below with a hard thud. Dropping down a couple feet more than I expect, my heart jumps in my throat. But I keep my mouth shut. The last thing I need is to scare Jess as I hang there, bobbing on the rope.

I know the tree anchor will hold. There's no one I trust more than Louis to help with a big wall descent. After all, he and I have free climbed some crazy shit together. Down lower, the wall evens out, and I rappel more smoothly. Every time I test the wall for handholds and footholds, the rock crumbles beneath me. *How could anyone survive a fall from this cliff?*

Scanning the canyon below with my headlamp, I find Jess. My heart plummets. She lies on a rock face tilted downward with an outgrowth of trees barring her from sliding over the edge. It's a miracle they stopped her fall. One inch more, one wrong move, and I could lose her.

She's got to be at least one hundred feet down, and my stomach twists as I imagine what kind of injuries I may soon be dealing with. Louis is right. I'm too close to this call, but I'm also the most experienced mountain climber and SAR officer in this crew.

I look again, using the headlamp's light to see her. She's got a significant injury to her left leg, but beyond that, I can't tell. I hear her take in a frantic breath and stir.

Fuck, I was afraid of this. Sometimes, with rescues, people get so excited that they do unimaginable, stupid things. Like drown the lifeguard who's come to save them or grab onto a climber only to fall to their death.

I stop, hearing a cascade of small pebbles and dirt tumble down the gulch. This cliff face is sketchy as hell, eroded and brittle. I can't let my emotions get in the way. Taking a deep breath, I scold, "Baby, you've got to hold still for me."

"I know," she replies, her voice shaking, and I can hear her sob.

I continue rappelling until I'm on her level. She starts to move again, frantically, and I order, "Stop! You have to hold still."

She nods, fisting her trembling hands at her sides. She's breathing so hard, I can tell she's panicking. Shit goes south when panic sets in.

I command, "Take a deep breath. Slow down. You hear me?"

She nods again.

I search my mind for some way to help her. "You ever do yoga or meditate?"

She lets out a whimper.

"Stay with me, Jess."

"Yes," she chokes out in a quivering tone.

"Good. So, I want you to close your eyes and take a deep breath through your nose and out through your mouth." I hear her try, but it sounds more like hyperventilating. I don't need her unconscious on top of everything.

"You've got to slow down that breathing. I want you to inhale on a count of eight, hold it for eight more, and then exhale on a count of eight. You got me?"

She doesn't respond, but I hear her breathing slow. It

193

gives me a moment to assess her leg wound. Her thigh came down on a tree limb, and there's blood on her skinny jeans. Clearly, it's punctured, but I don't know how deep it runs. The tree staunches some of the bleeding, but we need to speed up this rescue.

Her eyes flash open frantically, and she lifts her head, looking in my direction. "Slow and easy," I remind her, and she sinks her head back, sighing.

I need to distract her. "You know, I've been thinking about it, Jess, and it might be time to try conventional dating. I mean, last night was fucking amazing, but I'm not digging this second date. Maybe we could settle for a restaurant or a bar next time?"

Her laugh is strained and almost inaudible. "Yeah, I guess I've kind of left you hanging."

I chuckle. "Your sense of humor's still wack, I see."

"Yep," she whispers on an exhale. "Falling off a cliff won't change that."

Her face scrunches, and her fists tighten until her fingers turn white.

"What's your pain level on a scale of one to ten?"

She sighs almost imperceptibly. "Like a five." But she grimaces, telling me she's putting on a brave face.

"Just your leg or anything else?"

"My head. I think I hit it, too."

I let out a sigh of resignation. There will be no buddy rappelling with her. I get on the walkie and order Louis, "We're a go on Hawk. You good coming down behind me? I'll need a hand to stabilize her."

"Sure thing."

"Set up a second tree anchor to the left of where I came down, that way you'll avoid abseiling into the undercut. You're going to get into some dihedrals, that way, and there's choss everywhere. So, I'd recommend body belaying to avoid the fun ride I had."

"Sounds like a fucking chop route."

"Roger, that."

"Maybe I'll get some dry-tooling in?"

"If all goes to plan, Hawk'll lift us out of here. Believe me, you don't want to go back up the way you're coming down."

"What's the fun in that, boss?"

I shake my head.

Returning my attention to Jess, I command, "You're going to hold perfectly still while I head in your direction, okay? Don't move a muscle or try to grab onto me."

She nods, but her face twitches with panic.

"Promise me."

"I promise," she sobs. "Just please don't leave me."

My heart sinks in my chest. "Never. I will never do that again. But I need to make a few things happen for your rescue, okay? I'm going to hand you a blanket and some water. I don't want you to move more than you absolutely have to, baby girl. Especially your left leg. Got it?"

"Yes." Her voice sounds more resolute, and I move towards her on the line, unfolding the blanket and draping it over her. I place a bottle of water by her right hand, noticing more blood.

"What's wrong with your hand, Jess?"

"My hand?" There's a long silence before she replies, "That's not my blood."

As the picture of what happened to her continues to emerge, I'm confused as hell. But I'm also seeing red. Somebody will pay for this.

I hear Louis at the top, heading down. "Jess, I'm going to get you out of here. I promise. But you have to trust me. I know you don't like taking help from others, but you've got to let me help you, and that starts with more slow breathing, okay?"

The full moon shines directly overhead now, providing extra light, which I'm thankful for. "If it helps, baby, look up at those gorgeous stars I showed you last night. Keep looking at them, and don't fall asleep."

"Don't leave me," she pleads, holding her head up, and her tear-streaked face is a punch to my gut.

I have to level with her. Attempting to steady my voice, I say, "Jess, listen to me." She's sobbing harder now. "Listen to me."

She presses her lips together, stifling another sob, and I explain, "Louis and I may have to drop down below for a while. We've got to find a good place to get you up in the helo. But I swear I won't leave you."

"Helo? Like helicopter?"

"Yes, baby. You're not afraid of flying, are you?"

"Compared to this cliff? No."

"Good. I need you to be brave. You've got to be tough, and trust me. Louis and I will find the best spot, and then we'll climb back up for you. I promise."

"I trust you, Logan," she replies, taking another shaky breath.

CHAPTER
SEVENTEEN
JESS

I close my eyes, replaying the last few hours in my head. The moon and stars shining overhead, and Logan's voice, keep me awake and calm. I remember how the light from Logan's headlamp dashed across the cliff walls as he climbed back up towards me. He took a long time, accompanied by noises like metal hammering.

"What is that sound?" I ask.

"Anchors, babe." The other man starts up behind him, and now two sets of lights flash up on the cliff above me. Logan shouts occasional directions to Louis, and I only understand half of what they're saying. Mountain climbing speak is like another language.

I tilt my head down carefully, watching the muscles ripple in Logan's arms, shoulders, neck, and legs each time the other man's light glints off him. Logan's skill is undeniable, unbound by gravity.

Above my head, the whir of a helicopter sounds, and I look into a bright searchlight. A rope with harnesses descends towards me. Logan and the other man, who I later learn is Louis, make their way toward me.

After dropping below me, they never found a decent spot to lower and stabilize me. So, they decided to hoist me from the trees. Carefully, Logan straps me into the harness while Louis steadies us. I stifle a scream as Logan pulls my left leg free of the branches, tying something tightly around it. He takes my cheeks in his hands, resting his forehead on mine. "Hang on, Jess. Everything's gonna be okay." Then, Logan straps into the other harness to ride up with me. "I'll send this back down in a second, Louis. You good?"

Nodding his head, I watch the man's kind face fade away as we head skyward. I've never felt anything as good as Logan's arms around me, making me secure even as we float through the air towards the helicopter.

Once inside, he sits on the floor, working on my leg to staunch the bleeding. Next, he assesses my head injury and other cuts and bruises. Then, he pulls me between his legs, wrapping his arms tightly around me, and refusing to let go. Soon, the other man joins us, and with a call to the pilot, we move forward. I later find out the pilot is Hawk, Logan's brother.

On the Ophir City Hospital landing pad, Logan carries me, ignoring the protests of nurses pushing a gurney. He stares fiercely at them until the lead nurse yells, "One thirty-two."

That's where he heads, gently depositing me on the emergency room bed. Only then, seated across from me in a chair, does he let out a long ragged sigh, allowing the fatigue and worry on his face to show. His hands shake, and he rests his head in them, exhaling sharply.

Medical professionals bustle around, assessing my condition. They tell me I couldn't have gotten luckier. No broken bones and the sharp tree branch that stabbed into my left thigh missed my femoral artery by mere inches. Yes, the gash required over twenty stitches, and I'm going to have a nasty scar. But I'm alive.

My luck runs other ways, too. Apart from one other woman, I'm the only person to survive a Ted Wesley Craven attack. Good Luck Gulch lived up to its name, after all. Even my concussion is minor, although doctors want to monitor it.

I feel nervous, wondering what Logan will think of my stitched gash, if he will still find me attractive. But he laughs when I confess my concerns. Leaning down to hold me, he fingers the scar on his neck, saying, "Now we've both got matching good luck scars."

"Good luck? How do you figure?"

"Because we both survived and now we can be together."

My eyes fill with tears at the answer to a question that's been on my mind ever since the cliff. He leans in, whispering, "I know what I agreed to, but the strings are attached, and I'm not cutting them...*ever*. So, you better get used to me."

"I can do that," I reply, grabbing him around the neck and pulling him towards me for a kiss.

CHAPTER
EIGHTEEN

JESS

It feels like months since Alex and Maksim's wedding, even though little more than forty-eight hours have gone by. Drawing the shades of the hospital room window closed, Logan lets down the railing on the side of the bed, perching on the edge next to me. He's a big man, and it's a tight fit. But I need his arms around me desperately.

I dissolve into the warmth of his firm body, letting my muscles fully relax for the first time since learning Craven was released from prison, and he rests his chin lightly atop my head. Earlier, he slipped out for a couple of hours to feed Max, take a shower, and change his clothes. Now, he smells like the evergreen soap he keeps in the shower. Taking a deep breath, I'm moments away from sleeping when he says gently, "I've got a couple of things to tell you."

"Yes?"

"First, a body was found this afternoon. There's been no official announcement, yet, but forensics has confirmed it's Craven."

My body jerks at the sound of the name, and Logan pulls me closer, whispering in my ear, "It's okay."

"How do they know?"

"Dental records."

"And how do you know this if they haven't announced it?"

"Perks of having a sheriff for a brother."

Yes, that's right. Christian. The words sink in slowly, eliciting a tremendous sigh as I feel a massive weight lift. One I didn't even realize was pressing me down. "Where did they find him?"

"The bottom of Gold Run River. Looks like he ran off the cliff in the dark."

"Wow."

"Are you okay?" he asks, pressing his lips to the top of my head.

"Relieved." But it's more complicated than that. Feelings pass through me in a tangle. I've never wished someone dead before, and I don't even now. I'm just relieved I don't have to face Craven again. And that he'll never hurt anybody else. What a terrible way to die, though. Even for a monster. I shiver at the thought of how close I came to a similar fate.

Logan kisses my cheek.

"Second, you need to start working on a grocery list. That way, I can make sure my— I mean, *our* fridge is fully stocked and ready for you when you get discharged. It's still a few days out, but I'm guessing Cricket will want to take a trip into Ophir City to go to an actual grocery store. The local mercantile won't cut it." Logan's told me Cricket works at the sheriff's office. I haven't met her, yet, but she sounds nice.

Our fridge. I let Logan's words sink in. Just a few days

ago, talk like this would've made me feel trapped, terrified. But now I've never felt more hopeful—hopeful for a future with my handsome mountain man and savior.

"You're awfully quiet. Am I moving too fast?"

I realize he's misread my silence. My mind's racing a mile a minute. I have so many things to tell him. *Where to start?*

"Jess?"

I open my mouth but then close it. How do I describe the warmth radiating from my chest throughout my body? What words can I use to describe the way my heart feels like it's growing, expanding?

Only three will do: "I love you."

His breath catches in his throat, and I shut my eyes, realizing I've said too much. I'm not the only one with relationship issues. And maybe his remain unresolved. There's a big difference between sharing a fridge and sharing a life. Maybe I've read him wrong. After all, there's only one way to reply to what I just said, and silence isn't it.

I keep my eyes closed, frantically wondering if I should fake fall asleep. Maybe I can play it off and pretend I never said it?

He lifts his head, and I can sense him looking at me.

I squeeze my eyes more tightly, wanting this awkward moment to pass.

"Jess," he begins, his voice thick with emotion, "I love you so fucking much, it hurts. The thought of losing you... ever. I can't even—" He buries his face in my hair, exhaling hard.

A sigh escapes my lips. *Thank God.*

We lie in each other's arms, and nothing has ever felt more perfect. Our breathing syncs, our bond stronger than words or even thoughts. Just the pure exhilaration of existing in this moment—together.

How long do we stay this way? I don't know. But I can't sleep now. The sheer bliss of those words on Logan's lips has my heart thumping against my ribs. And I can feel his heart racing where his chest covers my back, too.

Finally, he breaks the silence. "Marry me, Jess."

Stunned, I blurt out the first word that comes to mind, "When?"

He hesitates. "Is that a yes?"

I shift in the bed, twisting at the waist towards him. I don't want to move my hurt leg, but I have to look him in the eyes. "Yes, that's a yes."

His face transforms from unreadable to overjoyed in a heartbeat. Flashing an extravagant smile, he confirms, "Seriously?"

"Yes, seriously, Logan. But when?"

He chuckles, leaning in to kiss me. "When? Let's see. I don't know. As soon as you're discharged. I need to get an engagement ring. I'm sorry, I know, I'm doing this whole thing ass backwards. But the last few days have been...well, you know, hectic. As for a wedding, we could make it a third date in Reno or Vegas, picking up bands there? I don't know."

"Third date?" I laugh, remembering what he said to me on the cliff.

"Well, technically it could be the third date. After all, what would hold a candle to the last two, except you becoming mine forever?"

I giggle, nodding. It feels so liberating to quit guarding my heart and finally be honest with him about the over-powering emotions I feel for him...and that he obviously feels for me, too.

"Besides rings, what else would we need for a wedding anyway? Clothes, I guess. Witnesses." He shrugs, "Unless you want to do something over the top like Alex and Maksim?"

"No way. I vote elopement. One hundred percent. But are you sure about this? I mean, it was only a few days ago you were paying off Alex's cousin to catch the garter."

"Only because I knew if I had to slip it on your leg, there'd be no going back. I'd be a goner. And was I wrong?"

"I don't buy that for a moment. You were afraid of commitment—"

"And so were you, which makes this pretty fucking ironic and pretty perfect at the same time, future Mrs. Caples. That is, if you want to take my last name. You don't have to."

My pulse quickens. "I like the sound of that—Jessica Caples."

"It's perfect," he replies, covering my mouth with his.

NINETEEN

JESS

Logan's pants pocket vibrates, and I jump a little. He digs for his phone, pulling it out and taking a look at the screen.

"Alright, next thing. Don't get mad at me, okay?"

"Okay..." I reply, waiting.

"Alex and Maksim are here to see you. Can I let them in?"

"But they're supposed to be on their honeymoon... "

"They postponed it. They couldn't go without knowing you were okay."

I cover my face with my hands, breaking into a sob as a wellspring of hot tears cascade down my cheeks. All of the emotion of the past few days finally crashes into me. I feel terrible, beyond terrible, that I ruined Alex's honeymoon. And I know it's something I can never make up to her.

"Hey, baby, it's going to be okay," Logan comforts in low tones. "There was no way Alex and Maksim could go on their honeymoon until they were sure you were okay. You'd do the same for her."

"I know," I manage before another sob grabs hold of me. "But I just want her to be happy."

"Jess, she's happy because you're okay."

I take a deep breath, wiping the tears from my face with the backs of my hands.

"Can I let them come in to see you?"

I nod, taking another deep breath to pull myself together. Logan starts to get up, but I grab onto him. "Text them. I'm not ready for you to move yet." Without hesitation, he types something into his phone before snuggling next to me and gently kissing the back of my head.

A few minutes later, the door opens, and footsteps shuffle into the room.

Alex rushes to the side of the bed, grabbing my hand. "I had to see you with my own eyes...to make sure you were okay."

"Thank you," I reply, my throat tightening. "I'm a terrible friend. I'm so sorry I ruined your honeymoon." I barely get the words out between sobs.

"Jess, how could I go on vacation knowing you were in danger? You would do the same for me. And it's only a short postponement. It actually works out better because our travel agent got us a suite upgrade with the change of dates."

I stop crying, taking another deep breath. "Really? That's great." I try for a smile, but it's difficult with my lips still trembling.

Alex strokes my cheek, smiling. "Sweetie, you've been through so much. But it's all going to be fine. I'm just so glad you're okay!"

Up to this point, Alex has averted her eyes from Logan, looking narrowly at me. But now she raises her gaze, taking in the full picture.

She opens her mouth but says nothing, chewing on her lip instead. I know it's a lot to take in, and it'll take time for her to get used to the idea.

I reply, "Still, I feel terrible about messing things up for you two."

Maksim breaks the silence, coming around the other side of the bed, "You're a part of the family now, Jess. If you're not okay, we're not okay. That's how family works, and you'll have to get used to it."

I nod, feeling more loved than I thought possible.

"Does this mean I'm going to be seeing more of you around Rough & Ready?" Alex asks, hopefully, with an ambivalent sweep of her eyes from Logan to me.

"You've got that right," Logan grumbles from behind me. "I'm never letting this girl go again."

"And I'm never leaving," I reply, basking in the pleased growl that escapes his lips.

Alex's eyes say it all. I have a lot of explaining to do. But then, her gaze falls to her engagement and wedding bands for a long moment. Her smile grows relaxed, knowing, and she comments, "Crazy what love can do, right?"

Maksim puts his arm around her, smiling.

She levels her gaze directly at Logan. "Thank you for everything you did to save Jess. It sounds like you put it all on the line for her."

"It was a team effort," he replies.

Maksim asks, "Can I let everyone else in now?"

Logan lifts his head again, looking at me, and I give a nod, unsure of what I'm getting into. He orders, "Family first."

Within minutes, the room floods with his other brothers and their cowboy patriarch, Wyatt, in the lead. He sits in the chair next to the bed, grabbing my hand and squeezing it.

"You gave us a good scare, young lady." The old cowboy removes his hat with his other hand and passes a wrinkled hand through his thinning hair.

"I didn't mean to," I reply, softly smiling.

He winks. "That's okay. You can make up for it by staying here with my son."

From behind me, I feel Logan's voice rumble through me. "I swear I didn't send him in here to say that."

Wyatt's eyes are gentle as he continues, "When Logan first came to live with us, he didn't speak for a long time, and it took him even longer to trust again—"

Logan lifts his head, interrupting, "Pop, you sure this is the right time for this story?"

The wizened cowboy raises his hand, looking directly at me. "He went through a lot young, and I've always worried about him. It took a while, but he finally started opening up to my wife, Ruby Jean. Eventually, they got along like two peas in a pod, and I couldn't believe how much he blossomed around her. Started acting like a kid again. But then cancer took her early, and he had a fresh set of wounds to deal with." The cowboy sags under the weight of the story.

Logan adds in softly, "I miss Mama all the time, Pop. I wish she could be here now. To meet Jess and Alex and Maksim and see we turned out okay."

"Mostly okay," Wyatt says, and I know there's more to the story. But now's not the time or place.

Alex shoots Maksim an inquisitive look, and he whispers, "I never got to meet Ruby. I came into the picture later." She nods.

Wyatt isn't finished. "Logan has a big heart but doesn't like everyone knowing it. And he needs people, certain people, more than he lets on. Now that he's found you, I will worry a lot less about him."

"You know, worrying goes two ways, Pop," Logan mutters under his breath.

The old man nods, his face growing stern. His eyes narrow as he looks directly at me. "And just know, if he ever causes you trouble, come see me, and I'll straighten him out. Isn't that right, son?"

"You won't get any trouble from me, Sir," Logan replies automatically, and I can't help but grin. I can tell by how he delivers the line it's a well-worn phrase.

Christian steps forward in his tan and black uniform, resting his hand on Wyatt's shoulder. "Some day, when you're ready for it, ask me what Logan's first words were when he finally started talking again."

"Not in front of the lady," Wyatt warns, closing his eyes.

Logan clears his throat, adding, "Let's just say Christian was the family bully, and I had to stick up for myself."

Christian shakes his head. "You sure did that, although I wouldn't call myself a bully. I was more breaking you out of your shell. Anyway, I'm not sure what you've done, Jess, but my brother's wrapped around your finger so tight I don't think he'll ever spring loose. Thought I'd never live to see the day, but he's all yours."

"Good thing," I reply, kissing Logan's hand. "Because he's all I want."

Alex shoots me an intrigued look. I know my bestie. She's going to want concrete details...sooner than later.

"Now, why don't you do something about Cricket?" Logan challenges, clearing his voice. Christian grimaces as every pair of eyes in the room turn his direction. Mine follow.

He warns, looking agitated, "She's my employee. And

she's about to come in here. So, you better keep your mouth shut."

Logan laughs, shaking his head.

Raven-haired Hawk, with his high cheekbones and bronzed skin, steps forward, clasping my hand. I feel Logan's muscles tense, and I swear he's jealous. Ignoring the exchange about Cricket, Hawk says, "I hope the next time you ride in my helicopter, you'll get to enjoy it a little more."

"Thank you, Hawk, but it may be a while before I take you up on that offer.

The fact isn't lost on me that I don't have any immediate family here. Honestly, there's no one to call. Well, no one to care, that is. But the loving people assembled here are like a balm on old wounds. *Is this what family's supposed to be like? If it is, I want more.* After speaking with each brother, I give the okay to let non-family members into the room.

Louis steps through the door, leading a group of search and rescue officers and sheriff's deputies. He jokes, "Just so you know, there are better ways to get down a mountain. But I'm sure Logan will show you that." He winks.

Then, he introduces the crew, including the mythic Cricket. She's curvy and petite in her sheriff's deputy uniform, with hazelnut-colored locks and large gray eyes. I can't help but notice how Christian, who's retreated to a corner of the room—as far away from her as possible—lets his gaze follow her.

She's oblivious to it, though. Smiling warmly and taking my hand, she says in a tiny, adorable voice, "I'm so happy to finally meet you. And I'm happy you're okay. Logan is a good man. You couldn't do better."

Christian sighs audibly, leaning his head back against

the wall. Cricket's the only person in the room who ignores it. *My, my. It doesn't take being a journalist to see there's more to this story, too.*

I meet so many people I can't keep their names straight, and the room fills with flowers, cards, and stuffed animals. My eyes droop, and I need to rest. Logan senses the change because he orders, "Time to go, everyone. My girl needs sleep."

CHAPTER
TWENTY
LOGAN

Calls from reporters and freelancers flood the hospital. As a journalist, Jess understands the need for a good scoop, but I can tell she's not ready to tell her story. And I'm not about to let anyone pressure her into it. She's my woman now, and I'm determined to protect her.

A few more days pass, and we get closer to discharging from the hospital. The intravenous antibiotics are almost finished, and there's nothing else holding us back. I'm straightening up the room and getting all our belongings together. I guess I'm hoping if we look ready to go, the doctor will give her okay.

Out of the blue, Jess says, "I'm ready to talk to a journalist."

All I can think about is keeping her safe. "Why put yourself through that, especially when you're still recovering?"

"I need others to know what happened. Just in case my story could help somebody else."

I understand, but I still don't like it, and I know she can

read the expression on my face.

She insists, "I want an AP reporter so that the story gets wide distribution. Maybe it'll help with the crowd outside, too."

"It's a shitty trade off you shouldn't have to make."

She lifts her chin defiantly, "It's journalism, babe. "

Once she's made up her mind, there's no talking her out of it. I exhale sharply, still not pleased by the idea.

"And I'm going to have to get used to it. This could go on for years, you know. So, I need to start managing it now. Wait until 20/20 and *Dateline* reach out. Maybe even Lifetime. I know how true crime works, and I've profited plenty from it throughout my brief career."

I don't have the heart to tell her 20/20 and *Dateline* already have. So, I ask the next obvious question, "Lifetime? Like a cable TV movie?"

"I hope not, but it wouldn't surprise me. Craven," she shudders at the name, "was a serial killer, after all."

Considering what I've seen outside the hospital and when I flip on a TV, it's tough to argue with her. Resigning myself to life in a media circus isn't something I want to do. For Jess, I'd walk through fire, though. So, I resolve to see this through to the end for the woman I love.

Since Jess went missing Sunday, I've tried to avoid the news, because from local to international, Ted Wesley Craven remains the top story. Up until now, I'd only heard of the guy in passing—loosely related to a string of abducted women. I never thought in a million years he'd come after the most precious thing in my life. Or that I'd ever have anyone so precious to call my own.

The AP reporter is all business, and he keeps the questions professional. I guess that's a relief. But I get an earful during the interview that shakes me to my core and makes my blood boil. Thank God Craven's dead. When push comes to shove, I could be a violent man, something I never wanted to accept about myself but can no longer deny. Nobody better fuck with Jess again. That's all I have to say.

Throughout the interview, I hold Jess's hand. As she goes over the timeline of events, images flash through my mind. The cell phone broken by the side of the road. Her red Camry wrapped around a tree. The blood and the footprints, the obvious places where the forest floor attested to a struggle. How Jess survived can only be described as a miracle, and by the end of her story, I alternate between rage and anguish, my jaw clenched as I stare at the wall. The reporter asks me for a comment, catching me off guard, and I refer him to the official statements of the Sheriff's Department and Sierra Search and Rescue.

"Are you okay, Logan?" Jess whispers after the reporter leaves.

"How could I be okay knowing you went through that?" I ask in a voice so quiet she has to lean forward to hear my words.

Silence shrouds the room, heavy and palpable. I know I should say something, but I have trouble forming a sentence. Still, something's been gnawing away at me for days now, and I need an answer. "Why didn't you tell me about Craven before? I could've protected you. I could've—"

"I didn't want to drag anyone into my problems. Remember, we agreed to no complications? Just sex."

I shake my head, choking out, "Fuck, Jess." I look down, trying to keep the simmer in my voice under control. "You can't ever keep something like that from me again. Ever. You understand? I don't know what I'd do if something happened to you."

"I promise," she reassures me.

I sink my head into her lap, mindful of her sore leg. Wrapping my arms around her waist, I hold her tightly, possessively. She's mine, and I'll never let anyone hurt her again. She runs her fingers through my hair.

I turn my head towards her so I can speak without sounding muffled. "The real question is are you okay? Retelling all that...has to be tough." My mind flashes back to my six-year-old self, fingering the bandage on my neck, and sitting in a big room with spare furniture, surrounded by cops, CPS workers, and social workers.

I couldn't say a word—not even to ask for my teddy. I stopped speaking for more than a year after what my father did to my mom and tried to do to me before offing himself. If it wasn't for Wyatt and his wife Ruby Jean, I don't know what would've become of me.

Jess strokes my cheek, her eyes overflowing with tenderness as she holds my gaze. "It was tough. But there was also something liberating about getting it out. And knowing Craven can never hurt another person."

EPILOGUE

LOGAN

I bring Jess home the next day, and my heart is overflowing. I honestly never thought I'd feel like this about another human being. And I never dared imagine a future with someone like Jess. Now, I can't fathom life without her.

I want everything to be perfect for her. The press continues to dog us, and I fear they'll be at the cabin when we arrive. But Christian handles it, setting up a perimeter around the property. Just as I thought, Cricket makes the trip into Ophir City to shop at the supermarket for our groceries. Working for the sheriff's office means she can slip past the barriers, no questions asked. She touches bases with me about what time we'll get back, and when we arrive, the kitchen's filled with the smell of marinara sauce and garlic bread. There's chilled Pellegrino on the table, attested by the sweat on the bottle. Cricket really outdid herself, but I knew she would.

"Something smells amazing," Jess exclaims. I hold her in my arms, barely wrapping my head around how far we've come in such a short time. After the wedding, when we went stargazing, she refused my help while crossing the stream. Now, I'm carrying her.

"Yeah, it does smell good."

Max whines, sniffing at my legs, and I set Jess down carefully on the couch, whistling for him to follow me outside. But first, he greets her with a wagging tail and sloppy dog kisses.

"If it isn't my rescuer!" she says, rubbing him behind the ears. He closes his eyes, letting out a contented sigh. You'd think he was about to purr or pass out.

I whistle again because I don't want him to paw all over Jess and hurt her leg. It's going to be tender for a while. He goes outside.

"That dog deserves some serious treats," she orders, and I stride into the kitchen to grab them from the pantry.

As I walk past the kitchen counter, I see a note in big, bubbly handwriting on the table: "Try to get some rest, you two." It's from Cricket, and she signs her name with a heart over the "i." She's done that since high school, and I can't help but laugh. I'll have to call and thank her for all the extra help later. Besides groceries and cooking, she straightened up the kitchen and ran a load of dishes and clothes. She's always been like a little sister to me and my brothers, which I'm guessing is part of the reason Christian won't step up. *But who knows? He's also a stubborn son of a bitch.*

I hand the dog treats to Jess, and let Max back in. "Don't let him jump on your leg," I sit down next to her, protecting her from the exuberant canine. He relishes getting showered with affection and treats, and I apologize to him. The night we found Jess, I doubted Max's skills. But he pulled through, helping me save my woman.

At the hospital, Jess filed police reports and got everything squared away, and it's a relief to be back here, away from the crowds of reporters. Jess contacted the *Chronicle*, and they're transitioning her to a remote position. But first, they want her to rest up and get better.

"I'm so ready to be done with hospital food," she says, and I have to agree because I've stayed with her the whole time, eating plenty of it myself. Thankfully, the Sheriff's Department, Sierra Search and Rescue, and local volunteers stepped up to cover my shifts over the past few days so that I could recuperate and spend this time with her.

I still have so much to say to Jess. So much to tell her, and at the top of my list is letting her know this relationship — *there, I said it* — is about so much more than mind-bending, earth-shattering sex. Although I'll take that, too.

"Your crate," I order Max while I head to the kitchen to dish up the pasta and garlic bread. I don't want him begging while we eat.

After putting plates, silverware, and glasses of Pellegrino on the table, I pick her up, gently moving her to her seat. I pull my chair next to her because I can't stand to have anything between us, even a table. *Maybe I understand Maksim more than I realize.*

We laugh through dinner, and then she snuggles into me, yawning.

"Don't do that yet," I scold. "I've got a surprise for you."

"Really?"

I head into the bedroom where I've dropped off her luggage and search through it looking for a warm jacket or sweater or anything resembling fall wear. "Don't you San Franciscans use coats?"

"Yes, when it's foggy. But it's been pretty nice in the Bay Area, lately, not to mention here, too."

"That doesn't answer my question," I grumble, heading to my closet to pull out one of my hoodies. I've been secretly jonesing to see her in my clothes. It's another way to show the world she belongs to me.

I help her into the hoodie, and we both have a good laugh as she disappears into the fabric. "Where did your hands go?" I ask, and she shakes her head.

When I lift her, she wraps her arms around my neck. Outside, it's getting dark, and I set her down in an Adirondack chair while I get the campfire going. I place the kindling and stack the wood before lighting it.

Once it's started, I settle Jess back in my lap. She nuzzles into my chest, and I kiss her tenderly, holding her close. Then, I confide everything I've felt over the last few days. I tell her how out of my mind I was when I thought I lost her. How I've changed my mind about the whole relationship thing, and I'm never looking back. She's my woman, a fact that will never change.

We watch the fire turn to glowing embers, and she whispers, "Take me to bed, Logan."

Without hesitation, I carry her inside. I help her get what she needs out of her luggage and leave her in the bathroom with her nightgown, toothbrush, and toothpaste.

Back outside, I drown the fire with Max at my side and then put him in his crate in the living room corner. Opening the bedroom door, I see she's made her way to the bed, and I can tell by the look on her face she's in pain.

"You should've let me carry you," I scold.

But she shakes her head. "I'll never walk again if I let you have your way."

"You may be right."

I get ready for bed, and it does me good to see her curled up under our blankets, waiting for me. I pull her into my arms, kissing her forehead, and her hand reaches down to my cock. I can't control the throaty growl that comes out of my mouth, and I warn her, "Baby, you've been through so much, and I don't want to hurt you. This can wait for another night."

"No, it can't," she replies. "I need you so much, Logan. Just be careful of my leg."

"Do you need another pain pill?"

"I just took a Tylenol."

"What about the stuff the doctor gave you?"

"It makes me feel terrible. I'd much rather stick with the over-the-counter stuff. Now, quit playing doctor and make love to me, Logan."

"Not fuck me or screw me or any of those other things people say when they're trying to sleep with someone and still keep their distance?" I tease, but my voice is dark with emotion.

Her eyes burn with a longing I've never seen before. "No, *make love to me.*"

I take her face in for a long moment, a knot forming in my throat, before admitting, "I've never done that before."

"Really?"

I already know the answer, but still counter, "Have you?"

Her smile softens as the realization hits her. "You're right. You'll be the first man I've ever made love to."

"And the last, dammit."

"Yes," she says, a slight tremor in her voice.

I turn her gently so her leg is safe, hovering over her carefully. Covering every inch of her body with kisses, I linger over the dark bruises from her ordeal.

When I can't take it anymore and absolutely have to be inside her, I reach for the nightstand. She stops my hand.

"Don't use a condom. I want to feel you as close to me as possible."

I catch my breath.

"What?" Her eyes narrow.

"I have another confession for you," I say with an embarrassed grin. "I've never gone without a condom before, either."

"Neither have I. You'll be my first, Logan."

I look at her expectantly, pausing until she says it.

"And my last."

"That's more like it."

Our eyes meet, and the moment is electric. Slowly, gently, I savor every sensation as I claim her, becoming one with her.

Gazing into her stunning mint green eyes, I confide, "Now I know what all that romantic shit means. I get it."

And she smiles, her eyes overflowing with tears. I wipe them away with my thumb, cupping her cheek in my hand, and touching my lips to hers. Together, we find the perfect rhythm, staring into each other's souls and giving ourselves completely to one another.

BONUS SCENE
JESS

TWO YEARS LATER

THE ROOM IS dark, and Logan's at my side, peering into the screen. "How the heck do you know what you're looking at?"

Polly, the radiology tech laughs. "Experience. Lots of experience." Hollister is small, and Logan went to school with her. I can tell she's impressed to see him so domestic. And I can't blame her, having heard the local rumor mill about him. But Logan couldn't be a more devoted husband.

I ignore the weird feeling of cold goo on my stomach and narrow my eyes, looking at our baby. I can hear his heartbeat, and it's the most wonderful sound...since the day I heard Logan's voice on the cliff.

"Wait, what's that?" he asks, pointing at the screen. I can no longer hold back a giggle.

For months now, he's told me we're having a girl. But I know better. The little boy I dreamed about on the cliff remains buried in my heart. I can't explain it, but there's a certainty about him. I know I'll see him again soon. I even know what his name will be—Oliver Wyatt.

I haven't convinced Logan of the name, but we have a deal. If I'm right, I get to name our son. If he's right, he gets to name our daughter. Opal Jean is his choice. I haven't told him that he'll get to use that one in a few years. The man who scales rock faces and drops out of helicopters in his free time remains overwhelmed by all this baby stuff.

And I get it. There's a part of me that worries, too. I don't want to repeat the mistakes my parents made, and it's hard to know where to start after growing up in a dysfunctional family. Add to that Logan's concerns about his father and not wanting to pass on bad genes (as he puts it), and it's taken us time to feel comfortable about having a baby.

"What do you think that is?" The radiologist asks with a laugh.

Logan peers at the screen, and then he turns to me. "What would that be on a little girl?"

I can't take it anymore. "Baby, it's a boy. That's his penis."

After all we've been through, I'm shocked to see his cheeks darken slightly. Have I finally found something that embarrasses my husband?

"You need to put a Post-it over that or something. I don't want everyone ogling our ... *our son*." The last two words come out pinched.

I laugh again, and Polly joins in.

"He'll be wearing clothes soon enough. By the way, how's the baby shopping going, Mrs. Caples?" she asks.

"There's still a lot to do," I reply.

Logan shrugs. "We're taking our time. The nursery's done, though."

"Done but about to get a remodel," I correct.

He lets out a sigh. "I was sure it was a girl."

Polly laughs.

"I don't want to say this," I reply. "But I told you so."

"I still don't get it. How did you know?"

I shrug. "A mother's intuition."

He sighs, squeezing my hand. "Time to stock up on blue paint."

"Or we could go neutral since the next one'll be a girl," I blurt out before slapping my hand over my mouth.

He shakes his head. "Wife, stop it with the psychic revelations already."

Polly wipes the jelly from my stomach, pulling down my shirt. She slowly increases the light in the room and heads to the printer as Logan helps me up.

Retrieving the strip of sonogram photos from Polly, he thanks her as we head out. I notice him stealing glances at the images on the way to the truck, a huge smile plastered across his face.

I can't help myself as I say, "You know, he's going to look exactly like you."

"Is he now?" The handsome mountain man asks, boosting me into the Chevy before kissing my lips tenderly. He looks at the photos again and then places them carefully in my lap.

"I know you lost the bet, but are you happy?"

"Happier than I ever thought possible," he replies, placing a hand on either side of my belly and leaning down to kiss it. The baby kicks, and he laughs.

"We may have a football player in there, after all." His lips cover mine again—deep, penetrating.

"What's up next, husband?"

225

He cocks his head to the side with a smile. "Sex, more sex, more sex, and then maybe some sleep."

I laugh, slapping his shoulder. "What's gotten into you?"

"Everyone keeps telling me we've got to catch up on sleep before the baby comes. I figure the same thing's true with sex. Are you on board, baby?"

"Strings attached?"

"I wouldn't have it any other way."

Logan turns the radio up as we drive towards the cabin, and I steal side glances at him. From his black hair to his well-trimmed beard and rugged chin, the sight of my husband still takes my breath away. And his virile, masculine smell sets me on fire, all woodsy and soapy from our morning shower.

Morning shower. The thought of that steamy, slippery, wonderful episode makes my whole body vibrate. I let go of Logan's hand, sliding mine until it cups his cock.

"Fuck, Jess, you make me the worst damn driver. You know that?" I massage his hardening length, and he lets out a dark, thick moan, barely able to finish his statement.

"I can't wait. I need you so badly, husband. It's crazy. I feel like an animal. Besides, you're the one that brought up 'sex, more sex, and more sex.' I believe those were your exact words."

"Leave it to a true crime reporter to quote me," he pants. The feel of his unyielding arousal behind the zipper of his Levis puts a thick lump of desire in my throat. I try to unzip his pants, thinking about sinking my lips over his cock and what his driving would look like then. But the zipper won't budge against the strain of his manhood, and besides, I've got a prominent stomach, affecting my flexibility now. "Fuck," is all he manages as he turns onto the road to our cabin.

My pussy is already tight and throbbing, and I need him more than breath.

"I'm going to crash, baby. Seriously," he growls, removing my hand. He reaches over to my side, his hand trying desperately to find the bottom of my skirt. "Help me, Jess. Please. I've got to know what's got my girl so horny."

I pull up my skirt, and he sinks his hand beneath the waistband of my dripping panties, letting out a sharp exhale. "Oh, that's what it is. You're fucking soaked for me, baby. I'm a bad husband. I shouldn't have let this go so long."

His rugged fingers slide through my folds until they feel as silky and slick as I do, and he finds my pearl, teasing me. "Bad husband? How could that be? Remember what you did to me in the shower this morning?"

"Yeah, bad husband because I made you wait too fucking long, and now we're never going to get inside the house. Be forewarned. I'm eating out your pussy in this damn truck as soon as we park, so get ready to spread your legs, baby."

"And then what?" I challenge.

His cheeks darken, and he shoots me the most adorable look. "What, that's not enough for you, lover?"

"Not nearly enough," I reply in a sassy tone. His finger penetrates me, finding my G-spot, and I can barely breathe.

"Normally, I'd pull you up into my arms so that you can wrap those thick thighs around me and ride my cock. But, no offense, our baby's starting to get in the way."

I laugh breathily, shifting in my seat as his fingers

227

continue to intensify my need. "None taken. This belly's your fault anyway."

"And you know I love it, and every other thing about you, wife." He pulls his fingers out of my panties, bringing them to his mouth and greedily licking them.

I'm shivering with desire, my lower core tense, my legs shaking.

The tires of his truck squeal down our driveway, and he stops abruptly. His face is hot with desire, and his voice is shaky. "You stay right there."

He jogs around to the passenger side, unceremoniously opening the door and taking off my seatbelt. He grabs my knees, turning me to the side, and lifts up my skirt, letting his fingertips stroke up and down the length of my legs.

"Seriously? In the middle of the day? Outside?"

His featherlight touch leaves goosebumps. "These legs are the two sexiest things in the world. And I'm the luckiest man in the world." He smiles up at me, parting them.

"Really? Here?"

"I warned you. Now, get comfortable," he replies darkly, sliding my panties to the side and swiping his tongue through me. I'm already so close to orgasm that the sensation nearly kills me. I arch my back, letting out a high-pitched cry. He growls, diving into me and laying his claim.

"I could do this all damn day," he moans, devouring every inch of me, sucking on my pussy lips, and making all sorts of naughty, wet noises.

I can feel the roughness of his beard on me and the contrast of his soft, hot mouth. He plunges into me again, fucking me with his tongue and circling my clit with his thumb until my body writhes. He stands up with a pleased look on his face, rubbing his hand over his beard and mouth.

I feel wonderfully sated and lazy under his burning gaze as I recline back on the truck's bench seat. But despite the release, my core instantly re-tightens as I hear the zipper of his jeans.

"Oh, Logan," I barely manage before he grabs onto my ample hips, pulling me towards him. "Right here? Right now?" I sit up so that I can wrap my arms around his neck.

"Don't give me that shy act, Jess. Right here, right fucking now," he commands, swiping the head of his cock, already dripping pre-cum, through my wet folds and sending me into more convulsions.

"What's the matter?" he asks thickly.

"I'm so sensitive," I manage on a ragged exhale.

"You don't even know what sensitive is, yet, baby. But you're about to find out," he promises, teasing the head of his cock over my engorged clit until I scream. I feel every slick, thick inch of him as he claims me.

He doesn't stop until he's seated completely inside me, and my pussy clenches and throbs around him. Pausing for a moment, he tries to calm his breathing, looking to the side to distract himself.

Then, he starts moving, drawing his massive rod all the way in and out of me so that I feel every second of his slow, demanding stroke, from his hot tip on my pussy lips all the way to his full girth at the center of my core.

Digging my nails into his muscular back, I scream, hearing the cry echo off into the distance. Thank goodness we're on ten acres, although I hardly care now as my husband drives into me again and again until I'm thoroughly wrecked.

"I love the smell of your cum," he growls.

I'm a panting, sweaty mess. With another needy pull of my hips, he comes into me, leaning against me as I feel tremors of desire rock his core and his heat fill me in waves.

"Damn, woman. You are so dangerous," he breathes into my hair, covering my face with kisses. I can still smell and taste myself on him.

"Am I worth it?" I ask seductively, palming his bearded cheeks and staring up into his big, warm, mahogany eyes.

"Worth every minute of every day for the rest of my life."

"That's a long one-night stand," I tease, and his soft lips capture mine tenderly.

"This is all I want for the rest of my life," he declares fiercely, wrapping me in his warm, safe embrace. "You forever, baby."

LOVE AT FIRST RESCUE

A SMALL-TOWN SHERIFF
/ CURVY GIRL ROMANCE

PROLOGUE

CHRISTIAN

My hands shake as I look at the folded letter again. Written on a stained piece of binder paper with the edges ragged where someone tore it from a spiral notebook. The handwriting is scrawling, irregular, and came addressed to my high school. The words still shake me to my core, five months after receiving them:

Dear Christian,

I read about your winning touchdown with the Hollister Bobcats, and all I can say is "Wow!" I had no idea you would turn out to be such a successful athlete. I'm proud of you—for whatever it's worth.

I made the right decision all those years ago when I gave you up for adoption. There was no way I could have provided for you the way your adopted parents have. But you're still my son.

If you ever want to talk or find out more about me and your family, feel free to call or come by. I'll know exactly who you are when I see you because you're a dead ringer for your father.

Your mother,
Mazie McLeod
751 False Creek Road
Ophir City, CA
555-0199

I CHECK the address on the letter one more time. I'm definitely on the wrong side of the tracks, staring down a white doublewide trailer with peeling turquoise trim. The yard's overgrown with bushes and old car parts and piles of junk I can't identify, and the chain link fence around the place has holes, making an imminent attack from two mixed-breed canines barking ferociously on the other side a high probability.

I hear a low gravelly female voice scold, "Shut the fuck up!" My stomach knots.

The cursing does nothing to stop the dogs, and I'm about to lose my nerve, hop back into my vintage pickup truck, and drive away, when the woman comes out.

She's skinny as a rail, and the skin on her face is leathery. Her hair's long, dishwater blonde, and disheveled. She's bare-footed and missing a front tooth and looks like a poor person out of a National Geographic magazine. She stares directly at me, twitching. I don't know if it's from surprise or drugs.

"Christian!" she hollers my way. "It's about time you showed up. I was starting to wonder if you got my letter."

I nod, holding it up for her to see. I can't make words come out of my mouth. She motions for me to step towards the gate of the fence, but my feet won't move.

"Don't let these motherfuckers scare you. Come on in."

I take a deep breath, making a mental note of how strange I must look in this neighborhood. I've got on my blue-and-white high school letterman jacket, a pair of Levis, cowboy boots, and a spotless white T-shirt. My dark blond hair is clean-cut with a preppy vibe.

"Are you gonna stand there all day?"

A second deep breath helps me start moving again. I tell myself I can leave whenever I want to. I'm just here for some answers.

Mazie wears cropped jean shorts no son should have to see their mother in. That's to say nothing of her torn, stained lavender tank top. She holds a dog collar in each hand as I pull back the squeaky gate and step into the yard. Both dogs have black and brown brindle fur with the occasional white patch, and they look like siblings. Once the canines see me enter the yard, they go crazy, pulling and barking until white foam and drool pour from their mouths. Mazie digs in her heels, but they drag her towards me anyway.

"Go inside," she orders. "I'll be right there. I've got to chain these two shitheads up."

Climbing the half-rotted steps to the front door, I don't know which is worse—taking my chances with the dogs or the trailer. The doorknob is sketchy as hell and shows signs of a break-in.

Inside, I'm greeted by a wall of clutter. Boxes stacked from floor to ceiling against a backdrop of ancient brown shag carpet. The smell of cigarette smoke and weed hangs heavy, and I can hear heavy snoring coming from a room down the trailer's one narrow hallway. The kitchen smells like something's been sitting out too long, and the orange and brown linoleum has large holes in it. Dirty dishes fill the sink, and the refrigerator is buried under magnets and papers. A small cockroach scurries from the kitchen sink towards the island, disappearing.

Behind me, I hear the door push open with more than a little effort, and the woman who greeted me in the yard shuts it, breathlessly. "Don't mind the mess. You shoulda warned me before coming. I'd have straightened up the place."

Everything about this is a bad nightmare. I want to run out of the trailer screaming and never look back.

"Can I get you something to drink? A beer maybe?"

The question alarms me. I'm no prude, but having your estranged mother start by promoting underage drinking? Just plain weird. The pit in my stomach grows.

She talks in hushed tones. "Let's try to be quiet so we don't wake up Ralph. He's coming off a two-day bender, and the last thing we need is him all fired up." Leaning on the kitchen counter, she stares at me for a long moment, and I feel the awkwardness ratchet skyward.

Shaking her head, she clarifies, "Ralph's not your father by the way. Haven't seen that man since before you were born. But you really do look just like him." She doesn't hide her disgust.

Covering her hands with her face, her shoulders shake, and I realize she's crying. I don't know what to do. But standing still isn't an option thanks to my upbringing, so I step around the kitchen counter to lightly pat her on the shoulder. She snorts loudly and wipes the tears from her face. Her head twitches and darts around, and she chews on her bottom lip, which bears an angry sore. She's also got sores on her cheeks that look like she's taken her own fingernails to them. She cranes her head, looking around nervously before settling on a used dish towel to blow her nose.

Done trying to comfort her, I drop my hand to my side where it fists like the other one. The letter crumples in my hand.

She motions me to sit at a barstool at the kitchen counter, and she heads to the fridge for a can of beer.

"You sure you don't want one?"

"No, ma'am."

She laughs, "Ma'am. Your adopted parents must be uptight." The criticism makes me fighting mad, but I try to give her the benefit of the doubt. Maybe it was her attempt at a joke. Her eyes widen, sweeping from the top of my head to the toes of my boots as I perch atop the stool, trying not to touch anything. Her eyebrows raise.

This experience needs to end. "Look, I came because of the letter. I guess I wanted to know a little more about you and my family. But if this is a bad time, I'll go." I motion with my head towards the snoring in the back.

"It's hard looking at you. The picture in the paper wasn't so bad. But, up close, you're a spitting image of your father."

I shrug, not especially impressed by the pronouncement. "Basic biology."

She laughs. "You're a smart boy. You must get that from me."

I nod politely.

"What would you like to know about your family?" She sits on the stool next to me, turning so our knees face each other.

My mind goes blank. Uncrumpling the letter, I take another look, hoping it'll spark something. My eyes fall to the signature line. "The name McLeod. I'm assuming that's my blood father's last name?"

Her eyes round. "Oh no, no, no. That's my maiden name."

"Okay, so what was my bio dad's name, then?"

"Coach Wheeler. Matthew Wheeler." Her face twists, and she looks near tears again.

I can't stand to see a woman cry, and I send up a silent prayer she'll calm down.

"Sounds like you two never married?"

"Never."

"Hmm. My name could've been Christian Wheeler instead of Christian McLeod. Weird." I frown, staring at the stained vinyl countertop.

"Yeah, but you don't want to use that name."

"Why not?" I ask, curiosity growing.

She shakes her head, trembling. "Because he was a bad man, Christian, and you don't want to be anything like him."

Melodrama's obviously her thing, but I'm not buying it. I shrug my shoulders, "Yeah, I get it. You guys broke up or whatever, and you're still pissed over it."

Her mouth drops open. "You don't know?"

"Know what?"

"I had you when I was sixteen."

Sixteen doesn't surprise me. Wyatt has always been forthright about us being foster kids and knowing what we need to about our bio families. Like the fact I was abandoned at the Ophir City Hospital as a newborn. Up until this point, it's been no skin off my teeth as I can't remember any of it. I guess I got passed around to a couple of foster homes before ending up at Rough & Ready Ranch. My memories begin with Wyatt and Ruby Jean.

Still, I try to sound understanding. After all, I want her to know there are no hard feelings. "I see why you gave me up. That's pretty young to be taking care of a kid." At eighteen, I'm barely capable of remembering when to change my truck's oil.

Speaking so low I have to lean forward to hear her, she says, "Matt Wheeler was my high school PE teacher. He raped me. That's how I got pregnant with you."

"What?" My pulse races, and I can hear the blood rushing through my ears. "You've got to be kidding." I shake my head, unable to grasp what she's saying.

"I wouldn't joke about rape, especially of an underage girl." Her face scrunches.

"I'm sorry," I say reflexively. But I can't catch my breath. "Is that what you wanted to tell me? Seriously?"

"I thought you already knew. It's just uncanny. You look so much like him. You have many of the same mannerisms, and you're a football player, too. I hope that's all you have in common with him."

The words slap me in the face, and I reel back nearly losing my balance on the stool. I jump to my feet heading for the door.

"Wait, I have something for you."

I don't want to wait a second longer. I want out of this suffocating trailer. My head spins, and a cold sweat breaks out on my skin. The spaghetti I ate for lunch at the Ophir City Cafe is suddenly in grave danger of reappearing.

"I don't want anything from you," I reply, putting my hand on the doorknob.

"But I have a photo of him, if you'd like it?"

I choke out, "There's no way I want that."

She breaks into another round of sobbing, burying her head in her skeleton-thin hands. "It's just I thought you would stay longer. I thought we could get to know each other better."

My gut tells me she contacted me for other reasons. I wait patiently for her crying to stop.

Finally, Mazie continues, "Ralph and I have been down on our luck lately. He got fired from the mill right before Christmas. Can you believe that? And we haven't been able to make ends meet." She starts itching her skin, and I immediately know where the sores on her face come from. "I just need something to help with my nerves, and I was thinking maybe now that you're a big football star and probably getting recruited by colleges, you might be able to help your mom out a bit."

I want to tell her she'll never be my mom. That role fell to Ruby Jean, who embraced it with enthusiasm before fate took her from us. But I can't stand the thought of seeing her cry again. Or of dragging this out any longer. I've got five twenties in my pocket that Dad gave me for prom tonight, and I pull them out of the wallet in my back pocket, handing them to her.

Her eyes light up, and she takes them greedily.

"I have to go," I say, turning the doorknob. But she's not paying attention. Instead, she remains transfixed by the green paper in her hands. Muttering a full on lie—"I wish I had more"—I strain against breaking into a run away from the trailer and back to my pickup.

Mazie follows, standing at the gate and waving as the dogs growl, snarl, and pull on their chains. My hands shake, and I need a moment to pause and think. But I'm sure as hell not going to prolong my stay in this neighborhood. I hop into my truck, shift into first, pressing my foot to the gas so hard the tires squeal. Behind me, I hear Mazie let out a shriek, but it's too late to stop. And I'm not turning back.

Looking in my rearview mirror, I see her waving the newspaper clipping from my big game. I don't know when, but it must've fallen out of the letter.

The clock on the dashboard says three forty-five. I have plenty of time to get back to the ranch, take a shower, and put on my tux for tonight. I even have time to pick up a corsage for Cricket. She said to make it pale pink or lavender to match her dress. The thought of seeing her in her prom dress makes my heart soar. Well, at least it did an hour ago. But I've just given away every cent I own, and after this meeting, I can no longer look Cricket in the eyes.

CHAPTER
ONE
CHRISTIAN

EIGHTEEN YEARS LATER

"What's the word?" I ask rolling down my window as I pull up next to three of my deputies, Stacey, Conner, and Kirk. Standing in their tan and black uniforms in the parking lot of the Last Chance apartment complex, their faces look shaken. Kirk leans against my black Ford F-250 filling me in on the situation. "More trouble from Patrick McConnell."

"No surprise there. What's the old timer up to this time?"

"According to Ophir City Hospital, he got discharged two days ago following a stroke and hernia surgery. But neighbors report he's been acting really belligerent and waving a gun."

"That's a hell of a way to recover from surgery." I let out a long sigh. "What kind of meds is he on?"

"Doctors discharged him with a prescription for

Percocet and some antibiotics. But we don't know if he's taking them or not."

"Has home health followed up with him?"

Kirk shakes his head. "No, he's refused it."

"Getting no less stubborn in old age, I see. How bad was the stroke?"

"Apparently, they caught it within the first four hours and were able to reverse most of the damage."

I frown. "What kind of firearm was he brandishing?"

"A handgun, but he's got a whole arsenal registered in his name." Things have always been exciting around here, despite the fact Hollister only has about 2,000 residents. But we get a lot of tourists and transients, which can mean trouble. And some of the locals, especially the older ones, are particularly ornery. It keeps me on my toes.

I'm still not used to all that happened this past year. My younger brother, Maksim, dug a girl named Alex out of a snowbound car during a freak March blizzard, saving her life and getting a bride in the process. They married in October and then honeymooned in Alaska in November. Not my cup of tea. But both are into huskies and dog sledding, so I guess it makes sense. I think Alex also mentioned going to see the Anchorage Symphony while they were there. She's a classical musician, although I can never remember the instrument she plays.

Anyway, during Maksim and Alex's October wedding, another of my brothers, Logan, got tangled up with the maid of honor, a true crime reporter named Jess. Unbeknownst to her, a notorious murderer, Ted Wesley Craven, followed her to Rough & Ready Country, resulting in a media circus I haven't seen in ten years of working at the Gold County Sheriff's Office.

To top matters off, Sheriff Clyde "Roughneck" Colletti

died unexpectedly in August, resulting in my appointment as the interim sheriff. A special election in December secured me the position, for better or worse. Everyone knows me in these parts, so I didn't have to do much campaigning. But I still feel the weight of my new role as I consider my next move with Patrick McConnell.

Eyeballing Kirk, I ask, "Anything else I need to know before going in?"

"You're going in?" Kirk's eyes widen. I get where the surprise comes from. After all, as sheriff I should send deputies in my place. But they're my responsibility. I know their families personally and what each stands to lose if something goes south. As for me, I haven't had anything to lose for a long time.

Besides I'm the only combat-tested Marine in the group, having done three tours of duty in Iraq and Afghanistan. I'm steady under fire, something the rest of my deputies can't say for sure. And I don't want any mistakes made in this situation. Patrick's always been a problem, having spent years alternating between the town indigent and town drunk. He requires a careful hand, and someone he knows he can trust.

"Yeah, I'm going in."

Kirk looks apprehensive.

In response, I shrug, "The guns may complicate things a bit, but for all we know, this is just another wellness check." There's something I have to do before going to the door. Dialing the office, Cricket answers. Her tiny voice makes my heart jump, and I instinctively rub my hand over my chest. I've resigned myself to the fact she will always do this to me.

Clearing my throat and steeling my voice, I say, "Can you get Ophir City Hospital on the phone and see what you can do about home health services for a recent discharge? Patrick McConnell? Apparently, he refused their services, but I'm gonna go out on a limb and say he needs them."

She's silent for a moment before responding, "If he refused home health, there's nothing we can do about it, Chris. Unless somebody has a medical power of attorney on him?"

"Doubtful."

"Is he going to be okay?"

"I'll know in a few minutes. Hey, do me another solid and get a hold of Birdie. I think Logan's the one who told me she's working as a home health nurse now. Maybe we could get her help moving forward?"

"This is well beyond your sheriff duties," Cricket scolds in her soft, smoky voice. But she knows me better than that. The people of this county are like family to me—even the assholes—and I'm not about to let anyone in need go without care.

She asks, "Do you know if he has insurance to pay for any of this?"

"Don't worry about that. I've got it covered, either way."

There's another long pause. "If people only knew how caring you are ..."

"Cricket, keep this between you and me, okay? Last thing this county needs is a weak ass looking sheriff. Now, get back to work and show me what the people of this county are paying you for."

She exhales loudly. I have to keep it this way with her, being an interminable asshole. I have no other options.

I end the call without waiting for her response.

Getting out of the truck, Kirk tells me, "We've tried

banging on the door three times in fifteen minute intervals, but McConnell isn't answering."

"Let me handle the bastard," I reply dismissively. "What's the apartment number again?"

"Two thirty-seven."

"Thanks. Oh, and see what you can do about getting a key from the landlord, in case I've got to let myself in."

"Sure thing, boss."

A flight of cement stairs with a black metal railing leads to the second floor and his apartment, smack dab in the middle of the second-floor row. I bang on the door for who knows how long, calling through it for Patrick to open up. But there's no response. The adrenaline starts flowing as I grow concerned he may be incapable of opening the door. Kirk appears with the key, and I tell him to provide back up while I head inside.

Unlocking the front door quickly, I pocket the key and start to open it when a shotgun barrel appears in the crack. I can barely react before the son of a bitch fires, nearly taking my head off and leaving my ears ringing. Instinct takes over, and I shoulder my way into the door gap, wrestling the gun from the old man. After securing the firearm, I glance around the room. Indeed, he has an arsenal, and it's all piled up in this living room.

Before I can catch a breath, Patrick reaches for a nearby handgun, and I growl fiercely, "Don't even think about it, McConnell." Thankfully, it's enough to make him hesitate, giving me time to put my body between him and the weapon. After I've got him secured, I carefully handcuff him and read him his rights. I help the old man off the floor onto a chair to await transport. He's frail and old, and I could break him with my hands. While I sure as hell don't want to get shot, I also don't want to fuck up an old man in need of medical treatment.

Kirk comes in behind me followed by the other two officers. They secure the scene while I assess Patrick's condition. The bandage around his abdomen is covered in blood, and he seems confused and disoriented. "Call for an ambulance," I order, looking in Stacey's direction.

"Yes, sir," she replies.

I finally let out the breath I've been holding, rubbing my hands over my face. The last thing this town needs is more drama with firearms. And between the brandishing and discharge at an officer, McConnell will be looking to do some serious time. A sad way to live out the last few years of his life. But not a huge surprise. People make shitty mistakes, and then they live with the consequences.

CHAPTER
TWO
CRICKET

Doing double duty is finally catching up with me. My mom owns the Sweet Rush Bakery in Hollister, right next to Delilah's cafe, The Human Being. Things have been crazy ever since she set up her online shop in December. It all started when she baked the cakes and cupcakes for Alex and Maksim's wedding. A whole bunch of people showed up from San Francisco, and they couldn't get enough of her baked goods.

I can't blame them. Mom is an amazing baker and has been keeping the family going with her secret recipes for decades. Crazy to think we started out here in Hollister homeless. My parents had a bad divorce, and mom and I lived out of our car at first. Thankfully, it was spring, which meant temperatures weren't too low. She sank every dime from the divorce settlement into this bakery. I remember sleeping on the floor. But as the business took off and her reputation grew, we soon had enough money to move into a small house next to Rough & Ready Ranch.

As Valentine's Day approaches, I can't believe the tally of orders she's got in the works. The great thing about living in a small town is finding reliable long-term employees. And the bad thing is never having enough of them. So far, mom and her two employees have managed to cover baking demands, but packing and shipping have stretched the operation thin. That's where I've stepped in. Currently, I'm putting the finishing touches on a box of flower cookies and chocolate-dipped hearts shipping to a cafe in Sacramento, and I've got to hurry because the UPS driver will be here momentarily.

By the looks of the bakery's Quickbooks account, mom's in for the most lucrative year of her life and will finally be able to pay off the house and think about retirement. The last thought puts a knot in my throat. She wants me to take over the business. Until last night, I refused. But then everything changed as I watched the local news.

Maggie Waters, a brunette female reporter who recently started working for KXAM-4 stood outside the Sheriff's Department interviewing Chris. My heart jumped in my throat at the sight of him in his tan and black uniform with his sheriff's badge and white stetson. Despite seeing him daily at work, he still puts a lump in my throat.

During the broadcast, Maggie asked him about almost getting shot in the head during an afternoon wellness check. He replied, "I'm just a guy doing my job." *Classic Christian.*

But when she pressed him on why he went in the apartment instead of sending in one of his deputies, his answer floored me. "I'm responsible for my deputies, and I know what each one has to lose. As for me, I've got nothing to lose, so making the call about who should go in was easy, actually."

Nothing to lose. About six months ago, I broke up with my on-again, off-again boyfriend of four years, John. If I'm going to be honest, a big part of the reason for this was because he just couldn't compare to Christian. And when John proposed to me, I knew I couldn't pretend I'd moved on any longer. It was a horrible break up, painful on both sides for so many reasons. Still, ending a four year relationship hurt less than hearing these words come out of Christian's mouth.

Nothing to lose. Honestly, I know I've always meant nothing to him. He made that abundantly clear the day he stood me up for prom. But over the years, I held out hope, a stupid hope that somehow, some way, things would change. That he and I were more than water under the bridge.

"Baby girl, what's wrong?" Mom asks, leading the UPS driver over to the mound of boxes I've been working on all morning. As the young man in the brown uniform loads his dolly, Mom takes me aside, running her fingers through her short brown curls. "You look exhausted. You need to sleep more. Maybe you should take a raincheck on coming in early to help. I can find another way to get orders out."

I shake my head. "You've worked yourself to the bone, too. I said I'd help you through Valentine's Day. I just had trouble sleeping last night."

Her eyes narrow, and she guesses, "Christian again, huh?" Instant shame stings me as I realize how predictable I've been over the years because of this man.

Mom leads me to her office where expense reports and tax documents lay piled up on her desk next to a personal computer. We sit on the comfy, burgundy loveseat that faces her desk, and for the first time in I don't know how long, I don't burst into tears over Christian. The shock of his words last night have pushed me past the point of hope.

I'm not about to sit around watching him kill himself through recklessness.

"Did you see the news last night?" I ask.

She nods, stroking my long hair and looking at me warmly, her eyes filled with compassion. "Sounds like he had a close call. But the man knows what he's doing. Don't forget, he spent six years in the Marines."

My heart pounds as I remember seeing him for the first time in Rough & Ready after so many years, wearing his Marine dress uniform. He was breathtaking, even with his hair buzzed. But he showed me no interest then, and he still doesn't now.

When he worked as a deputy with the Sheriff's Department, I didn't see or speak with him that much, apart from morning briefings and when he called in to dispatch. But now that he's been elected sheriff, I have to report directly to him—day in and day out. A part of me hoped the close proximity might make him realize how good we are together. I also thought it would mean worrying less about his safety in the field. I was wrong on both accounts.

"I still can't believe Patrick shot at him."

Mom shakes her head, "Patrick's been trouble for a long time. Remember when he tried to steal from the bakery?"

"Geez, I'd almost forgotten about that." I look down, fingering my half apron quietly. "You know what upset me the most about what happened? What Christian said afterward in the interview with Maggie. 'I've got nothing to lose.' How could he say something like that?"

"Oh, baby, we're back to that again?"

Well, there goes not crying over Christian. I wipe the hot rush of tears flowing down my cheeks with the backs of my hands. "Not back to it. Still on it."

"I had hoped you'd figure it out after he stood you up for prom. You realize how many years ago that was?"

Letting my head fall back, I take a deep breath. "Yes, Mom, thank you for making me feel even more pathetic than I already do."

"You know what you need?"

I already know the next piece of advice before she says it.

"Read that book I gave you for Christmas a few years ago—*He's Just Not That Into You*. Or watch the movie if you don't have time for reading."

I let out a sigh. "Okay, I'll read it."

"Now, speaking of Chris, I've been meaning to ask you. What are we doing for his birthday cake this year?"

I put my head in my hands, and Mom pats my shoulder. I answer, "I don't know."

"What do you mean you don't know? I was thinking we could do something with the department's colors and the star now that he's officially the sheriff?"

"No, I don't know if I should bring him a cake. I've been doing this for more than ten years without so much as a birthday card in return. I'm so tired of looking pathetic ... "

"But don't you do this for all of the staff at the Sheriff's Department?"

I nod. "Yes, I do."

"And are you keeping track of whether they bring you cards or gifts in return?"

"You have a point, although Sheriff Colletti's wife was always good about bringing me cookies. I wonder how she's doing these days. I need to go see her again."

"We both do." Mom replies, still stroking my hair. "His passing was such a shock."

I nod in agreement. "Things were much better at the Sheriff's Office when he was still in charge."

"Are things really that bad with Christian?"

Pausing to think about her question for a long moment, I'm shocked by my answer. "Yes, they are. I'm tired of being the doormat he steps on day after day at work. It's ten times worse now that he's sheriff. At least when Sheriff Colletti was still there, he would send Chris out on patrol and give me a break."

With an expectant look on her face, Mom asks, "So, what are you going to do about it?"

I close my eyes, taking a deep breath. Finally, I look up at her and say, "You're right. I need a career change. I can't do this anymore. I think I'm finally ready to take over the bakery."

Her face lights up, and she claps her hands together. "Are you serious? Hawaii, here I come!"

I can't help but laugh at the exuberance of her response, and there's a peace about this decision that I haven't felt before. My mom's secret recipes are legendary, and she's absolutely refused to entrust them to anybody but me. She's even got NDAs on both of her bakers—jealously guarding her intellectual property.

Up until this moment, I think she'd resigned herself to permanently closing the bakery when she retired. Hollister would be a lot less sweet without it, though. Although I'm nervous about taking the helm at a time when she's so busy, we hash out a schedule that makes sense and by the end of our talk, she's on Priceline researching tickets to Maui, while I gather the nerve to walk into Christian's office and give my two weeks.

CHAPTER

THREE

CHRISTIAN

When the lights go out in my office, I know what's up. I let out a gruff sigh as candlelight fills the room, and the office staff and deputies milling around after our morning briefing start singing. The mixture of voices is a veritable cacophony, and I'm going to need more coffee after this. But it's been Cricket's thing ever since I started working in the same office with her. And I don't have the heart to tell her I quit celebrating my birthday a long time ago.

This time, she carries a large tray filled with cupcakes each decorated to form a large sheriff's gold star badge. My eyes linger on her candlelit face longer than they should. She still takes my breath away, after so many years. I rub my hand over my heart, thanking everyone for singing, and then I blow out the candles. The lights come back on, and I watch the smoke from the extinguished candles twirl in the air, dissipating upwards.

In all honesty, I'm not the only target of Cricket's birthday celebrating obsession. And it probably has a lot more to do with her mom owning Sweet Rush Bakery than any one person. But the cakes and cupcakes she brings for me are always ... well, extra extravagant. Over the years, all I could do is humor her begrudgingly.

"Thanks, folks. A few more years, and we'll need to call out Travis and his buddies to extinguish all of these candles." I'm referring to my brother who's a wildland fire-fighter. Being such a small town, everyone in this office knows him well. "Cricket, you've gone overboard as usual. Everybody, grab a cupcake ... or two. Then, get your asses back to work. We've got a county to protect."

The crowd disperses, and I'm about to dive into morning paperwork when I realize Cricket's still standing in front of my desk. By the look on her face, she's upset.

"Yes?" I ask raising an eyebrow in annoyance. If she only knew how hard I have to work to be like this with her. But I can't leave even the slightest room for hope. God knows, she deserves better than me.

"Chris, I need to talk to you."

I turn around apprehensively, following her curvy silhouette in a black cashmere cardigan and gray-and-black leopard-spotted pencil skirt as she shuts my office door and takes one of two leather seats in front of my desk, crossing her legs.

"What's up, Cricket?" I ask slowly, trying to control my voice. But the skirt's not helping one bit.

She takes a deep breath, her face flushing and then spits out, "I'm giving my two weeks notice."

I lean across the desk, barely believing my ears. "What?"

Inhaling loudly, she repeats, "I'm giving my two weeks notice. I have a new job, and they want me to start as soon as possible."

"You're leaving me?" My jaw hangs on the ground.

Her eyebrows shoot up, and her eyes narrow. "Leaving you? What do you mean?"

I shake my head, not ready to answer that question. "Where are you going?"

"I'm finally taking over Sweet Rush Bakery."

"I thought you decided against it because of the lack of benefits? May I ask what made you change your mind?"

Her steel gray eyes cut through me, and she raises her chin defiantly. "Do you want the truth or the official story?"

I sit back with a laugh. "Hit me with it."

"Here goes the official story. My mom refuses to give anyone her secret recipes but me. She'd rather let the place close when she retires than trust somebody else with it. And I can't imagine Hollister without Sweet Rush, so I agreed to step in. Besides, I baked for her for years in high school, so it'll be kind of like riding a bike, hopefully."

I nod, interrupting, "Yes, I remember."

She looks floored by my response. "I didn't think you remembered that."

I shake my head. Have I been that good at my act all of these years? Trying to keep her at arm's length, pretending she doesn't matter to me? A wave of guilt hits me. All I've ever wanted was for her to be happy. I was never trying to negate our history.

"Now, you ready for the truth?"

I nod, intrigued by her firm tone. This is a side of Cricket I don't often see.

"First of all, I'm not leaving you. I'm leaving the Sheriff's Department. Second, the bakery's doing better than ever but needs some new energy. I know I can provide that. And third, I'm tired of putting off my life for other people. It's time I put myself first."

I couldn't agree more, and I've always wanted nothing

but the best for her. But the thought of coming to the office and not seeing her puts a lump in my throat. I look down, licking my lips as a mountain of regret crushes me. I don't even know what I should've done differently with Cricket. After all, she's always made it clear that she wants a white picket fence, family, and the whole nine yards. That's not a future I can give her. As far as I'm concerned, the McLeod and Wheeler lines should die with me.

"Fourth ..."

I look up. "Sorry, I thought you were done."

"Fourth, I'm tired of working for an asshole who treats me like less than nothing. But then as you said on the news last night, you have nothing to lose, right?"

Her unassuming voice has gone from firm to ferocious in a flash, and her cheeks flush red to complement the emotion. Anger radiates from her, and now I'm totally confused about what's going on.

"Are you mad at me?"

"No," she spits out.

"Well, you could've fooled me," I reply drily, sitting back in my chair to the crisp sound of shifting leather.

"Christian, you almost got shot at point blank range in the face yesterday. You put yourself needlessly in the line of fire, and all you can say is, 'I've got nothing to lose'? Am I nothing? Are your brothers and dad nothing?"

The suggestion that she's nothing to me sends my heart into free fall. But isn't that what I've spent my adult life trying to convince her of? And it's been a lot tougher since she broke up with John six months ago, although that bastard was never good enough for her. I've had to be even colder and ruder now that she's single. Getting the job as sheriff forced me to double down even more. After all, I can't let personal feelings get in the way of my job.

But I never anticipated how much all of this would still hurt her. I look away, composing myself. If only she knew the truth. One thought of the way Mazie looked at me that day in the trailer fortifies my resolve. She has to move on. I have to let her go. Looking at her, my face scrunches as I ask, "How soon does your mom want you to start?"

"Honestly, as soon as possible. But I told her two weeks since I need to give you notice."

I shake my head. "There's no reason to work for an asshole any longer than you absolutely have to. The county can get a temporary dispatcher in here until I can properly hire for the job. As far as I'm concerned, you can start tomorrow."

Her face blanches, and she stares at me, unblinking for a long moment.

"Is there something else you want to say?" I ask.

"I just have to know. Did you really mean it when you said you have 'nothing to lose'?"

I nod, "Yes, Cricket. I'm a single man with no attachments. What do I have to lose compared to my deputies?"

She sits back defeated, and I watch her face working out the emotions my answer has caused. Her expression anguishes me. But I know I'm doing the right thing for her. There's no future with me, and if that means leaving the Sheriff's Office, then that's what she needs to do.

"The night you stood me up for prom. You never treated me the same way after that, Chris. What happened? You've still never explained."

I'm glad I'm sitting because her words blindside me. I lean back in my chair instinctively, as if dodging gunfire. We've only talked about this twice in nearly twenty years. I'm astounded it still means so much to her, and even more surprised at the acute ache it lodges in my chest. But I can't let her know that.

I grumble, "I've already apologized about the whole prom thing, and I'm not about to rehash it. Especially at work. Truth be told, I grew up, Cricket. That's all I can tell you. I grew up."

FOUR
CHRISTIAN

"Alright, then." Cricket's breath catches in her throat. She struggles to get up but never makes it to her feet. Instead, she buries her face in her hands. Before I can even think, I round the desk, kneeling in front of her. I turn her chair so that she's facing me. Cricket's small hands flash pretty pink-tipped nails. I hesitate for one moment before stroking her hair gently. My mind rushes back, thinking about all the times I played with her shiny locks in high school. Back when no girl existed for me but her.

"Hey," I whisper, transforming instantly from the Gold County Sheriff into a man hollowed out by long-buried feelings for a woman he can never have. I feel her shoulders shaking, and between the sadness and the tears I've caused her, I'm undone. I wrap my arms around her, taking in the scent of vanilla musk and burying my head in her hair. "I'm sorry, Cricket." I haven't held her like this since high school, and I know I'm treading on dangerous ground.

She finally looks up, her eyes round and bewildered. I

cup her cheeks in my hands and wipe the tears away with my thumbs, trying for a half-hearted smile.

"Please don't cry," I plead, staring into her eyes more attentively and deeply than I've allowed myself to do in years.

She stifles another sob, and I tuck her head back onto my shoulder, enveloping her in my arms. My heart's beating out of my chest, and my throat's so thick I can't speak. Through another sob, she manages, "It's just letting go is hard."

I swallow loudly. "I know." Softly stroking her hair, the silky locks feel so good, so natural in my hands. I wonder how I've gone so many years without this simple pleasure. I can feel her warm breath where it falls on my uniform, directly over my heart. For far too long, I've played a careful game of ebb and flow when it comes to my resolve to keep Cricket at arm's length. Now that resolve feels dangerously close to crumbling.

I open my mouth, ready to beg her to stay. And I don't just mean at work. But my bio mother's caustic voice fills my head. *He raped me, and that's how I got pregnant with you.* I could spend a lifetime fighting the enemy as a Marine or arresting perps as a sheriff, but I can never outrun the shadow hanging over my conception. Spilling the sordid details to Cricket would destroy me.

Cricket looks up from my shoulder, and before I have a moment to react, her warm pink lips cover mine. She leans forward into me, and I have to steady her in the chair to keep her from toppling onto me.

Her kiss is wild, savage as she angles her head, deepening it with the kind of abandon that only comes from years of denial. It's world's away from the innocent make-out sessions we had in high school—more lip balm and nerves than passion.

But she's all woman now, which her lips and tongue make abundantly clear. I can't hold back, letting out a ravenous groan as my tongue mates with hers, seizing the lead in this sensual dance. My cock jumps at the potential of something I've hopelessly fantasized about for far too long. I need her so badly my entire body throbs at the mere suggestion.

Fuck, not in the Sheriff's Department. Not in my damn office. But I can't hold back. I lean into her, claiming her mouth until she gasps for breath. My heart pounds against my ribs, and I barely let her breathe before I devour her lips again, pulling her into me with a ferocity that scares me. I could hurt her if I'm not careful. The swell of desire in me feels inhuman, unrestrained. It's totally different than the lust I've felt with random women I've taken home over the years. Those feelings have always been easy to control.

But this? This is so overwhelming, so all-consuming, I can't trust myself. The heart I've forced to feel nothing for so damn long comes thrumming back to life, and God help me, tears fill my eyes. I can't let this happen. I can't let her see me like this, and I can't let this go any further.

I pull away, dazed as I stare at her for one long, unguarded moment. Her eyes are red from crying and her lips puffy from kissing. I let out a ragged breath, disgusted by my lack of self-control. Swiping my eyes with the back of my right hand, I sit back on my heels before standing up.

"Dammit, Cricket. I can't do shit like this at work," I growl looking over my shoulder in her direction.

She sits back, visibly shaken by my words, but a realization lights her eyes that has me worried. I turn back around to face her, crossing my arms over my chest so she can't see my shaking hands. My cock's rock hard in my pants, but I don't even try to hide it. She's always been able to read me like a book, and I know she understands how desperately I want her.

She replies, "You can't deny it. You want me as much as I want you."

I lean my weight back against the front of my desk, making my face as cold and rigid as possible.

But she's not buying it. "Say you don't want me, Chris."

It's an impossible ask. Instead, I answer, "I want what every other dumb brute on the face of the planet wants—sex. It's that simple, Cricket. But I'm not about to ruin our friendship or taint my professionalism over it. You know me better than that. Now, you better go before one of us says or does something we regret."

She raises her chin defiantly, leveling her storm gray eyes at me. "I'll never regret what just happened."

Before I can catch myself, I rapid-fire back, "I guarantee, if you knew everything about me, you'd regret it."

Her brows furrow, and she opens her beautiful pink lips to say something. But I stop her with a hand. "You need to go before this gets any more out of hand. I'm at work, and unlike you, I don't have a new job waiting in the wings. I've got deputies and county residents depending on me for their safety. What just happened was totally inappropriate, especially during work hours and on the taxpayer's dime. What the hell do you think this would do to my re-election campaign? This is just the kind of thing my political enemies would love to get a load of."

Her eyes narrow as she takes me in for a long moment. I can tell she's noticed my eyes and the damn tears still making them moist. I'm desperate for her to leave because if she stays any longer, I won't be able to control myself. I'll fucking claim her in this office. My mind's already picturing it—locking the door, pulling up her skirt, and burying my cock balls deep. *Damn work. Damn my past. Damn all of it.*

But being out of control like this, impetuous and focused solely on instant gratification disgusts me. It also drops me a few rungs closer to scum like Matthew Wheeler. Maybe Mazie was right when she warned me I was too much like him.

Trying to steady my breath, I beg, "If you've ever cared about me, please go, Cricket. Please. Just take the day off. Put in two weeks of vacation, however you want to do it."

She stands up slowly, giving me a hesitant look. Smoothing her skirt and straightening her back, she says firmly, "You know where to find me, Chris, when you're ready to talk. And just for the record, there's nothing you could say or do that will ever change my feelings for you."

"Alright, bro, what's the fucking deal?" I bark, taking another drink of hot black coffee from my thermos. Last night, it snowed at least fourteen inches, and now the fog's set in, making the winter landscape look eerie, devoid of life. I haven't slept in days, and my office has gone to hell without Cricket. The temporary dispatcher can't keep it together, and even if he could, it wouldn't matter. The sexy woman with curves for days that I want to see running around my office is gone, and I'm the fucking reason. To top it off, without her, the coffee's pure shit. I should've stopped at The Human Being on the way over.

Zane, the ranch foreman of Rough & Ready, gives me a hard, long look before declaring, "You look like shit, dude. What the hell happened to you?"

I rub the stubble on my chin distractedly as my mind wanders back over the past two weeks. How could I begin to sum it all up? And why would I want to fess up to so many mistakes? Not ready to do either, I retort grumpily,

"You're no easier on the eyes. Now tell me what's got Dad up in arms."

Leaning against the fence with a piece of straw dangling from his mouth, he replies, "Amestoy's back at it with those sheep of his. Course this snow'll put a temporary cramp in his style." Ever since he stopped rodeoing, Zane's been trying to kick his smoking and chewing habits. I guess, he's finally settled on straw instead.

"You've got to be kidding me."

"And, of course, Dad's pissed as hell and ready to start a fucking land war over it."

I laugh, looking down at the spot where my boot tip works a hole in the fluffy snow. "Stubborn old men, the both of them."

"Yep, but then things got complicated when we found three dead cattle."

"Two cows and a calf, you said? Surely, you don't think it's Amestoy and his crew?"

"I don't, but Dad does, and right now that's all that matters."

"What are you thinking? A mountain lion? A bear?"

"Hell, it could be wolves for all I know. You know, some of the tagged ones from Yellowstone have been tracked around here?"

"Only way to know for sure would be to plant your asses outside and stay with the herd."

"My cowboys would shit bricks if I made them do that this time of year. Can you imagine how fucking cold it would be?"

"There's not a real cowboy left on this ranch," I challenge in reply.

Zane laughs. "Now, they've all unioned up and want

three weeks of paid leave. Not quite like when this operation started."

"Maybe you should go back to the circuit."

He stiffens next to me, adjusting the white brim of his hat. "You know I'm too old for that shit." He pauses for a long moment, "But if Logan and Maksim keep insisting on Birdie as Dad's new live-in nurse. Well, I may just go back to bulls."

"It's that bad, huh?"

He eyes me seriously, setting a firm line to his jaw. "Hell, yeah, it's as serious as you working around Cricket for all these years. Only you two actually like each other. Birdie can't stand me, and I can't stand her."

"I remember when you two couldn't keep your hands off each other."

"That was lifetime's ago," he replies, looking more pissed by the minute.

"Cricket doesn't work for me anymore," I reply morosely.

"Well, good for her. She's a saint for putting up with you for as long as she did."

"A saint that left me high and dry when I needed her most," I grumble.

"I'll let you work that out. I didn't call my fucking brother over here to look at dead cattle. I called the Gold County Sheriff. Now, pull it together, man."

I take his words in stride. He's always been an ornery son of a bitch, just like Dad. "Let me get saddled up then, and we'll head out."

He nods. "Take Hell or High Water."

"What about the new Appaloosa?" I counter.

Zane shakes his head, rubbing a leather gloved hand

over his unshaven face. "Last thing I need is your ass with a broken neck today."

I laugh. "That's the nicest thing you've said to anyone in years. You going sentimental on me?"

He clenches his jaw tightly, quipping, "No, I just don't feel like breaking through the permafrost to dig your fucking grave."

"I love you, too, bro," I reply, heading towards the expansive white and green stable.

Hell or High Water's my favorite horse anyway. I stroke the nose of the black Mustang with white socks on his back legs, and he nickers for treats. I broke the gelding years ago, and he broke my ribs in return. But over the years, we've come to an agreement of sorts.

"You ready to go?" I ask, stroking the soft pink part of his nose. People might think I'm crazy, but I've always talked to my horses. They're intelligent, intuitive animals, and I'd wager they understand far more than they let on.

My cell phone vibrates in my pocket, and I flip it out instinctively, taking a look at the message notification that lights up my screen. I don't recognize the number, but when I open it, I read, "Congrats on your new sheriff position! Anyway, you could send a little help Chuck's and my way?"

It's from Mazie. I don't know how many cell phones and numbers the woman's gone through over the years, or how many men. But she always comes back around to ask for money when I make the local news. Just like clockwork. She's been polite about it, though, asking for modest amounts and feigning momentary interest in my life. And after seeing her at the trailer, I've never doubted her desperate need for money. I figure, spotting her a fifty or one hundred here and there is the least I can do, considering what she endured to have me. Assuming she's after some grocery money, I reply. "Tell me where to send it."

Hell or High Water's pawing back and forth in his stable. I've got the blanket on him now, and I can see the excitement twitching in the muscles under his black hide.

"Venmo?"

"Sure. Give me a figure," I reply.

"Fifteen hundred."

I let out a sharp breath, typing back, "What the fuck? You behind on rent or something?"

"I just figured you'd feel generous now that you've got the fancy job as an elected official. It's not like you want people in Hollister knowing about your past."

Okay, now her texts have my full attention. "It's illegal to blackmail a law enforcement officer," I reply, gritting my teeth.

Hell stamps his foot impatiently on the ground.

"Geez, your mother just needs a little help over here."

"Chuck?"

I wait for God knows how long, holding my breath as I watch the three dots on my text messages alternate. Finally, I get the following message, "Just think about your reputation." I shake my head. My bio mother may be a desperate and sad woman, but she would never cross this line. Considering some of the other characters she's allowed into her life, though, I've got a long list of suspects. "I'll get back to you."

"Don't take too long."

"Don't fucking threaten me."

I'm ready to scream at the top of my lungs with frustration, but the last thing I want to do is spook Hell. Shaking my head, I put my phone back in my pants pocket. My stomach's knotted, and I don't know how things could get any worse today. Cricket's left me and will likely never talk to me again. Dad's about to stage his own version of a shoot-'em-up with the elderly Basque neighbor and massive extended family, and I've got some asshole impersonating my bio mother for money. Zane doesn't have to dig my grave. Honestly, I already feel like life's piled six feet of trouble over my head.

CHAPTER
SIX
CHRISTIAN

Two hours later, I'm in a fucking standoff with Dad, Zane, Rough & Ready's ranch hands, and Amestoy's extended family. I told Dad he was making this ride over my dead body, and he took me up on the offer. Seems to be the trend today. I thought about leaving him behind but knew he'd just saddle up and ride out alone—a far more dangerous prospect.

Fierce Amestoy steps forward, his face red with rage or drinking or both. He shakes his black head of curls, yelling threats in a mixture of English, French, and Basque. Zane and the ranch hands are worked up and raring for a fist fight. This is the last thing I need as the new sheriff in town.

I step forward, putting a hand on Zane's chest and pointing at Dad's ranch hands. "You let me handle this."

I roll up my sleeves, stepping towards Amestoy, and he's literally spitting mad. "You need to calm the fuck down," I order.

"Oh, I see how it is. Now that you're the new sheriff, you're going to hide behind the badge."

"I don't need a badge to defend myself," I yell back,

stepping towards him. If I don't get this under control, it'll turn into a fucking cowboy riot. Besides, Fierce has always been a bully, and I've never much liked bullies.

Zane hollers, "Chris isn't hiding behind his badge, and neither are the rest of us. Isn't that right, Chris?"

Didn't he tell me just a few hours earlier that I was there in the capacity of a sheriff and not as his brother? I look over my shoulder to say as much, and Fierce clocks me hard in the jaw. He's caught me off guard, and I take a step back swaying a little before regaining my balance, just in time to have him charge into me headfirst, tackling me to the ground.

I've got to finish this before everything goes haywire. All I can think of is the number of guns kicking around this event. I get my hand back and manage a punch to Fierce's face and then a second to his eye. But he's not done with me. He gets me in the left eye, and I'm seeing stars like a Looney Tune before I finally get him in a hold, restraining him until he stops struggling beneath me. It reminds me a lot of fighting a rooster in the farmyard.

"Fuck!" I yell, letting off pressure slowly until I'm sure he's not going to retaliate. I've known him since high school. He was one of the Bobcats' linebackers, and I already know I'm not pressing charges. I hope it won't come back to haunt me later, though.

I stand up, facing Fierce so that I can watch his every move. I'm not making the same mistake twice. My head's spinning, and my vision goes black. I double over, putting my hands on my knees until the blood comes back to my head, and I catch my breath.

Fierce goes back to his side of the property line, getting pats on the back from his cousins and brothers. He's got blood pouring from his nose and an angry red spot where he's going to have a shiner. By the feel of my left eye and bottom lip, I don't look much better.

"Just for clarification's sake," I scream at both parties. "I'm now acting in my full capacity as sheriff, and I don't ever want to see a shit show like this again. I'm turning this over to the livestock commission, and that's that."

I grab my head, still feeling off-kilter, and Dad comes up next to me. "You should've let me at him, Chris."

"Fuck, Dad," I laugh, and he shakes his head. "Sorry," I say quickly. Even though he raised us rough and tumble, Wyatt is not a fan of swearing.

Zane pats me on the back, taking a good look at my face. "Well, you're uglier than before. I didn't know that was even possible." He grimaces, looking more closely at me. "Can you still see out of that eye?"

I feel it swelling. "Sadly, yes," I reply.

"Why sadly?"

"Cause I'm looking at you, asshole!"

Old Man Amestoy calls my way in his broken French-Basque accent, "You're not pressing charges, are you?"

I shake my fist, stepping forward and looking grimly at Fierce. "No, I'm not pressing charges. But this is your first and last free pass. Now, do we, or don't we have the property line figured out?"

After glaring at me long and hard, the group of shepherds nod their heads in agreement. I turn on my heels heading towards Hell.

CHAPTER

SEVEN

CRICKET

Happy Hour at the Five Star Saloon shouldn't be this busy. It's a Tuesday night, after all. But it's the Tuesday before Valentine's Day so maybe that has something to do with it. Honestly, it's probably more like the replay of the Supercross race on the big screen. One of the participants in the 250 class is from Ophir City, so naturally Hollister has embraced him as a local.

I've been officially learning the ropes of the bakery for two weeks now, and Alex and Jess invited me out to celebrate. We've had trouble syncing our schedules because we all have so much going on, but I'm glad we could make it work.

"How's the job treating you so far?" Alex asks.

"Honestly, I wasn't convinced I'd love it. After all, it kind of felt like taking over my mom's dream. But I'm really enjoying it. And I already have big plans for some upgrades. The place definitely could use some new furnishings and a paint job. I've even been talking to a Sacramento street artist about a mural as an accent wall. He came in this afternoon with some sketches, and I loved them."

Alex has a mane of untamed ebony curls and crystal blue eyes that glow in the dimmed light of the bar. Normally, her cheeks are flushed bright pink, but tonight she looks pale and tired.

I stop in the middle of my thought. "Are you okay?"

A huge smile lights up her face as she confesses, "Maksim and I are having a baby!"

Jess nods enthusiastically, her blond, shoulder-length hair shaking, and her green eyes beaming. I stand up rounding the table to give Alex a big hug.

"That is so exciting. I couldn't be happier for you two! Do you have a due date, yet?"

"We're going in Thursday for our first checkup and to hear the baby's heartbeat, so I think we'll find out then."

I've got tears in my eyes just hearing about it. I can't imagine what it would be like to be married to the love of my life and having his baby. I need to change the subject or I'll start legit crying, which isn't the right vibe for a celebratory night out. "I guess this is our last night out at the bar for a while, then?"

"True. Once I have more of an appetite again, I'll definitely want to hang out at Sweet Rush. Or if you need a change of pace, we could do The Human Being or the Silver Fork Diner?"

"I'm down with any and all of the above. You know the Silver Fork's Black Forest Cake is literally to die for," I reply. "I've got to get something similar on the bakery menu."

Alex smacks her lips, but Jess makes a face.

"What?" I ask.

"Cherries aren't my thing."

"Seriously? Well, then you're missing out," I declare,

putting my hand on the table for emphasis. To Jess, I ask, "And how's the wedding planning going?"

She shakes her head. "Crazy. Totally crazy. We're trying so hard to keep it simple and intimate, but these kinds of things have a way of ballooning out of control."

I put the hand I just smacked on the table over hers, reassuring, "Just remember this wedding is about you and Logan."

She nods.

"You've got a great guy," I say for the umpteenth time. "He and I went to high school together, which you already know. And he was always a good friend to me, even though I was three grades behind him. He always treated me like a little sister."

"And what was Maksim like as a kid?" Alex pipes up.

I take a deep breath, tilting my head to the side. "So, he came to live with Wyatt after Ruby Jean passed away. I want to say he was about eight years old. I was a sophomore in high school, and I just remember him being super moody and a total troublemaker."

"That's exactly what he's told me," she replies with a laugh.

"And what was Christian like?" Jess asks. A moment later, she presses her lips tightly together, looking like the cat that swallowed the canary. "Sorry, if you don't want to talk about him. I get it."

I close my eyes. Does everyone know about my feelings for him? How pathetic! I reply, "No, it's okay. How do I describe Chris? He was just this super happy, go-lucky guy. He was gorgeous, of course, and the Bobcats' star quarterback. But he didn't let it go to his head or anything. He was just a really nice guy, an amazing athlete, and very fun to be around …"

Jess nods. "Doesn't sound like much has changed."

Alex nods in agreement, but I counter, "Maybe for you guys, but not for me. He's downright morose around me. Has been ever since high school, and I don't know why."

Alex raises an eyebrow. "What do you mean?"

I look down at my hand, thrumming my fingers mindlessly on the table top. "One day everything changed—at least with me. First, he stood me up for prom, without ever explaining why. It couldn't have been more out of character for him. Then, he joined the Marines and disappeared for ten years. Even though he'd had countless college football recruiters after him. Around other people, he's still his old happy self. But with me, he never acts that way. It's like I bring out the worst in him."

"Weird," says Jess.

I shrug, "What's really weird is that I couldn't take a hint. I just kept thinking things would get better. But now I can see he's just not that into me."

Jess's eyes narrow, and she chews on her lower lip for a moment before saying, "Actually, I know that's not true. Christian is definitely into you. I've heard he and Logan go back and forth about it. But there's something holding him back. Obviously, you working for him was a big part of it …"

My heart pounds against my ribs, and I shake my head countering, "Well, I haven't worked for him for two weeks now, and what has changed? I haven't seen hide nor hair of him. And maybe it's for the best."

Alex licks her lips, looking down at her plate of food with something resembling disgust.

"Are you okay?" I ask again.

She lets out a shaky breath. "Yes, but I'm finding morning sickness doesn't seem to stick to the morning with me. You wouldn't mind too terribly if we cut out a little early?"

Her face looks as pale as my white purse. "Of course not, honey," I reply, standing to give her a hug. Jess stands with her, excusing, "We came together."

"Oh, gotcha," I reply, hugging her, too. "Well, this was fun, and we need to do it again. But I'm voting for the bakery next time."

"Definitely when I've got my appetite back," says Alex.

I sit down at the table to finish my beer and plate of nachos as they walk out. I've got nothing better going on tonight, so I might as well enjoy myself. After all, I've always been a fan of people watching, and the crowd here tonight is a lot more interesting than usual. My mind races back over the end of my conversation with Jess and Alex and her claim that Christian is into me. If it's true—and that's a big "if"—I only have one thing to say. Too little, too late.

CHAPTER
EIGHT
CRICKET

I feel a hand lightly squeeze my shoulder, and I turn looking up at the Sacramento muralist I met only a few hours ago. He's tall and lanky with a scraggly beard and long brown curly hair in a man bun. "Fancy seeing you here," he says with a warm smile, and I stand to shake his hand.

Instead, he gives me a big bear hug, swaying side to side, until my nostrils burn with his earthy, patchouli oil smell. I've only just met him today, and it makes me feel uncomfortable. I pull away, surprised. "Peter, what are you doing here?"

"Thought I'd check out what's happening in Hollister these days. It's not often I get over this way."

"Have a seat," I say pointing to a chair

"I don't mean to impose, if you're with someone else?" he asks, looking at Alex and Jess's uncleared plates

"Oh, no, my friends just left, actually. Tootie should be around to bus the table any minute."

"Alright then." He sits down, smiling at me for a long, awkward moment.

"So, how do you like Hollister?"

He shrugs. "It's okay. I must say, this bar is quite the happening place."

"It's not usually this busy," I observe with a nod. "Especially for a Tuesday."

"Looks like every good old boy and local yokel is out this evening."

His words make me defensive. I hate it when big city people show up here and get judgmental. But I try to give him the benefit of the doubt. Maybe he's just trying to break the ice.

"So, what's a smart, funny, sexy girl like you doing in a town like this?"

The question floors me. It's far from the professional tone I'd expect from a potential contractor. But then I have to remind myself that work's over and the contractor-business relationship is not the same as that between an employee and employer.

"My mom and I moved here when I was ten years old. So, you could say I'm attached to the place."

He nods. "You'd have a lot more opportunities in a bigger city, though. I mean, Sweet Rush makes some seriously good shit. I couldn't get enough of those angel food cake and strawberry cupcakes. They're like crack or something."

I laugh, feeling a little uneasy. "If I ever need a testimonial, you'll be the first person I ask."

"So, I've been thinking. About the bakery. I'd like to get started on the mural as soon as possible. I'll paint outside of your work hours so that it doesn't impact the clientele or anything. There will still be the smell of paint, which isn't especially appetizing. But I'll do my best to air it out in between."

"Sounds like a plan. I still need to run the sketches by my mom."

"It's going to be cool," he replies with a nod. "And it's a good excuse for me to hang out here for a while. I live out of my RV, and I was wondering if it'd be okay for me to park behind the bakery?"

I scrunch my face taken aback by his request. "I don't think so."

"Why not?" His face looks serious.

"There aren't any hookups, and overnight parking isn't allowed. There's not much room back there, which means you'd block the emergency exit. I don't want to break fire code. Besides, there are plenty of nearby campgrounds and RV parks where you can find hookups, electricity, and whatever you need."

"Wow, you're more uptight than I thought," he observes, leaning back in his chair, with his sprawled legs angled towards me.

I laugh, shaking my head. "Whatever you want to call it. I just wouldn't feel comfortable with that arrangement."

"I promise you won't even notice I'm there."

Now, he's starting to annoy me. I glare at him. He seems to finally get the picture.

"You want an edible or something? You need to chill out."

"No, thank you."

He laughs. "But it does look like you could use another beer."

I doubt he's paying, but it doesn't really matter. I'd planned on a having a second one anyway.

A few minutes later, Tootie swings by, looking back over her shoulder and saying, "I'll be right back to clear the plates, Cricket. Busy night!"

"We'll take two beers and two Crowns on your way back!" Peter yells after her.

She stops, looking a little annoyed before asking, "You having the same, Cricket?"

"Another Corona, thanks."

"Bud Light for me," he calls, and she nods heading back towards the bar.

Ten minutes later, we're each nursing a beer, and he's downed both shots of Crown.

"I'm sorry to ask about parking at your bakery like that. I'm just low on dough right now. I recently got out of the hospital, and I don't have the money to cover my bills."

"I'm sorry to hear that."

"Yeah, it's been tough, you know. I guess that whole starving artist thing isn't just a saying."

"Do you have any other way of making money?" I ask.

He shakes his head. "Nope, if this art thing doesn't work out for me, I'll be homeless."

I don't point out the fact that he kind of already is.

The Crown's catching up with him, and he moves his chair closer to mine, putting his hand on my shoulder. "Do you have a man?"

Taking a deep breath, I'm about to tell him I'm not interested when I notice Peter looking over my head, trepidation on his face.

Behind me, I feel a pair of warm hands grip the back of my chair, and a deep voice exclaims, "Yes, she does."

Peter pushes his chair back, his face a mixture of fear and confusion. His hands come up, palms facing me as if he's surrendering, and his voice shakes. "I'm sorry, officer, I didn't know." He stands up, staring regretfully at his unfinished beer for a moment, like he's thinking about whether or not to finish it. One more look over my head, and he thinks better of it, though. Digging into his pocket, he grabs a handful of coins and ones.

I put up my hands, refusing him. "No, Peter, it's on me. Consider it a travel stipend for coming all the way from Sacramento."

"You sure?" He stares past me again, and then turns tail and walks out.

"The timing on you!" I exclaim, throwing my hands up.

"Now, hold your horses," Christian says cooly, taking the seat Peter just left, and bringing it around the side of the table next to me. He sits, staring at me for a long moment, his jaw clenched so that I can see the muscle working.

"Christian? What happened to your eye? Your lip? Your uniform?" My hand comes up reflexively to touch the dark red spots on his collar, but then I stop.

Taking a deep breath, I steel myself. I've had enough of this. He only ever shows up long enough to keep other guys away. But he won't do anything himself. I'm done with his toxic, misplaced jealousy. Reaching into my purse, I grab my credit card, plopping it on the table. He tosses it back into my purse and pulls out a wad of cash, not even counting it, before slamming it on the table.

"No, I've got this myself," I protest.

"There's no way you're paying on my watch."

The skin around his left eye is bruised and swollen, and his lip is three shades of purple and thicker than usual. My heart floods with concern, and I have to fight the urge to reach up and touch his wounded face. Instead, I push down my feelings. I'm done with this. I'm done with Chris, no matter what trouble he's gotten himself into this time. I push my chair back from the table, standing up.

"Leaving so soon?" He asks. He reaches for the white cowboy hat he placed on the table when he sat down.

My eyes shoot daggers at him. "What are you doing here?"

"Just following up with Stonie about an issue with missing till money. Nothing serious but worthy of a report."

I hiss, "I mean here. At this table?"

He shrugs, ignoring my question. "That guy looked guilty, if you ask me. Quite a response at seeing the sheriff." He glares back.

"He's a down-on-his-luck artist. That's all. I had him come out to talk about a new mural for the bakery. But you didn't ask, so I'm not sure why I'm telling you this."

"And you had to meet him at a bar, during Happy Hour?" He rubs his face with his hand, wincing at the tender bits. Sitting stock straight in his chair, his body language couldn't be more opposite of Peter's. "Seemed an awful lot like a date to me."

"A date?" I laugh. I'm about to explain I was here with Alex and Jess, and Peter just randomly showed up. But then I remind myself I don't need to explain anything to him. Besides, there's something oddly satisfying about watching the way his face twitches with jealousy.

His voice raises accusatorially. "He came all the way from Sacramento, and he had his hand on your shoulder."

"Why do you care, Christian? Just leave me alone!"

"He's not good enough for you," he replies, frowning.

There are about a million ways I could respond to the last statement, but finally I settle with, "And how would you know that?"

"He's got a man bun, Cricket."

"So?"

"And he's dressed like a bum, and he didn't even have enough money in his pocket to pay for your drinks. I mean, he was fishing through coins and one dollar bills, which isn't gonna cut it, even at the Five Star."

"Like I told you, he's an artist who may be painting a mural for the bakery. Not that it's any of your business."

His gaze penetrates me as he proclaims, "He won't be painting any mural on your property. I don't like the look of him. He's trouble."

"Well, for what it's worth, you look like trouble yourself. Covered in blood, with a black eye, and a fat lip. What the hell happened?"

"Does it matter?"

I let my head fall back, staring at the dingy, dollar-bill-covered ceiling. Finally, looking his direction, I say, "I'm going home!"

Pointing to the mostly full beer in front of me, he counters, "Not after you've been drinking. I'll drive."

I head for the door. He follows. Dammit! If ever I wished you could get an Uber in this town, it's tonight. I don't know what to do. I'm not about to drive, even though I'm not even buzzed. But you can never be too safe. I really need him to leave me alone. So, I walk towards my car.

"Just leave me alone," I order, turning around so quickly he bumps into me. I nearly fall backwards, and he grabs a hold of my waist to steady me. He overcorrects, pressing my soft curves into his hard chest, and I let out a sharp exhale. We're nose to nose now, and I can feel his hot breath on my face. But I can't look at him. I'm too mad to make eye contact, so I drop my head to stare at the gravel.

For a split second, I think he might kiss me, but I should know better. Instead, he straightens up, dropping his hands from my waist, and I take a few steps back. "Give me your keys," he orders. I'm mad as hell but not in the mood to defy the sheriff of my county. Reluctantly, I dig into my purse and hand them to him.

CHAPTER
NINE
CHRISTIAN

This is the worst fucking Tuesday of my life. But everything that happened today pales in comparison to seeing Cricket with Man Bun. My chest still aches from the shock. I don't know whether I'm mad or disappointed or frustrated or heartbroken. I can't quantify the heap of feelings piled up inside me, like tangled ropes.

I open the passenger door for her, and she climbs in, her movements sharp and haughty. Leaning over her, I click her seatbelt into place, breathing in her vanilla musk. She lets out a testy sigh. I'm careful not to look her way as it would put our faces only a few inches apart, and I know I couldn't pass up that temptation again. Not after what I know about the way the woman version of Cricket kisses and tastes.

I get in the driver's seat and put the key in the ignition. The sound system comes blaring to life, and I hear the old man voice that comes at the end of each Audible audiobook recording. "Thank you for listening to this recording of *He's Just Not That Into You* ..." The words make me choke on my spit, and she rushes to turn it off, frantically clicking the power button.

"Hmm," I say, swallowing hard. I make a mental note to never again assume a day couldn't get worse.

She puts her head in her hands. I remember the last time she did that in my office. Next thing I knew, we were lip-locked. I rest my head on the back of the car seat for a long moment, letting out a sharp exhale. My face throbs from the fight. But blood rushes to my cock thinking about her mouth. I've always had it bad for her. Now, it's getting impossible to hide, even though it's the decent thing to do. The problem is the difference between the kissing Cricket and I did in high school and what happened in my office. I haven't been able to think straight since. It was sure a lot easier keeping her at arm's distance before getting a taste of that.

Two weeks of sleepless nights and shitty work days have me confused about everything. I thought I had it together. But then I saw her at the bar with that douche bag, and everything changed in a split second. I can't let a loser like that have her ... and all because I haven't had the balls to claim her myself.

If only she didn't want the fucking white picket fence and family, it'd be so much easier. I could get into a relationship with her, especially now that she's no longer an employee. Everything might work out okay. I'd even risk our friendship for the chance at something more. But the thought of having to tell her about my birth parents—and I would have to tell her since she wants kids—makes me sick to my stomach. I couldn't stand to have her look at me differently, her face filled with disgust like Mazie.

Still, I can't deny that every time Cricket enters my head, I get a hard-on. It's been very inconvenient on top of everything else going on these past two weeks. Now that I'm in this car with her, smelling her vanilla musk, I need a release so bad my hands shake. I wouldn't take advantage of her after she's been drinking. But I'll be damned if I let "Man Bun" or any other guy touch her.

Thankfully, Cricket's not crying this time. When she finally looks up, she sounds embarrassed as she orders, "Please just take me home, Christian. I'm so done with this day."

"Nuff said," I reply. If she only knew the half of it.

We drive in silence as I try to untangle the knot of thoughts in my head. Being in her presence again, unbound by my duties as a sheriff means every line is blurred. I can have what I want—what I've wanted for so long. But am I just being selfish? Unrestrained? Weak? *Fuck, I want her so bad*. I could keep my feelings under wraps as long as I thought she'd move on and find somebody better. But if she's just going to start slumming ... Well, I won't let her do that.

"So, how do you know he's just not that into you?" I finally ask, wincing as I try to raise my left eyebrow.

She lets out a ragged breath. "Christian, please."

"It's a fair enough question ... and I'm not talking about Man Bun."

She sighs.

I look at her out of the corner of my good eye. "You're doing a lot of hemming and hawing over there and not answering my question."

"You want me to answer your question, Chris? Alright then. Let's see. He's just not that into you if he doesn't call you."

"What if there are reasons he can't?"

She gulps. "Doesn't matter. If he was into you, he'd move mountains to make it happen. No matter what."

A cold sweat breaks out on my forehead.

"He's just not that into you if you have to constantly make excuses about why he treats you the way he treats you."

"How do you mean?"

"Like an asshole."

"That's a bit of an exaggeration."

"Is it?" she spits back. "He's just not that into you if he can't remember your birthday."

"April 11th." My words stun her into silence.

But she's not about to let her anger go, and I don't blame her. "Okay, he's just not that into you if he knows your birthday and does nothing about it."

I start to speak but grimace instead.

"He's just not that into you if he doesn't want to have sex with you."

I swallow hard. I can feel her glaring at me as I turn to the left, heading towards her house.

"What, are you a mind reader or something? How could you possibly know what he wants?"

Her voice sounds shaky as she replies, "I do know one thing. He has nothing to lose. Nothing."

"You're really not going to let that go?"

"Why should I? I mean, your current appearance illustrates my point perfectly."

I shrug. "I just got in a friendly fist fight with Fierce."

"Wait, Wyatt and Old Man Amestoy are back at it?"

I scrunch my face and regret it. "Back at it? It never ended. Now, back to that nothing to lose comment. Have you ever thought that maybe I didn't mean it like it sounded? It was a tiny soundbite taken out of a fifteen-minute interview with no context."

I pull into her driveway, and she jumps out of the car, running up to the front door and triggering the motion light before remembering I have the key to unlock it. She throws her head back in frustration and stands there waiting, her toe tapping.

I move slowly to the front door, trying to give my pulse a chance to settle back down. I unlock the entry, and she runs inside, forgetting to take her keys. I follow behind her.

She wheels around, planting a finger squarely in my chest. "I didn't invite you in."

"I'm just here to make sure you're safe. I'll check around the house, make sure all of your doors are locked." But I don't move a muscle. Instead, I stand there looking at her mouth and thinking about the last time we kissed. Fuck, I'm breathing hard now, just thinking about it. I kick the front door closed behind me, taking in her beautiful face and trying to communicate through my gaze how much I want her.

Tears swim in her misty eyes, and they fog with confusion. My hands come up, holding her cheeks, and I smile sadly, saying, "Honey, you know I can't stand to see you cry. Please stop."

Her breath catches in her throat, and now the tears flood her face. I wipe them away with my thumbs, still swollen and cut from the fight. She begs, "Please, Christian, don't do this if you don't really want me."

My hands are shaking now, and the blood is thumping so loud in my temples, I'm sure she can hear it. I've been thinking for two weeks about what I'd say the next time I saw her. What comes out surprises me. "I haven't wanted anything but this for years, Cricket. But I couldn't do anything about it because of our jobs. You know I follow the rules, and I wasn't about to break them even if I knew how happy it'd make me."

"Happy?" Her eyebrows knot, and she lets out a tiny sob, searching my face for answers.

"Yes, fuck, Cricket, how could you ever doubt that?"

"You've treated me like shit for years, Christian."

"And you've done the same to me. I had to sit there for four years watching you date that John guy who was never good enough for you. And if you're going to turn around and do the same thing with Man Bun. Well, I'm putting my foot down, dammit. You need to pick your men better."

She tries to wiggle out of my hands, but I won't let her.

"I'm no exception to that rule. You could do so much fucking better than me."

"No, I can't, and I don't want to," she replies defiantly.

I take one step closer to her, leaning down to rest my forehead lightly on hers. It's about the only part of my face not bruised. "Honey, you could. I know you could. There's so much I can't give you. I can't give you babies or a white picket fence, or any of that domestic shit you want. You may not think it matters right now. But I know you, and I know it will matter one day. And I can't give you a guarantee that something won't happen to me at work. You know how dangerous my job is."

Her hands come up to my face, touching it gently. "How about we just focus on what you can give me, Christian?"

I step back, swallowing hard. "I don't want to take advantage of you when you've been drinking."

"I had one beer with dinner and a few sips of a second one with Peter. I'm not even buzzed."

I shift my weight, torn over my next move.

"You want me to walk a straight line or do a breathalyzer test, officer?"

She looks so fucking adorable the way her pink lips part, desire written all over her face. I can't find any words. Instead, I step forward hoisting her into my arms. Her legs wrap around my waist, and she gasps as she feels my hard arousal. I grab onto her round ass, squeezing as our lips lock, and I can't fucking breathe or think.

So much pent up longing, so many years of wanting this make me insane. Her lips crush into mine, and I jerk my head back slightly, reminding, "Gentle, honey." But the next moment, I forget my own advice, thrusting my tongue into her mouth, claiming her with an authority that scares me. I don't know how long we make out in the middle of the living room, but it's the best fucking feeling I've ever had. I've crushed my busted lip to hell, but I don't care. There is something I do need to tell her, though. Letting out a growl, I finally pull back, breathing against her mouth. I beg, "Please don't let me hurt you."

"Hurt me?" she gasps. "I'm hurting you."

"Fuck that. I want you so much, Cricket. So fucking much. I can't stop myself. But you have to promise to stop me if I'm too rough."

Her gray eyes round as she reassures me, "Of course. I won't let you hurt me. But I know you never would, Christian."

I want to argue with her. Ask her how she could possibly know that, but I'm terrified of where the conversation could lead. And my head's foggy with want. I take her to the loveseat in the living room, which has a large ottoman the same height abutting it. It's perfect for spreading her out. And I can't wait another moment to make her mine. The bedroom down the hallway's too far. Kneeling in front of her, I order, "Lie back." My voice is dark and dangerous, and I barely recognize it.

Her breath catches in her throat as she obeys. I've crossed a line I can't retread. Unable to form a logical thought, I grab the waistband of her yoga pants, pulling them down over her shapely legs so that all she's wearing is a red lacy thong.

"Fuck me," I exclaim at the unexpected delight.

CHAPTER
TEN
CRICKET

Christian doesn't give me a moment to think or react. He's crazed with desire as he takes one look at my dripping wet scarlet panties, and raises both of my legs with his hands until his head is buried between them at my throbbing core. His mouth devours the slick wet panty silk, and pushes it to the side with a finger as his tongue urgently explores me.

"Fuck, fuck, fuck," he screams.

I look up surprised. "Did you hurt your lip?"

He shakes his head. "You taste so fucking good. I can't get enough of you," he says burying his head between my legs again. I arch my back, my hand instinctively going to his head, threading my fingers through his short blonde hair, and he moans into me as he spreads my legs wider, changing the angle of his approach.

His hands come up to the slip of silk between us, and he sighs, "These have got to go." Slowly, he pulls them down, leaving a trail of fire and arousal on my legs. Tossing the fabric to the floor, he dives into me again, his tongue devouring my pussy.

So many years of wanting this man, of longing for a moment like this have me ready to come. But I hold back, trying to savor the moment. I don't know what's gotten into him, but I have to enjoy it because it likely will never happen again. He strokes my pussy lips with his fingers, covering himself in my desire, and then he slides a finger slowly into me, his eyes dark with lust. His mouth covers my pearl, and he sucks and plays with it as he slowly strokes me, finding the rough spot near the front that makes me tremble.

He moans against my pussy, teasing my clit until it's so swollen I feel like I'll explode. "You're so responsive," he says breathlessly, looking up at me. "Fuck, I can tell you want me as much as I want you. You're drenched, honey." His head descends again, and he fucks me with his fingers and his tongue until I'm certain the neighbors will call 911 to report screaming.

I recline back on the couch, drenched and exhausted, and thoroughly pleased. And for a moment, I don't feel him touching me. My heart lodges in my throat, and I'm afraid he's leaving me or finding some excuse to go. Lifting my head, I see him scrambling out of his sheriff's uniform. He's got his shirt off, revealing sexy black and gray tattoos on his shoulders, chest, and arms. I've only seen the chest and shoulder ones occasionally when I caught him working shirtless at the ranch. Now, I admire them unhesitatingly as he hurries out of his pants, wearing only black boxer briefs tented from his desire. When he removes them, his large, thick cock pops free. There's a vein running down it, and it's so taut with blood, it looks angry.

He steps towards me, his face flushed with desire. Licking the fingers he just had inside me, his eyes roll back in his head for a moment. "I could take you on my tongue forever and never get enough." Kneeling in front of the ottoman, his face darkens and grimaces, and I don't know if it's because of his injuries or something else. If he rejects me now, after all of this, I won't be able to handle it. My body shakes.

"Do you have a condom?" he asks, staring at me pleadingly. "I wasn't expecting this, and I don't have any with me."

I sit up on my elbows. "No, I don't. But I'm clean, and I'm on the pill."

"I'm clean, too," he says, his face relaxing slightly. "So you're okay bare?"

I nod.

He grabs onto both of my legs, dragging me to the edge of the ottoman. It's the perfect height when he's kneeling for his cock to enter me. Grabbing onto his rod, he brings it to my throbbing core, swiping back and forth in my juices. I'm still sensitive from coming, and I writhe under his touch.

"What's wrong?" he asks, a teasing tone in his voice.

I can only moan in response.

This time, as he swipes the tip through my folds, he enters, closing his eyes in concentration. He's only tip-deep when he lets out a desperate exhale, saying, "Fuck, Cricket you feel so good."

Then, slowly with great control, he moves in and out of me, stroking deeper as he grabs possessively onto my hips. "Fuck," he moans again. "I've waited too long for this," he apologizes. "I'm sorry if I can't hold on that long." He lets out another exhale, putting his hand on my pearl and circling it until I feel like I'm floating into the ceiling. With any other guy, I'd close my eyes at this point and concentrate on the sensations in my body, but I want to see him. I want to see the man I've loved since high school make me come. The sight of his naked tattooed chest and gorgeous blue eyes ratchet up the tension, tightening my pussy. Even his bruised mouth and wounded eye are perfect in this moment as I arch my hips up towards his thrusting cock, taking him as deeply as I can before crying out. I writhe under him again, and he releases into me, squeezing my hips so tightly I wince.

In an instant, he drops his hands, apologizing, "Oh fuck, Cricket. I'm sorry. I didn't mean to hurt you."

"I'm fine," I say, smiling. But his face has gone dark, grave, and I know he's going to pull out. I wrap my legs around his waist, stopping him. Then, I put my arms out for him. "Please don't go, yet," I beg, sounding needy and definitely breaking all of the rules in the relationship book I just listened to. But I don't care.

His face looks ambivalent for a moment. "I would never hurt you on purpose," he says again, rubbing his hand over his heart.

"You didn't hurt me. I promise. Now, come lie with me, please," I command more than ask, and he climbs up the ottoman and loveseat, spooning me. I don't say anything and neither does he as he strokes my hair, kissing my neck lightly.

I almost fall asleep in his arms before realizing I need to get up and clean myself. But he stops me, saying, "Let me do that for you." A few minutes later, he comes back, holding a wash cloth wet with warm water and gently takes care of me. His eyebrows furrow as he looks at me and says, "Please be honest with me, Cricket. Did I hurt you?"

I shake my head, puzzled. "No, you didn't hurt me. But I'm pretty sure I hurt you," I point towards his swollen lip.

He shakes his head, but his eyes dissect me, as if there's more he needs me to say.

My voice catches. "You didn't hurt me. You made me happy, Chris."

"And you wanted it as much I did, right?"

"Of course," I reassure him. How could he not know that, considering the way my body reacted to him? But I can tell by the look on his face he needs to hear me say it, and so I add, "I wanted everything that just happened. It was perfect."

"Okay," he says, standing over me and looking down at the floor. I've never seen him so unsure of himself, and it surprises me. "If you want me to go, I can go."

A shield instantly pops up around my heart as I assume he's trying to excuse himself. But staring into his face, that's not it. His eyes are red. He's tearing up.

"Hey," I say, reaching my hand out to grab his. "It's okay." I honestly don't know what else to say.

He shakes his head, almost speaking but stopping suddenly.

"We don't have to figure it all out tonight. Why don't you just come and sleep by me? At least for a little while? I mean, if you'll stay?"

"I want to stay," he replies, but the stormy look on his face doesn't change. Is he feeling regret? I don't know, and I don't want to know. If he can't make up his mind, I'll make it up for him. At least, for tonight. "Come lie with me, Chris. We don't have to think about anything else." He looks torn, and I steel myself, preparing to wake up tomorrow in a cold bed. But I'll take his warmth next to me, even if it's just for a few minutes.

He looks towards the front door, and my heart drops. He's ready to leave.

"I forgot to lock up," he says, striding that direction, and I exhale relieved. I can't help but admire the way his muscles ripple as he moves, his chiseled build remains impressive, even after so many years away from football and the Marines.

Turning around, he catches me staring. "Are you ogling me, Ms. Walker?" The change in his tone of voice and expression catches me off guard. But I love it.

I tease back "Why, yes, I am, Sheriff McLeod."

"Well, you're gonna catch hell for that," he replies, chasing me into the bedroom for round two.

CHAPTER
ELEVEN
CRICKET

"Happy Valentine's Day," I hear a voice whisper in my ear—Christian's voice—and I let out a soft, satisfied groan, replaying last night. His warm body's still wrapped around me, and I can feel his rock hard arousal pressing into my back. It sends instant shivers of desire through me, and I snuggle back into him as he lets out a relaxed growl. "I'm sorry I didn't get you anything, but I swear I'll make up for it later today."

My heart races, and I feel his arms tighten around me. *He didn't go anywhere. He didn't leave me. He stayed ... all night.* My alarm clock confirms it: three thirty in the morning. Behind me, he yawns, pressing his hips demandingly against my ass.

"You're the best Valentine's Day gift I could ask for," I whisper, still wondering if I'm dreaming.

"You deserve better, and I plan on giving it to you. But first things first." His hand comes around to the front of me, sliding between my legs until he finds my clit, letting out a happy groan. He circles it slowly while his hips find a suggestive rhythm behind me. "I don't know how early you have to be to the bakery ..." he whispers, his voice deep and scratchy from sleep. Lightly kissing and licking my ear and neck, he sends shivers down my shoulders and back.

I swallow the lump in my throat. "I have time." I'm not exactly telling the truth, but I'm also not about to pass this up. I'll take anything Christian has to offer. Besides, the bakery's just down the street from the saloon, so I don't have to make a special trip to drop him off where he left his truck last night.

"Good," he says, letting his fingers slide through my folds, priming me for his entry. "Fuck, you're already dripping for me. I'm starting to think you like my cock."

"I do," I reply, my voice trembling at his touch.

"How do you like my cock, honey?" His breathing sounds restless, urgent, as his fingers slide in and out of me.

My cheeks flush with heat. I'm not used to voicing my desires, but I can tell by the dark desperation in his voice, he needs to hear this.

"Tell me how you like my cock, Cricket." His voice is steely this time, commanding.

"I like your cock inside of me."

"Do you?" he whispers in my ear, and I can feel the prickly stubble on his unshaven cheek.

"Yes, Chris, I need you inside of me now."

"And where do you want me? Always?"

"Inside of me." I whimper, pressing greedily into his arousal.

His chest rumbles with anticipation as he grabs my hips, tucking my ass up against him at the perfect angle to take me. He slides his cock into my pussy, slowly, moaning against its feel before finding a relaxed rhythm. His left hand returns to my clit, spoiling it with attention. His right arm is pinned under me, but he angles it so his hand can stroke my left breast, twisting and playing with my nipple. "How did I neglect these last night?" he asks, deepening his stroke. "They get all my attention next time."

I moan as his arms tighten around me, thrilling at the feel of his muscular abs and thighs pressing into my soft curves.

"How do you like my cock now, Cricket? Do you like me balls deep?'

I can't stifle a moan as he changes angles, thrusting into me. "Yes, baby," I whisper breathlessly, "Yes, I like your cock balls deep. I need it balls deep."

"Good girl," he growls, fucking me harder.

His pace quickens, and his hands drop to my hips before circling around to my pudgy tummy. I swat them away, self-conscious about anyone touching me there.

But he's not having it. Swatting playfully back, he covers my belly completely with his hot palms, pulling me into him with increasing urgency. Through heavy breaths, he commands, "Every part of you is perfect, Cricket. Don't ever keep any of it from me. Because it all belongs to me now."

I'm swollen and sensitive from last night, and his words push me over the edge. Trembling, I feel my pussy clench tightly around his cock. He shudders against my back, releasing into me with a deep-throated scream. My pussy milks everything he has to give, and I can feel him pulsing into me. Holding me possessively, he rides jerky waves of pleasure, his heart pounding against my back. Once he's got his breath back, he declares, "Fuck, why do we have to go to work today?"

I stretch, leaning back into him, and he yawns next to my ear. My stomach knots, and I ask shakily, "Will this ever happen again?"

He props himself up on his elbow, staring into my face. His eyes look sad as he says, "I'm sorry for all those years I made you think I didn't want you. Convincing myself of that was the hardest thing I've ever tried to do." He runs his free hand through his hair. Smiling sheepishly, he continues, "And you can see how well it worked in the end."

I don't want to ruin this moment, and I know we both have to get ready for work. But I need more from him. I need to understand what's going on between us, and why it's happening now.

"What?" he asks, searching my face. "I can tell your brain's working a mile a minute."

"I'm just trying to understand what this means. How this changes things? If it changes things?"

He stares at me long and hard before saying, "It changes everything, if you want it to. I'll be here every night, if you'll have me. And if you want this to be a once in a while thing, I won't be happy about it, but I'll put up with it. You get to call the shots. But I do have one rule: No other men. I don't want them talking to you, looking at you, smiling at you. Anything. You understand?"

"Chris, half of working at a bakery is customer service. I can't scare away fifty percent of my clientele by ignoring them or giving them the evil eye."

"Keep your customer service to a minimum, then. Or else I'll make you come back to the Sheriff's Department. The temporary dispatcher's shit, Cricket. Doesn't hold a candle to you."

I roll my eyes. I know better than anyone how hard Chris is to work for. But my heart thrills at his possessiveness, even as my stomach drops. This sounds so much like commitment, and yet, honestly, is it? Will he follow the same rules? I side-eye him, questioning, "Does the same go for you? Minimal contact with all females moving forward?"

"I can do that," he replies in earnest, and it makes me giggle.

"Why are you laughing?" he asks.

"I don't know. You're just acting so differently now." *I can barely wrap my head around the last ten hours.*

"Is that a bad thing?"

"No, I love it." *I love you.* I press my lips tightly together before saying something stupid.

He shrugs. "It's an easy ask, because yours is the only pussy I want in this whole wide world." It's not what I'm longing to hear from him. But I'll take it.

"You're all I want, too," I reply, re-forging his words into something romantic.

He smiles broadly. "Good, because I'll kill the mother-fucker that lays a hand on you."

I inhale sharply. "Chris!" Staring at his black eye and swollen lip, I don't doubt his words. But it's not a good look for a sheriff.

"I'm serious." He strokes my hair gently, his eyes roving over my face like he's trying to remember this moment forever. "I've wanted this—what happened between us last night and this morning—for a very long time. And I won't let anyone take you from me now that you're mine."

"I just don't understand why it couldn't have happened sooner," I say quietly, looking down. I realize too late, I've opened a Pandora's box. "I'm sorry. We can talk about this later. We need to get ready."

He puts a finger under my chin, pointing my face up towards his until our eyes meet. "I'm not leaving this spot until we straighten this out," he replies authoritatively. "Cricket, when we were in high school ... Well, you were just too young for me. I never should've stood you up for prom, but I never should've asked you out, either. Everything I did in the past to hurt you, I'll regret for the rest of my life. But I had reason to believe you were better off without me. And I thought that for a long time, until your shitty taste in boyfriends proved me wrong. The truth is, I'm still not good enough for you. But I know how to treat you right and protect you and pleasure you and make sure nothing comes between us ever again. And that's what I plan on doing, if you'll have me?"

I nod, my heart soaring at his words. But I don't agree with everything he says. "How was I too young? I'm only three years younger than you, Chris."

"That doesn't mean anything now, but back then ... Honey, I was eighteen by the time prom came around. Any fooling around we would've done afterwards could've gotten me statutory rape charges." His voice breaks saying the last two words.

For the briefest instant, he looks away, a darkness shrouding his face. *He's not telling me everything.* Years of waiting for this moment have made me patient. But they've also left me constantly preparing to be hurt by him again. My cheeks heat as I ask, "And did you plan on fooling around with me after prom?"

My question makes him raise his eyebrows, and he winces, saying, "Of course, I did. You were hot as fuck—and still are. You know what a horn dog I was in high school and still am," he growls wrapping his arms around me and kissing my neck. "Years later, I thought I had it together until the day you kissed me in my office. It was the last thing I expected, Cricket. And it unleashed something in me, for better or worse, that I can no longer control. I just hope you won't come to regret it."

He still doesn't understand how much I love him. As he nibbles my ear, all I manage is a soft protest. "How could I ever regret this?"

Christian leans back, staring into my face and smiling grimly. He opens his mouth. Then, closes it again. Finally, he peers into my eyes, asking, "Do you want me back here tonight?"

"You already know my answer. I want you here tonight, tomorrow night, every night."

"Good," he yawns, stretching. "I'm glad we can agree on something. Besides, I haven't slept this well in God knows how long. And the couple of times I did wake up, it was easy falling back to sleep knowing you were safe and in my arms."

Does that mean he's spent sleepless nights thinking about me, worrying about me the way I have about him? I don't want to jump to conclusions, so I bury the thought deep in my heart, hoping we'll return to it someday.

"Now, we're both going to be late if we keep fooling around. I'll go make coffee, and you should get a shower started. I'll be right behind you," he promises with a wink. "After all, I've got to keep my promise to those beautiful breasts of yours." My nipples instantly pearl at his words.

I pad across the plush beige carpet to my all-pink bathroom, more floating than walking. It's funny seeing such a rugged, hard man in my hyper feminine house. Everything's flowery and frilly and caters to a single woman. But Christian's all bronzed, hard, angular planes, and he sticks out like a sore thumb among the pastel and lace. My heart thrills at the thought of him leaving his stuff here—shampoo, aftershave, a razor, his clothes, his cowboy boots, his hat, whatever. I'll take it.

But I'm getting ahead of myself. *Way ahead of myself.*

Something tugs at the back of my mind. Reflecting on last night, I remember how concerned he was about hurting me. The way he emphasized never wanting children. So many questions remain. The tightness building in my chest lets me know he's not telling me everything.

TWELVE

"What's got you smiling?" grumbles Zane looking at me suspiciously. I'm whistling and can't hide how the last week with Cricket has made me feel. I've been at her place every night, and yet it's never enough. Every afternoon, the closer I get to seeing her again, the faster my heart thumps against my ribs. I thought things would calm down a bit. But I don't know if they ever will, and I'm okay with that, too. She's always ready for me when I come through the door, which has my cock throbbing with desire and my hands shaking each time I approach her house.

I think back fondly to Valentine's Day night. We were so newly together, and I was afraid she'd start second guessing all that happened with us the night before once she got to the bakery. When I rang her doorbell, leaning against the door frame, a dozen pink roses in my hand, she answered in a fucking lavender teddy, more lace than silk. Grabbing me by my tie, she pulled me inside, and made quick work of dropping to her knees to please me. I barely got the front door closed behind me. Believe me, I returned the pleasuring in spades, keeping her up most of the night, although we never managed to officially make it into the bedroom. Talk about the best fucking Valentine's Day ever!

I'm a moron for how long I went without claiming her. I wanted so badly not to hurt her but did it anyway, and then some. And the pit in my stomach tells me it may happen again. But I can't keep running from my past, no matter how much shame public knowledge of it stands to bring me. After looking up information about Mazie, I found out she's in an old folks home in Ophir City.

A quick call to the facility revealed she has advanced dementia, caused by years of drug and alcohol abuse. It's no surprise, but it has left me with many questions about who tried to blackmail me over text message. They haven't contacted me again, but the silence feels eerie. I had flowers delivered to Mazie's room, and the nurse told me she liked them. But she had no recollection of the name Christian. Maybe it's better that way.

Anyway, I know I need to tell Cricket everything. And after the week we've had, the way she shares herself generously and completely with me, I know even finding out about my past won't change her feelings. That realization has me regretting so many wasted years without her. And yet I still struggle to find the right words and time to level with her about my past.

Ranch hands are milling around, and I'm here to follow up and make sure there hasn't been additional trouble with the Amestoys. Apparently, the old man came down hard on Fierce and the younger men in the family, taking my threat as sheriff to heart. And there haven't been anymore dead cattle found, although I'd still put my money on predators over human interference.

"How's Dad these days?"

Zane looks perturbed as he replies, "Going downhill, slowly but surely. He definitely needs some extra help. I get it, but does it have to come from Birdie Jenkins, of all people?"

"What, you'd rather trust him with a stranger?"

'I guess not." He shrugs. "I just don't want to see her every day, you know what I mean?"

"Not really."

"Ever since you and Cricket finally sealed the deal, you've been annoying as fuck."

I go back to whistling and grinning, not about to hide my feelings from anyone. I've never been happier in my life, and I have a deep sense of peace that everything will work out. Even if I don't have all the details. The past seven days are shining proof of my theory.

Looking out across Rough & Ready Country, I watch the first rays of dawn touch the frosted ground still patched with snow. It sets the world on fire, glowing and glimmering like the gold nuggets that first brought pioneers up here more than a century ago. I can see my breath in the chill of the morning air as we prepare to ride out. I wish Cricket was here with me now. She would love watching the breathtaking transformation from grayscale night to this world of blazing color. All verdant evergreens, white-tipped with snow, and the towering Sierra Nevadas alternating between pristine patches of powder white and deep blue swatches of distant forest.

I make a mental note to bring her out here riding. She grew up around our horses, thanks to her home's proximity to the ranch. But she never had her own mount. I'm guessing she'd love another chance to experience this world we grew up in together. She's been living in Hollister too long. Savoring the splendor of this little slice of heaven, I know it's time to bring her home. As much as I've enjoyed fooling around at her place, I want her to take the next step and move in with me.

CHAPTER

THIRTEEN

CHRISTIAN

Two hours later, we're at upper camp, checking out the herd. Brands are in order, and the fences are mended and holding up despite recent snowstorms. We find one dead calf, but the babies born in January and February are never as robust as their warm weather counterparts. I don't see any signs of antagonism or trouble from the Amestoys, which is a relief.

Dad didn't come along today because he felt extra tired. I can't describe the pain of seeing the strongest man on Earth fade slowly away. It's different from when Ruby Jean passed. That was confusing because I was so young. I couldn't wrap my head around it, and I was angry with her for years for disappearing. Of course, as I got older, I came to terms with what happened. The situation with Dad comes with bittersweet awareness of how little time's left. But isn't that the thing with life? Never enough time. I know Zane doesn't want to admit it, but having Birdie around will be a relief.

My phone rings, and I see it's the office. "Sheriff McLeod here."

"Chris, it's Mike." I wince at the voice of the temporary dispatcher. When will the county get its act together and hire someone capable? More like Cricket? Although I know better than anyone she's one hundred percent irreplaceable.

"Thought you might like to know there's something weird going on at the bakery."

Something weird at the bakery? Fuck me. What's wrong with this guy? "What do you mean? Did they run out of doughnuts or something?"

"No. Everyone's saying the doors are locked as if it's closed for business. But there are people inside. One looks like an indigent … possibly with a knife."

"What?"

"Kirk and Stacey are on their way over there now. But I wanted you to be ready to answer your phone."

My chest hurts from where my heart's stopped beating, and I can hear ringing in my ears. I can't breathe, and I can't think straight. This has to be a sick joke.

Zane looks my way. "What's the matter, Chris?"

"It's Cricket," I reply, unable to catch my breath. "Something's happened at the bakery. Something about a guy with a knife."

"You need to head back!"

My head's on swivel as I look back and forth between Zane and the ranch where my truck is—nearly two hours away. There's no way I can wait that long to get to her.

My phone rings, and it's Stacey, "Boss, you better get down here."

"Tell me everything."

"We've set up a perimeter around the bakery. It's hard to see what's going on inside because the blinds are drawn. But it looks like a potential hostage situation."

The motherfucker that lays a finger on my Cricket will rue the day he was born. "Any idea how many are involved and what kind of weapons they have?"

"We've only heard about one man. Tall, long hair pulled back in a bun. Some witnesses say they saw him brandishing a knife before the shutters were closed."

"What about Cricket, her mom, the bakers?"

"Witnesses say they're all still inside."

"I'm on my way. Look, Stacey, if you or Kirk get a clean shot, take it."

"Yes, sir."

Shoving my phone back into my pocket, I turn to Zane. "You think Hell and I could get through the back way?" There's a much faster route into town. It would only take about thirty minutes from here. But after last year's bad winter, a mudslide washed it out. The trail's always been steep, and now, it's a mess.

He shrugs. "You're in for one hell of a ride."

Coming from a world champion rodeo rider, it makes me swallow hard. "But if you can stick to the right, you should be fine. Good luck with Devil's Gulch. If any horse can do it, I'd put my money on Hell. I know if I was riding him, he'd make."

Challenge accepted. I'm galloping off before he finishes the sentence, sitting low in the saddle, and urging Hell or High Water on to Hollister. Zane races up beside me, determination etched on his face.

"You coming, too?" I holler.

"Got nothing better to do. Besides I still don't feel like digging your grave!"

FOURTEEN

CRICKET

"Did you see the RV outside the bakery last night?" Mom asks, concern flashing across her face.

I wave the comment away, saying, "I handled that this morning when I got in."

"What did you do?"

"Remember that street artist from Sacramento that I told you about? The one I interviewed about painting a mural? That was his RV."

Mom folds the croissant dough on the table in front of her, adding more butter and working the rolling pin. "Did you tell him he could park out back?" she questions in a hissing whisper.

"Of course not. But he didn't take a hint. Anyway, I knocked on his door when I got in this morning. But he didn't answer, so I left a note. He drove off about forty-five minutes ago, I think."

"You should've gotten Chris involved. What's the point of having the County Sheriff as a boyfriend, if you don't ask for his help? Besides, I can't stand the thought of you out

317

there this morning banging on his door in the dark. You need to be more careful."

"He's harmless," I counter, looking down at the neat row of pastries I just finished readying for the oven. "Honestly, I feel a little sorry for the guy. He's down on his luck and needs some kind of a break, I guess. He originally asked if he could park here, but I told him to try one of the nearby campgrounds or RV parks."

We work in silence for a few minutes. Finally, she asks, "How are things going with you and Chris? Is he treating you okay?"

My face lights up with an ear to ear grin. "Things couldn't be better." But then I feel that subconscious tug that's been bothering me all week, and I bury my head in my work.

"Wait, what's that look for? Is there something wrong?"

I shrug. "No, not really. I just feel sometimes like Chris is holding something back from me. And it worries me. Makes me constantly feel like I'm waiting for the other shoe to drop."

Mom's eyes narrow, and her curly short brown hair shakes as she continues rolling out the dough. "I know how much you love him, Cricket ..."

I start to protest, but she cuts me off.

"Stop it. You're not fooling anyone. I know how much you love Chris and always have. But you can't let him walk all over you. You have to love and respect yourself, too. And part of a healthy relationship is showing him how you want to be treated and then holding him to it."

"If we're talking about how he treats me, it's wonderful," I say, thinking back to this morning before work.

"Sex doesn't count."

"Oh, Mom," I scold. "I don't want to talk about this with you."

"And I don't want to watch you get your heart broken. Just because you love a man doesn't mean you can let him walk all over you. You'll live to regret it. I learned that the hard way during my divorce. And I never want you to go through anything like that. So, set some healthy boundaries and expectations."

I cock my head to the side.

"Will you at least think about it?" she asks.

"I guess."

"I know I'll feel a whole lot better when he makes it official with a ring and some grand babies."

"Mom," I say, feeling my cheeks burn. My heart sinks as I remember how he stressed no kids.

"There's more you're not telling me, isn't there?"

I frown. "He told me he doesn't want to have kids."

"Not have kids? That's not going to work for you."

"No, Mom. I love him, for better or worse."

"He hasn't put a ring on it. Stop talking that way. And for heaven's sake rethink the whole kids thing. Did he say why he didn't want them?"

I look up at the ceiling, remembering the conversation. "Actually, he said he couldn't give me babies."

Her eyebrows shoot up. "Can't is a whole lot different than won't. Do you think something happened to him while he was in the Marines? Remember when everyone was talking about Gulf War Syndrome? As I recall it made it difficult for some service members to have children."

I shake my head. "I honestly don't know."

"See, that's what I'm talking about. This is your future, Cricket. Your future as much as his. You need to communicate your expectations clearly. After all, he's made you wait long enough for a relationship. How much longer do you really want to wait for a ring? And coupled with never having kids? Sounds like a bad deal to me."

I open my mouth to speak when I hear the door to the bakery swing wide and the bell tinkle wildly. I look at the clock, "Lillian's never this late. I wonder what's up?" There's scuffling at the door, and I hear a nasally male voice order, "Lock the fucking door!" Mom, the other baker, Mark, and I all jump simultaneously. Lillian lets out a squeal as we hear more commotion causing the bell on the door to chime.

All three of us rush from the kitchen into the store, seeing Lillian and Peter standing there. He's got a knife clutched over her chest. My eyes round, and I take a stunned step back. It's still early morning in Hollister, and there's not a bit of action outside. I'm guessing Chris is still at the ranch, sorting out the rivalry with the Amestoys. And it'll likely be hours before anybody's out on the street in Hollister, let alone noticing a problem at the bakery.

Peter shoves Lillian into a chair, sitting down next to her with the knife clutched so tightly in his hand his fingers look white. He stares around the room, wildly talking to himself. He's either strung out, schizophrenic, or a dangerous mixture of the two. Lillian exudes pure terror as she visibly shakes. I notice how Peter's holding the knife. It's obvious he has little experience with weapons. Still, I don't want to inadvertently trigger him, so I say in a low, quiet voice, "Peter, what's going on?"

His eyes flutter open, and they're vacuous. It looks like he hasn't slept, bathed, or changed clothes since I saw him at the Five Star. The smell that wafts my direction confirms it. "You should've just let me park here, bitch. Was it really too much to ask?"

My mother's hands are pressed into the dough on the counter, her entire body frozen. Years of working at the Sheriff's Department has one thing on my mind: de-escalation. But I'm no hostage negotiator.

"Why don't you let Lillian come over here and get to work, and you and I can talk about what's going on. Okay?"

He lets out a desperate sigh, tears pouring down his cheeks. "You know, I just can't catch a break." Lillian screams as he grabs her arm, pulling her closer.

"All I wanted was to make something of myself as an artist, and now I've lost everything. My family, my home, my life. I have nothing left to live for."

Everyone in the room is holding their breath as I take a step forward. "Can I get you something to eat? Some cookies or cupcakes?"

He relaxes the arm holding the knife, letting it fall into his lap as he wipes the tears from his cheeks with his other. His head lolls back as he talks to himself, and I wonder what combination of drugs and mental health issues might be expressing themselves at this moment.

Lillian seizes the moment to scramble away from him, running to stand behind Mark. Peter looks at her, suddenly very disinterested in her escape.

I take another step towards him, asking again, "When's the last time you ate? What can I bring you?"

He looks up, his face covered in tears. "Why couldn't you let me park out back? Was it really too much to ask? I just need a chance to get back on my feet."

"That's right," I reply. "Everyone needs that sometimes. But you're in a bakery now, and the best I can offer you is some food. What will you have?"

He raises the knife, shaking it back and forth in his hand as he thinks. He's not threatening us with it. But his actions are uncoordinated and erratic, and his mood could change in a heartbeat.

"Mom, could you bring me some cookies?" I ask, looking over my shoulder. She's clutching the rolling pin in her hand, ready to use it.

Mark takes my lead instead, quickly filling a box with unfrosted cookies. He walks forward carefully, placing them on the table in front of Peter.

I let out a shaky sigh.

"Thank you, man," Peter says, tearing up again. He shoves a dirty hand into the box, munching away. Leaning back and staring at the knife-wielding hand propped in his lap, he looks distracted. Mark walks backwards, never taking his eyes off Peter. On the way, he grabs me, starting to walk both of us backwards. But Peter stops him. "No, man, leave her there. I like talking to her. Even though you fucking woke me up, banging on my RV door this morning. The nerve of some people." He uses the knife to bark out orders, shooing Mark backwards. He stares at me unblinkingly, and I try to remain nonchalant.

CHAPTER
FIFTEEN
CRICKET

"Well, Peter, I know we got off to a rocky start this morning. But would you like to start in on the mural? Do you have paints and tools you'd like us to help carry in?" I'm trying to find any excuse to get him to open the door and let us outside. It feels like years have gone by since this ordeal started.

Lillian draws closer to me, whispering that she snuck into the kitchen trying to escape through the emergency door, even disarming the fire alarm. But there was something in front of the exit, so it wouldn't open wide enough for her to slip through. She's a lovely twenty-something Korean woman about half my size. If she can't squeeze through, none of us can. I'm guessing the RV's parked out back again.

Peter's voice brings the conversation to an abrupt halt. "You'd really still let me do the mural?"

"Why not? You're here. We're here."

The door shakes as someone outside tries to open it. They peer through the glass of the window, letting out a holler and pointing through the glass at Peter and the knife. Instantly, he gets agitated.

Soon, a small crowd of people have gathered outside, and he jerks with nervousness, screaming, "Close the fucking blinds!"

He's standing now, nervously swinging the knife around, and I'm weighing my options. Do I try to knock him to the ground and wrestle him for it? If I do it right, I'll have the element of surprise. But certainly not the upper body strength in a contest of wills.

Seeing nobody's going to pull the blinds for him, he runs to the windows doing it himself. But there's no blind for the glass door, so people continue to peer inside.

Glancing over my shoulder at Mark, I will him with my eyes to get ready. But he's frozen to the spot. So, I eye my mom, and she's still got the rolling pin in her hand with a determined look on her face.

I nod, and we both rush forward, trying to knock him to the ground as he messes with the blinds, his back to us. But the sound of my sneakers squeaking on the freshly mopped floor alert him to our plan. Turning swiftly, he brandishes the knife, ready to attack. Mom and I both step back.

"You're trying to trick me," he accuses, shaking the weapon menacingly.

"We were just trying to help with the blinds," Mom replies, breathlessly.

"You're lying!" he rages.

I put up my hands, speaking in calm tones. "Peter, it's okay. We're just nervous like you are. That's all. If you could put the knife away, I'm sure we could get this all sorted out, and you could start on the mural."

Outside, sirens sound, and I swallow hard. My heart jumps at the hope Christian is here to rescue us. But another part of me fears I'm about to watch Peter die. I stare at the desperate man, feeling both terror at his unpredictability and pity for his future.

Peter's sitting again, leaning forward on his legs, looking down and sobbing. "I'm in trouble. I'm in trouble."

"It doesn't have to be this way. We could make this end quickly and peacefully."

"Shut up!" he screams, his face anguished.

We stand in silence, but my eyes rove the room. There has to be some way to stop him. Mom's still got the rolling pin, and I get Mark's attention, using eye movement to draw his gaze to the ceramic baking dishes on the counter. Lilian stares towards the kitchen, poised to spring for the knives and pans the first chance she gets. Getting impatient, she makes a move, but Peter stops her, launching a barrage of threats her way. His voice sounds ferocious, inhuman, and it brings all of our plans to a standstill.

An eternity passes, and Peter finally stands up, pointing the knife in my direction. "You're coming with me."

"Peter, I don't think that would be safe for you."

I'm certain Christian has instructed his deputies to shoot to kill, and I know he won't hesitate. Despite the danger I feel, I want a peaceful resolution.

"Not safe?" He laughs, lunging unexpectedly in my direction, grabbing me by the wrist. "We're going to discuss where I parked and whether or not it's a problem."

"Cricket!" Mom screams as he wraps the knife-wielding arm around my waist, fumbling with the front door lock. As we pass through the doorway, I look down at his hand, assessing the hold of the knife. I think I can disarm him. But stepping from the dark of the bakery into the light of the curbside has me blinking furiously, frantic for my eyes to adjust. Two deputies, Kirk and Stacey, have their guns drawn, trained at Peter and me. I've never been on this side of a firearm before, and panic strangles my chest.

"Drop your weapon!" Stacey screams in a gruff voice, and I feel Peter's grip tighten around me. The knife cuts deeply into my arm, and I don't know if he's even aware of it. I try to struggle free, as he twists me around heading down the curb towards the back of the bakery. *Are we going to his RV?* My stomach drops.

Suddenly, the pounding of horse's hooves thunder in our ears. *What the hell?*

Peter wheels around, dragging me along, to see what's going on. In a flash, there's a black horse towering over us, front feet rearing into the air. I duck out of the way, and Peter falls, sprawling backwards onto the curb, his legs flailing. The stallion's front hooves come down mere millimeters from his crotch, and he lets out a high-pitched scream. In one fluid movement, the gorgeous sheriff of Gold County is off his mount and on his feet, a revolver pointed at Peter's head.

I scramble to Christian, and he uses his free hand to push me behind him for safety.

Peter lets out another hysterical cry. "It's your cowboy!"

"Yeah, it sure the fuck is," Christian growls through clenched teeth. "Didn't I warn you she had a man? That man bun on too tight to hear straight?"

Stacey and Kirk are at our sides in an instant, and the female deputy breaks into nervous laughter at Christian's man bun statement. It strikes her so funny, in fact, that Kirk has to read Peter his Miranda Rights. Her shoulders continue to shake as she handcuffs the guy. Christian's staring at my arm, and I look down to a gush of hot, dark blood. "Call for an ambulance," he orders firmly, pulling off his shirt to staunch the bleeding.

"Did he hurt you anywhere else?"

"No."

He's still staring at my arm, his face reddening and his nostrils flaring with rage.

"It's not that bad, Christian."

"The fuck it's not," he screams, grabbing Peter by the scruff of his collar, and screaming inches from his face, "You better thank your lucky stars you're still alive."

Mom has come out now, and her eyes dart to my arm and Christian's shirt, now stained burgundy. Finally looking around, she covers her chest with her hand startled at the unexpected sight of a black Mustang whinnying next to her.

"What happened?" she asks, her face awash in confusion.

"Christian rode to the rescue." As soon as the words leave my mouth, my vision tunnels and darkens.

Christian wraps a steadying arm around me, "Woah, there. Take a deep breath, honey. Everything's going to be alright."

CHAPTER

SIXTEEN

CHRISTIAN

Cricket and I sit in an ER hospital room together, taking turns getting medical attention. "Don't hurt her," I warn the doctor with a growl as he works painstakingly to put a neat row of thread in her arm.

"I'm doing the best I can," he replies as he works. He's younger and more handsome than somebody I want working on my girl. I'm tempted to tell him not to touch her more than he has to. But I don't want to distract him.

She almost passed out after looking at her arm, and so I try to distract her now, patting her leg comfortingly. Thoughtfully, she remarks, "I still don't know how you got from the ranch to the bakery in thirty minutes."

"He's a good horse," I say, shrugging. As Zane predicted, it was one hell of a ride. The many lacerations and abrasions on my face and arms attest to it. I want to tell her about jumping Devil's Gulch. When Hell landed it, his back legs struggled on the edge for purchase. There was a tottering moment when I wasn't sure we'd make it. But I should've known better than to doubt a Mustang. Pulling up the reigns to watch Zane follow, he took one look and started sweating. But the mare made the final decision, coming to a frantic halt before jerking backwards, spooked. We both knew it was no good.

Zane screamed, "No fucking way this mare'll make it. Don't wait on me. Give 'em hell, and go save your girl!" Sitting up in the saddle, he removed his hat, letting out a cheer, and I urged Hell on. Although the worst of it was over, we still took a beating, plowing headlong through rosehip bushes and manzanitas on a descent steep enough to make an airplane pilot's toes curl. Hell flew over large boulders and toppled logs, finding footing only a spirit horse could manage, charging furiously until forest floor gave way to pavement and the chance to rescue my woman. Cricket's not ready to hear this story—maybe she never will be. And I'd like to avoid a scolding about my recklessness. So, I keep the details to myself.

A nurse comes in, fussing with my face and arms, cleaning my wounds. Cricket looks my way as the redhead in scrubs teases, "What the hell did you do to yourself, cowboy? We're going to be here all night patching you up."

My woman's face looks testy as she orders, "Don't touch him anymore than you have to, and keep the talking to a minimum. He's *my* cowboy."

The nurse's jaw drops, and Cricket gives her a steely look, her chin raised defiantly.

"Shit, I like it when you're possessive," I grin, squeezing her free hand.

"It's stressful working on you two," the doctor muses, completing his last stitch. He looks at Cricket. "You're going to have a scar, but it should be minimal. I'm a plastic surgeon if you ever want to revisit this work."

"Thank you," she says, looking down worried.

"You're perfect, Cricket. Scars and all."

329

Her face beams at me, and I wonder at the fact she needed such reassurance. Doesn't she know she hung the moon and stars of my world? I'm determined to spend the rest of my life showing my devotion to her. Undoing the hurt of the past. I just wish I could give her everything she wants. But I'll give her everything I possibly can, starting with my heart and my future.

CHAPTER
SEVENTEEN
CHRISTIAN

I talk Cricket into coming back to the ranch with me. Zane transported Hell back to the stables earlier, but we go out to visit him. Bringing extra carrots and crab apples for him to munch while we pet him, comb him, and tend his scratches and scrapes. He's had a big day, and he deserves king treatment.

"I never thought old Hell or High Water would save me," she says, rubbing him down with her palm.

"You remember him from when we were younger?"

"How could I forget? He was little more than a foal when he first came here. A Mustang rescue. And the first time you got up the nerve to hold my hand was after we'd been out riding all day. We were combing him together. Our fingertips kept touching, and finally you grabbed my hand and wouldn't let go." She launches a seductive look over her shoulder, making me shiver with desire.

I take her hands now. "Yeah, and I remember talking you into making out with me in this very stable. Only you were so startled by every sound the horses made I couldn't get you to hold still."

"I didn't want your dad or brothers to catch us. Besides, I held still years later in your office, didn't I?" She sends another sizzling glance my way.

"You keep looking at me like that, and I'll make you hold still this instant."

"You think you have that kind of power over me, Sheriff McLeod?"

"That and more," I reply with a knowing smile. "But before we get back to the finer things in life, I have something I want to show you."

I grab her hand, leading her out to my black truck. After boosting her into the seat and leaning in to fasten her seatbelt, I feel so nervous I can't even kiss her.

My hands tremble as we drive in silence back to the cabin, and she looks somber. I guess she can sense I've got a lot on my mind. Some of it good. Some not.

Inside my cabin, it feels cold. Countless clues point to the fact I haven't been here in days. I turn on the lights, and she admires the rich dark wood of the living room and dining room, accented by Native American patterned blankets and fabrics and Western art.

"The floor plan is simple but lofty thanks to the high ceilings," I say pointing up. I hope she'll be comfortable here. I hope she'll stay forever. I kneel in front of the hearth to make a fire, while she explores. She's been here before, to pick up work documents and shit like that. But never as a friend, let alone as my woman.

"Can I get you some hot chocolate?" I ask after the fire's crackling warmly.

"Only if you've got a candy cane to stir it with."

"Of course," I say, heading to the kitchen to get a pot of water boiling. That's how she's drunk it for as long as I can remember. I've always kept a few around my kitchen, just in case.

"Get comfortable," I order from the stove, pouring steaming hot water into her mug. "Because you're staying here a while."

"Am I now?"

"Yes, ma'am."

She kicks off her shoes and reclines back, hugging a burgundy and black tribal pillow. Gazing down at the bandage on her arm as I walk into the living room, I still can't wrap my head around the day. I hand her the mug with a candy cane in it, and she asks, "You're not having any?"

"I may have a shot of whiskey in a few minutes. But I need to show you something first."

Her face tenses, and my heart jumps in my throat. "Do we have to do it tonight?" she asks. "This moment's so cozy and perfect. I don't want to ruin it."

I rub my hand over my heart. "Every moment with you is perfect. Now, hold that thought." I head into the back room, appearing a few minutes later with a shoe box. My breath's coming fast now, and I feel like my chest might cave in. But I can't put this off any longer.

"I know we've had a long day, but I'm not sure I'll get the nerve to do this again."

She laughs anxiously, remarking, "Please. The cowboy that jumped Devil's Gulch and rode into a hostage situation? What could make you nervous?"

"Who told you about Devil's Gulch?"

"Zane."

"Of course."

I sit down next to her, pulling her legs into my lap.

Setting the box on the other side of me, I take the top off and start shuffling through it. She sits up, putting her mug on the side table. I narrate, "I think you'll like this first part. Or else you'll think I'm a fucking stalker. I'm not sure which."

Her eyebrows knit as I pile letters and cards in her lap. She turns the first one over, sees her name neatly printed on the envelope, and lets out a little squeal of surprise. She looks at another and another, and soon her eyes well with emotion. "What are these, Chris?"

"All the birthday cards and letters I've ever written to you but never sent," I say quietly, looking down at the box. I feel fucking vulnerable. I'd rather jump the gulch again or stare down the barrel of Patrick's shotgun.

I explain, "You'll see, there's one for every birthday. Even this year, although it hasn't come yet. Don't worry, I plan on doing more than a card now that we're official. And there are some letters in there from when I was serving overseas. Even some from boot camp. But take those with a grain of salt because I was a real pussy back then."

Her hand is over her mouth, and her cheeks are wet and shiny.

"Honey, you know how it hurts me when you cry," I whisper, cupping her face in my left hand.

"These are happy tears," she excuses. Her eyes round as she dives into the cards and letters heaped in her lap. Some are happy. Some are sad. Some are hopeless. All are colored by intense longing.

Hours pass, and I have to throw a couple logs on the fire as she pours over every word. Sometimes, she settles on a phrase, a sentence, or even a whole paragraph, reading it aloud. Her voice catches, and she looks up at me, equal parts puzzled and moved. Other cards and letters make her smile as she reads them, laughing at a funny story or shared memory from our youth.

The words flood me with an overpowering mixture of memories and emotions as I remember the despondent man who wrote them. A man driven by sadness, desolation, despair, and shame. No wonder I never sent them to her. Even now, I can see the confusion on her face. Because none of the letters explain the reason for my hopelessness.

Reflecting back, I realize that despite all those torturous feelings, Cricket has always been my North Star. Subconsciously, she drew me back home to Rough & Ready. Drew me to her. One letter that I wrote during a sleepless night at a military hospital while recovering from an IED-related concussion in Afghanistan makes her break down sobbing. In it, I try to describe the anguish of possibly dying overseas, without ever seeing her face again. Without ever getting the chance to tell her how much I love her.

She shakes her head, fighting back a sob. "You loved me? Why didn't you tell me?"

"Honey, I can't remember a time I didn't love you, and I still do, more than ever," I stare at her hand, threading my fingers through hers. But when I look at her face, I see a swirl of emotion—sorrow, rage, bewilderment. *I knew this was coming.*

Her voice rises as she asks, "But I don't understand. All these years. All this pain. All this loneliness. You know, I was going through these same feelings, Christian. And you were so damn good at convincing me you didn't care. I don't get it. Why didn't you send me any of these cards or letters? Just one could've saved us so much lost time."

"Because of this," I answer, holding up a piece of crumpled notebook paper with a rough edge where it was torn from a spiral notebook. I never thought I'd have the nerve to do this. But I know I have to because I don't just want today with Cricket. I want forever.

Her face clouds as she looks at the stained paper, the messy handwriting, reading it silently. "This is from your birth mother?"

"Yep," I nod, shifting on the couch to face her. When I tell her this, I need to do it like a man. I need to look her in the eyes. "The day I was supposed to take you to prom, I finally got up the nerve to drive over to Ophir City to meet her."

She leans forward.

How do I put this? Each sentence brings me closer to the one I dread most. "She lived in a rundown trailer in the worst part of town. I think she was coming down off something when I arrived. And I could hear a man snoring down the hallway, but I never met him. She said he wasn't my father."

Cricket squeezes my hand tightly. I feel close to crying, which I didn't expect, as I pause for a long moment. I don't know how else to say it: "She got pregnant with me when she was sixteen."

Cricket nods.

"And my biological father, Matthew Wheeler, was her PE coach ... He raped her, Cricket." My voice falters over the last phrase, yet I will myself to hold her gaze. In her eyes, I read shock, sadness, pain. But I never see disgust. Not even for a split second. I exhale sharply, realizing I've been holding my breath.

She leans forward, both of her hands coming up to my face, and she kisses me. The kiss is tender, innocent, over-flowing with love. It's the balm my heart needs. She stares deeply into my eyes, saying nothing. Just showing me her feelings haven't changed—haven't even been shaken.

I sit back against the couch, explaining, "You can see what Mazie said for yourself. She said I looked just like him. And in person, she told me I played football like him, I acted like him, and I needed to be careful about not doing other things like him. The way she looked at me. She was just so disgusted by me. I'll never get that look out of my mind."

"But none of this is your fault, Christian. You had nothing to do with any of it. And no power to change it. You're a good man. You always have been."

I look her in the eyes. "Because of you, because of this last week together, I'm finally starting to realize that. But you've got to understand, at eighteen years old, it fucked hardcore with my mind. Hell, at thirty-five, it still does. I couldn't handle the shame, the grief. Feelings that have haunted me for years … that still nag at me. But my worst fear was the possibility of you looking at me the way Mazie did. That's why I could never tell you. Or let you know how much I loved you. Because, honestly, you deserve so much better."

"I deserve you, and you deserve me. You're the best man I know. And you'll never convince me otherwise. But I have to ask again: How could you think any of this was your fault?"

"It may not have been my fault, but I still have his blood running through my veins. And Mazie was no fucking saint, either. If you saw how she lived, you'd think twice about me."

"No, I won't," Cricket replies, raising her chin defiantly. "I want you to promise me you'll stop saying that because it's not true."

I look down.

"Promise me."

"I promise."

She continues, "We don't have control over the things that happened to us as kids. Much less things that happened before we were born. Don't you remember when Mom and I first came to Hollister? We were homeless. The kids at school made fun of me because I wore the same clothes every day, and my hair was unwashed. But that situation didn't make me unworthy. In fact, it made me a stronger, more caring person."

"It's not the same thing. It's not in your genes."

"And it's not in your genes, either. Yes, you can get personality and physical traits from your parents. Maybe work ethic or a tendency to like certain foods. But there's no rape gene."

I've never thought about it that way, and I feel lighter and freer than I have in nearly two decades. I should've told Cricket sooner. Regret floods me, and I have to ask, "Is that what you would have told me if I'd confided this in you in high school?"

"I don't know, Christian. We were both so young and stupid back then. I can think of about a million things I would've liked to do differently with you. But all of those mistakes we made and regrets we carry have still brought us to this moment. And it's the happiest moment of my life —every moment with you is."

I pull her into me, kissing her tenderly, soulfully. We sit lazily on the couch, savoring each other's lips and touch as the firelight warms the room.

Finally, Cricket observes, "There's something else bothering you. What is it?"

Taking a deep breath, I confess, "What Mazie told me ... Wyatt and Ruby Jean had to know about it. Why in all these years did he never tell me? I don't understand."

"That doesn't sound like him. Have you asked him about it?"

I shake my head.

"The only way to find out is by asking him. Promise me you'll do that."

"I promise."

"Is there anything else?"

"Over the years, I've regularly sent Mazie money. Recently, I got contacted by somebody else impersonating her who tried to blackmail me. They said they would tell everybody in Hollister about my past and demanded fifteen hundred dollars for their silence. I refused. I'll prosecute the bastard for blackmail if I ever find out who it is. But you need to know going into this relationship that there's a distinct possibility my dirty laundry will get aired publicly ... maybe very soon. Are you ready for that?"

"It's not your dirty laundry, Chris. You have nothing to hide, don't you see that? Your story is the story of a survivor. Don't ever let anyone make you feel ashamed about it. Honestly, I think you should do an interview about it—just put it out there to the public and let it go. It might even help others struggling through similar things. Besides, you're the best man I've ever known and ever will know. I know that and so do the people of Hollister."

I take her in my arms, kissing her passionately, and she returns my love stripe for stripe, showing me with her lips and tongue and body that nothing has changed. Nothing will ever change between us. It'll only grow deeper and stronger. We belong to each other now and forever.

"I love you, Cricket," I whisper, stroking her cheek and staring deeply into her eyes.

"And I love you, Christian."

EPILOGUE
CRICKET

The wind whips my hair, and I feel like I'm flying as the ground races beneath me. I'd almost forgotten how much I loved riding horses, and how much I love the Rough & Ready Ranch. For years, I thought I'd never see it again. At least not like this, galloping next to Christian, his face rugged and tanned, his dark blond hair wild and untamed without a cowboy hat. I chose a beautiful little American Quarter horse mare named Minnie for today, and of course, Christian selected his favorite black Mustang.

We've been riding since he got back from breakfast with Wyatt in Hollister, and I thought at first he was taking me to the gulch where he and Hell made what's become a legendary jump among the ranch hands. Instead, we end up in a secluded aspen grove with a small stream cutting through it. The white and black trunks and branches are just starting to bud back, sprinkled with tiny green shoots. It's a beautiful March day with the promise of spring thrumming in the air.

After watering the horses and tying them up, we dive

into cold cut sandwiches, sitting on one of the thick wool saddle blankets. I watch the way Chris chews his food and licks his lips, fantasizing about other naughty things he does with his mouth.

"What are you thinking about, honey?"

"How much I want your cock inside me."

He nearly chokes on his sandwich, turning a shade darker.

"You weren't expecting that?'

"Nope, but I'll take it."

"Will you?" I ask seductively, stroking the warm skin just beneath the collar of his flannel shirt. It's warm enough outside that he pulled off his beige Carhartt, making a pillow with it to rest his head on while he eats.

"Absolutely," he replies, breathing harder. "But first, there are a couple of things we need to talk about."

"Okay ..." I say, leaning back against a fallen tree log. When he tells me we have to talk, it still makes my heart jump a little. After all, we've had some very heavy recent conversations.

He begins, "Remember how you made me promise to ask Wyatt about my past?"

"Yes."

"Well, I finally did this morning when Dad and I were at the Silver Fork. And he was as surprised about the whole thing as you. Turns out, he never knew the full story. I was just a baby who'd been abandoned at the hospital by a teen mom, and the only piece of evidence she left to claim me was my last name."

"So, who gave you your first name?"

"One of the nurses who took care of me in the nursery. She told Wyatt and Ruby Jean I needed a name that would inspire me to do good things."

"But I thought you went to a couple foster homes before ending up here?"

"The nurse was the first home I went to, and she included a letter with me that went from home to home until I ended up at Rough & Ready Ranch. But it said nothing about the circumstances of my birth."

"She wanted to give you a fresh start."

"Maybe."

"I'd like to see the letter."

"Me, too. Dad said he'll find it the next time we're at the house."

I shift, moving towards Christian to lie on my side next to him. "You know, it worked," I muse, stroking the beginning of afternoon stubble on his cheeks and chin.

"What did?"

"The name the nurse gave you. It worked like a charm. You're a good man, Christian McLeod. The best."

"Dad told me that a man isn't made by his genes or blood. He's made by his actions."

"He's right."

"Wanna know what else he said?"

"Sure."

"He told me we need to hurry up and start having babies, before it's too late for him to spoil them rotten."

I take the handsome cowboy's face in for a long moment. But instead of looking distressed or worried, I see a new peace on his face. One I haven't seen before.

He continues, "And you know what I told him?"

I raise an eyebrow inquisitively.

"I told him I better hurry up and marry my future babies' mama, so we do things right." Sitting up, cross-legged, he pulls a small box out of the front lower pocket of his Carhartt, flipping it open to show me a large, sparkling diamond ring on a rose gold band.

I cover my mouth with my hands, stunned speechless.

"What do you think, Cricket? Will you have this asshole cowboy as your lawfully wedded husband? Will you have his babies, too?"

"Yes, Christian, yes!" I whisper. A thrill runs through me as he slips the sparkling band on my finger, and I realize so many years of dreaming and longing have finally become my reality. I wrap my arms around his neck, kissing him wildly, like that day in his office. My exuberance catches him off balance, and he rolls onto his back, laughing and clutching me tightly in his arms.

His hand comes up to my cheek. "I hope those are happy tears."

"The happiest." But I have to ask, "What made you change your mind about kids?"

"Everything about you is so beautiful, Cricket. That's why I know I'm ready to start a family with you. Because our children will be half you."

My eyes pool. "They'll be half of both of us, which is perfect."

Bringing his head up, he captures my lips, savoring them slowly, sensually, as his hands rove across my back and hips and ass, the urgency of his touch growing. He tangles my legs with his, making it clear I'm going nowhere. Of course, there's nowhere else on Earth I'd rather be.

In low tones, he asks, "Now that we've got that figured out, how about we start working on those babies, Mrs. McLeod?"

I answer with my lips, my hands, my whole body, giving myself to him completely, unreservedly.

BONUS SCENE
CRICKET

FOUR MONTHS LATER

MY PULSE RACES as I watch Christian walk up the long driveway to our cabin—tanned, tall, and breathtaking in his crisp sheriff's uniform and white Stetson.

The front door swings wide, and he strides in, his face unreadable. If anything, there's a grimace. My heart sinks into my stomach.

What Christian confided in me after the rescue lightened his spirit, but a shadow still loomed. The shadow of wondering when and how the person who texted him for money would make another move.

I encouraged him to go public with the story surrounding his birth. After talking it out and weighing the pros and cons, he decided on a sit-down interview with Jess, Logan's wife, who freelances for the Chronicle.

The article came out over the weekend, but this was the first day Christian had to face the people of Hollister after its publication. His face tells me more than words ever could.

I step forward. He wraps his arms around me, and the world stops.

"How was work today, baby?"

He shrugs. "Didn't get much done, if I'm being honest."

I put a hand on his cheek, feeling the rough stubble that shows up in the afternoon. "Did anyone talk about the article?"

He nods almost imperceptibly. "Everyone, actually."

I wait.

Silence.

Finally, I ask, "What was the response?"

He looks down to the right, thinking for a moment. Then, leveling his eyes on me, he replies, "Supportive ... and surprising. The office got some calls for interviews with other publications. I'm not sure I'm up for that. And Jess texted, saying she's received lots of positive feedback, especially from others with similar stories."

"You're my hero, Christian. Always giving of yourself to others. This story is just another example of that."

He shrugs. "I'm just a guy trying to do my job. But one thing's for sure. I've taken the wind right out of the black-mailer's sails. Haven't heard a peep from them even though this story has turned into a bigger deal than I imagined."

I nod gently, taking in his face, trying to read what's really going on inside his head and heart. "Are you still okay with everything? I hope you don't feel like I pushed you into this."

He threads his arms around my waist, pulling me tightly into him. Bringing his forehead to mine, he replies, "You were right, Cricket. I needed to man up and do this for myself, for you, for Gold County, for our future family." After a pause, he repeats something I recently said to him. "Darkness flees at the sight of light ... goes for dark secrets, too." Despite the words, his face bleeds exhaustion.

"Did anybody act differently with you?"

He lifts his head, kissing the crown of my head and breathing me in. "Not really. But honestly, the only person I care about not treating me differently is in my arms."

I tilt my head up, covering his mouth with mine, relishing the relaxed way we can bask in each other's touch now.

"Can I get you a beer or something? You want to kick off your boots and watch some TV?"

"Nope," he sighs, his mouth moving to my ear. I shiver at the feel of his hot breath on my cheek and neck. "Everything I need and want is right here."

I giggle as his mouth descends to my neck, covering it with open-mouthed kisses that curl heat low in my core. "I could get into this."

"Oh, could you now?" he murmurs into my shoulder, pulling my pale pink crocheted cardigan down over my shoulder with one hand, making a pathway for his lips to follow while he traces a trail of fire down my arm with the fingertips of his other.

"You know how much I like a man in a uniform."

He teases the sensitive spot behind my ear before showering my earlobe in more kisses, sucking and nipping until I let out a whoosh of air.

"There's only one man in a uniform you're allowed to like." Bringing his other hand beneath my apron and tank top, he squeezes my breast possessively, stroking my pebbled nipple.

My voice shudders. "Yes, only one man. Christian McLeod."

"You know," he growls. "I've been thinking about it, and

I like a woman in a uniform, too. Too bad I didn't take more advantage of it while you worked for me. But this'll do. And it is much sweeter."

He grabs the front of the pink half-apron I still wear from the bakery, pulling me against his firm arousal. My panties are dripping, thoughts of last night only compounding my need. When he ripped a lacy pair off me, smelling and licking them before diving into my arousal.

"Cricket, I need you so bad." He's got his hand in the ties of my apron, locking my soft curves against his hard, angular planes. "The only thing that got me through today was you—*this*. I don't want to think about anything else but making you scream."

His hands fumble with the apron, pulling up my shirt with a neediness that thrills me. His warm fingers rove over my back and ribs before settling on my breasts. He squeezes them while his thumbs tease my nipples until I gasp.

My hand cups his cock, and I pant, "And I had to work all day through a throb between my thighs because ... *last night*."

"Last night?" he says, slow and steady, eyebrows arching.

"Last night was inspired."

"You're my muse." He lowers his head to suck my nipple. My back arches against the silky heat of his tongue and lips, and I grind against him, begging for release.

Suddenly, he stops, turning me around and ordering, "Put your hands on the couch and bend over."

"Oh," escapes my lips on a sigh.

He comes up behind me, pressing his heat against my lower back as he finds the front of my pants, unbuttoning them. In one move, they pool around my ankles.

"Step out of your pants and spread your legs," he orders, and my heart flutters into my throat.

I obey, and he lets out an appreciative groan as he stops to admire my choice of underwear—a purple and black lace G-string. Smacking my ass, he slides his other hand between the front of my legs and beneath the slick, wet lace.

"You weren't lying when you said how wet you were."

"No," I exhale over my shoulder. "And it's all your fault."

He's past words, letting out a throaty moan. Circling my slick clit with his finger, he finds the rhythm and speed I need, his hot breath dancing across my back as he promises, "I've got to get inside you, Cricket. Right this fucking second. But after that, I'll take my time, spend the whole night worshipping your body."

"Yes, Christian. Please," is all I can manage.

He pulls my G-string to the side, plunging into me. "Fuck, fuck, fuck," he whispers.

"What is it, baby?"

He's motionless for a moment, holding his breath before he thrusts again. "You feel so good, Cricket. So very good. You're going to make me come, you naughty girl."

He pounds into me again and again. Until I'm submerged in a dizzy ecstasy, until every frustration of the day winds into a tight ball of desire. I exhale sharply when I break, spasming around him.

My legs shake, my hands gripping the couch for balance.

With a throaty groan, Christian explodes, pulsing heat with each wave of release. He grabs me around the waist, resting his head on my shoulder—taut, raw, sweaty.

"Thank you, Cricket. Thank you for always giving yourself to me, never holding anything back. I don't know how I'd get through a single day without you."

His words catch me off guard, and I bite my lower lip, fighting back tears. He stands up, steadying himself by holding my hips and slowly slides out.

Turning to take him in my arms, I reassure him, "And you'll never have to find out." My burly, tough-as-nails cowboy wraps himself around me, burying his head against my neck.

No matter what life throws our way, together we can stand against any storm.

What happens when Rebecca "Birdie" Jenkins, Rough & Ready's new live-in nurse, crosses paths with her old flame-turned-enemy Zane Mackey?

Insults fly, sparks ignite, and passion burns like wildfire in *Love at Second Chance.*

Hungry for more cowboy grit, mountain man heat, and small-town spice? Devour the next box set in the series, *Rough & Ready Country: Books 4-6*, today.

JOIN THE ENGRID EAVES COMMUNITY!

ALPHA-EMOTIONAL HEROES.

HEADSTRONG, CURVY GIRLS.

SAVAGE ROMANCE.

GIVEAWAYS. FREEBIES.

NEW RELEASES. LATEST NEWS.

Subscribe to my newsletter today to never miss out on a new steamy, small-town read.

SIGN UP FOR MY NEWSLETTER

ALSO BY ENGRID EAVES

ROUGH & READY COUNTRY

Love at First Blizzard - He's a reclusive mountain man who runs a husky rescue, but his world gets turned upside down by the curvy classical musician he saves from a freak March blizzard.

Love at First Campfire - She's a headstrong, curvy true crime reporter who's never needed anybody until a handsome search and rescue unit lead risks everything to save her.

Love at First Rescue - He's a small-town sheriff who plays by the rules until his sexy dispatcher changes up the game, initiating a rescue that sets long-time passions ablaze.

Love at Second Chance - She's the new home health nurse in Rough & Ready Country, but miles of history with the grumpy ranch foreman are in danger of reigniting, despite her best intentions.

Love at First Baby - He's a wildland firefighter who refuses to settle down for anyone until the curvy hometown sweetheart and an unexpected baby make him reconsider what and who he's living for.

Love and Forgiveness - She's a museum director trying to move on until her estranged husband's security company wins her facility's contract, resurrecting long-buried passions.

Love at First Relationship - Everything about Flynn's paralegal, Jasmine, is off-limits as his much younger, inexperienced employee. But a fake relationship proposal quickly blossoms into much more.

Love at First House - A marriage of convenience is the only way to help Turner's neighbor keep her family together. He tells himself it's a practical arrangement, but his heart has other plans.

Love at First Night - He's a helicopter pilot crushing on his best friend's little sister, Roxy. A cataclysmic night gives them a glimmer into a world of possibilities, but will love or heartbreak prevail?

Love at First Beat - Army cardiologist, Fletcher, excels at healing... But matters of the heart are another thing. Until he meets Drew, a romance writer, who specializes in happy endings.

Love at First Doubt - Kindergarten teacher, Effie, knows the town bad boy, Rock, is trouble. A tattoo artist and rockabilly musician, the cowboy's all wrong for the wholesome curvy girl. Or is he?

Love at First Wild - Ridge is a wild outdoorsman mountain man who goes viral with survival videos. Paige is a TV show producer determined to make him famous. But first, she has to tame him...

Love at First Secret - When Aspen and Axel meet on the Mountain Mates dating site, sparks flame and walls go up. Both hide secrets and lack trust, threatening to crush their blossoming feelings...

Love at First Revenge - When a paralegal and whistleblower hellbent on justice saves a rough-riding cowboy bounty hunter, worlds collide, hearts ignite, and vengeance finds a partner...

Love and Redemption - A decade apart hasn't cooled Holden's need for Delilah. She's his first love, his only, and he's back to claim her with the devotion he's carried every single day behind bars.

ROUGH & READY: COWBOYS AND MOUNTAIN MEN

Possessed by the Bounty Hunter - A six-figure bounty draws me back to my ex-fiancée and her mafia-linked Creole family. Soon, a centuries-old curse blurs the line between hunter and hunted.

Gifted to the Mountain Man - Farzad's first Christmas stateside is lonely until the woman he can't stop thinking about needs protection. As sparks fly, will his cabin and heart be big enough for two?

Mountain Man Santa - A blizzard leaves Jerry snowed in with his curvy server, Stacey. She may not be ready for commitment...or the secrets of his dark past. But naughty or nice, he won't stop until she's all his...

Hunted by the Mountain Man - Passions sizzle when an ex-military mountain man saves an innocent, curvy backpacker from unspeakable evil, in this high-stakes romantic suspense adventure!

ALPHA RIDGE CREEK MOUNTAIN MEN

Curves for the Mountain Man - Worlds collide, hearts ignite, and a rescue fraught with peril forces a wounded, ex-military, mountain man to envision a life beyond his reclusive existence...

The Mountain Man's Retribution - A nighttime escape sparks hot-blooded emotions, sizzling questions, and the drive for revenge...

Marked by the Mountain Man - A tattoo artist and mountain man's first look at his employee's younger sister becomes his last surrender ... if he can save her before time runs out.

Follow me on Amazon to explore the rest of my catalog, including cowboy and hockey romances!

About the Author

Alpha-emotional heroes.
Headstrong, curvy girls.
Savage romance.

Bestselling author Engrid Eaves writes steamy, fast-paced romances featuring gruff alpha male protectors and the headstrong, curvy girls they fall head over heels for.

Her heroes may have painful pasts, but they always find forever with their soulmates. Sexy, satisfying, heartfelt happily ever afters guaranteed!

If you'd like to stay in touch or get your next delicious cowboy mountain man, curvy girl romance fix (and who doesn't?), sign up for her newsletter: www. engrideaves.com.

amazon.com/author/engrideaves

goodreads.com/engrideaves

bookbub.com/profile/engrid-eaves

instagram.com/engrid_eaves

tiktok.com/@authorengrideaves

facebook.com/EngridEavesAuthor